SPECIAL MESSAGE

THE ULVERSCROFT
(registered UK charity
was established in 1972 tc
research, diagnosis and treatment of eye diseases.
Examples of major projects funded by the
Ulverscroft Foundation are:

- The Children's Eye Unit at Moorfields Eye Hospital, London
- The Ulverscroft Children's Eye Unit at Great Ormond Street Hospital for Sick Children
- Funding research into eye diseases and treatment at the Department of Ophthalmology, University of Leicester
- The Ulverscroft Vision Research Group, Institute of Child Health
- Twin operating theatres at the Western Ophthalmic Hospital, London
- The Chair of Ophthalmology at the Royal Australian College of Ophthalmologists

You can help further the work of the Foundation by making a donation or leaving a legacy. Every contribution is gratefully received. If you would like to help support the Foundation or require further information, please contact:

THE ULVERSCROFT FOUNDATION
The Green, Bradgate Road, Anstey
Leicester LE7 7FU, England
Tel: (0116) 236 4325

website: www.ulverscroft-foundation.org.uk

ISLAND IN THE SUN

When Cass is asked by her father to take on an unusual photography project in the Caribbean Island of Dominica, she really can't see a reason to say no.

But the remote island has just been hit by a severe hurricane, leaving destruction in its wake. Cass is travelling with Ranulph who is searching for the rare stone carvings her father wants her to photograph.

Their hunt leads Cass down a path of bravery and self-discovery, and she soon falls for Ranulph, who has been by her side every step of the way.

But does he feel the same way about her?

KATIE FFORDE

ISLAND IN THE SUN

Complete and Unabridged

CHARNWOOD
Leicester

First published in Great Britain in 2024 by
Century
Penguin Random House UK
London

First Charnwood Edition
published 2024
by arrangement with
Penguin Random House UK
London

A catalogue record for this book is available from the British Library.

ISBN 978–1–4448–5245–5

Published by
Ulverscroft Limited
Anstey, Leicestershire

Printed and bound in Great Britain by
TJ Books Ltd., Padstow, Cornwall

This book is printed on acid-free paper

This book is dedicated to my cousins,
Dr Lennox Honychurch, Sara Honychurch,
Petrea Honychurch Seaman and
Marica Honychurch,
and also to the beautiful island of Dominica.

1

Cass had been travelling all day. There had been an early morning flight from Bristol to Glasgow, two long bus journeys, a largish ferry and now this tiny ferry that took a dozen cars at best. She was nearly there.

Cass hadn't seen her father since he'd moved to the remote Scottish island she could see across the sea loch; she had deemed it just too difficult to get to. But she had loved this journey. The scenery was spectacular and her bus trips had given her a chance for a nap after her very early start. She had also managed to FaceTime her best friend, who was studying in Spain. It had been lovely to catch up with Rosa and try to show her how beautiful Scotland was on an unusually sunny day.

Cass hadn't expected the glorious weather; she had always associated Scotland with wild winds, driving rain and perhaps snow. But in late May the sky was blue and the majestic hills and mountains were reflected in the almost glassy sea loch.

She sighed, drowsy but happy to be seeing her father in such a wonderful place. Then she heard someone clear their throat and she turned, pulled out of her reverie.

It was the striking man she'd seen getting out of an ancient Land Rover earlier. He was very tall with a lot of almost white hair, but while his hair was prematurely light his eyebrows and eyelashes were still dark. Now she could see that his eyes were greeny-grey.

'Are you Cass?' he said.

She didn't answer immediately.

'Short for Cassiopeia?' he went on, his head inclined in query.

There was a heartbeat and then she said, 'That's me.'

'Howard — your dad?'

'Yes?' She was tempted to add something about him knowing her father's name, but she didn't.

'He knew I was on this ferry, and he asked me to give you a lift to Corriemore — where he lives.'

Cass nodded. She was trying to hide it, but she was taken aback by this man. He was so striking, so — she struggled for the word — attractive. But attractive didn't really cover it.

'I'm Ranulph Gregor. I've known Howard for a few years, before he moved here.'

'Well, your credentials seem to check out. I'll take the risk and let you drive me home — to my dad's house.'

Ranulph laughed. It was deep and musical and no less attractive than the rest of him. 'You haven't visited before, I know. But it's a wonderful place. Eleanor —'

'Eleanor?' Howard hadn't mentioned an Eleanor but as he never seemed to be without a woman, her presence shouldn't have been a surprise. He was dashing, a famous wildlife photographer, and could be very charming.

'She owns the house Howard lives in. She has a few properties in the area.'

Cass could picture her. Over-tanned, and so a little bit wrinkly, dyed black hair, and a lot of gold jewellery and a lot of teeth, set off by scarlet lipstick. Her father had a type.

Her feelings must have shown because Ranulph said, 'She's not what you might expect. Wait and see.'

Cass managed a smile. 'Well, I have to, don't I?'

Inside she was disappointed. She'd so wanted to see her dad, share a bit of the father–daughter time that used to be important to them both. She didn't want to do the sharing with one of his women, who would either desperately try to be her friend, or patronise her.

But Ranulph was a bit of a consolation. She longed to tell Rosa about him. He was so different from her last boyfriend, picked, she realised now, because he was about as unsuitable a boyfriend as she could find. He and Rosa hadn't got on when she came home for a week's holiday from Spain. Even then Cass had realised that she didn't much like him either.

The island was nearing and people were getting back into their cars. Ranulph gestured with his hand to the Land Rover. He opened the door and Cass clambered in.

'It's old but sturdy,' he said. 'It's never let me down.'

'Jolly good,' said Cass. She found herself unnerved by his looks and his bearing. It made her feel childish and resentful. She hoped she didn't appear as spiky as she felt.

'You're very lucky to visit while we're having such amazing weather,' said Ranulph. 'There's high pressure stuck right over us. It's rare but it shows the island off at its very best.'

Aware she was about to say 'jolly good' again, Cass nodded. 'My father will be pleased. He'll want me to see his new home in the sunshine.'

'Of course.'

They spent the rest of the short journey in silence. But after she had got out, Cass felt something weird had happened to her, more than just a short drive up a bumpy, stony track.

'I won't come in,' said Ranulph. 'If it's all right, I'll just drop you off here.'

A few steps from the parking place and Cass was at the door of the house, where her father was waiting for her. With him was a woman — Eleanor, presumably. Howard came towards her and took her bag, then dropped it so he could give Cass a long hug.

It was lovely to have her father's arms around her again, smell his expensive aftershave and feel like the favourite daughter she knew she was. It had been far too long since she'd seen him, she realised. Although he had invited her for a special reason, she remembered. There was something he wanted her to do.

'This is Eleanor,' he said. 'She owns the house.'

Eleanor's smile was diffident. 'Hello, Cass. Lovely to meet you at last. I've heard so much about you. All of it good!'

'Hello,' said Cass. She regarded her thoughtfully. Eleanor was so unlike any of her father's previous women. She was an appropriate age for a man in his seventies, for a start, nearer her mother's age than Cass's. And she wasn't overly tanned and was only wearing a bit of make-up. Her hair, an attractive dark grey, was done in a messy bun at the nape of her neck. She wore an interesting necklace of silver and sea glass and a loose linen dress. She was, Cass realised with a shock, someone her mother could easily be friends with. Maybe her assumption that she and Howard were together was wrong.

'Now I'm going to leave you and Howard to have

some father and daughter time. I know it's long overdue.'

'Eleanor,' said Howard, as if to stop her leaving. 'You don't need to go —'

'I do. I have a lot to do and you two haven't seen each other in far too long. I'm off! But I'll be back to cook dinner.'

Then she hoisted a straw basket on to her arm. 'Oh — Cass probably needs some tea. There's homemade shortbread in the tin.' Then she set off down the drive towards the cars.

'Does Eleanor live here?' Cass asked.

'She owns the house, but yes.' He didn't say any more which told Cass what she needed to know. He and Eleanor were together but she was being tactful and giving Cass a chance to get used to the idea.

She put her arm through his. 'Let's go in, shall we? I'm longing to see where you live.'

'And I'm longing to show it to you.'

Cass was also keen to find out why she had been invited. It was more than just a casual visit, she knew.

'Would you like tea or the tour first?' Howard asked.

'The tour, but tea quite quickly afterwards.'

Her father laughed. 'I'll put the kettle on. It's not a big house.'

But it was luxurious, not the 'but and ben' — dark and stony, full of draughts, possibly lit by sooty hurricane lamps — of her imagination. Although she should have remembered her father was someone who always fell on his feet. If he was going to rent a house so he could finish the book he had been writing for years to go with the photographs he'd taken in the Galapagos, it would be a good house, far better than anyone else would end up with. And he'd get some sort of deal. Maybe Eleanor was part of the deal, Cass thought.

When her father had telephoned, asking for Cass to come and stay, she'd been on her mobile, on a bus. Apparently, he needed her help. Cass found this hard to get her head round. Why was he asking her for help? She was the youngest and least educated of the family. He could easily have asked his stepchildren, older, cleverer, with strings of letters after their names. What could little Cass, the baby of the family and Howard's only biological child, possibly do for him?

Her mother, divorced from her father for many years, already knew about this request. As parents, they got on well, and had discussed the matter. Besides, having left the squat she'd shared with her now very ex-boyfriend, the alternative to the Scottish idyll would have been going back to her mother's house. Cass loved her mother very much and they got on well up to a point, but she did not want to live with her. The remote Scottish island seemed a much better bet. Besides, although Howard had been a fairly absent parent, she had always spent time with him over the summer.

And so Cass had decided to go. Howard had put money into her account for the journey, her mother had driven her to a bed and breakfast the night before the flight, where being driven to the airport before dawn in a battered van, along with other travellers, was part of the package. Once on the plane, Cass's long journey north had begun.

Now, Cass followed Howard as he showed her his current home.

The house had been designed by an architect and made the most of the stunning if rugged views of the sea and a couple of other islands. Pale wood floors matched the pale wood walls and made the house full of light. There were huge glass lamps in case the power went off but there was no soot. The kitchen had granite surfaces and a coffee machine that would probably play music in the hands of the right barista.

The tweed-covered sofas looked inviting and hand-woven blankets were laid over every furniture arm in case a stray draught managed to penetrate the huge, triple-glazed windows. Cushions, pouffes and foot-stools abounded. It was the height of tasteful luxury.

'Eleanor has put a lot of time into making sure all her properties are absolutely perfect,' Howard said. 'The beds have sheets with very high thread counts, which I gather is to be desired, and the pillows and duvets are like clouds. Hungarian goose down is the key, apparently.'

Cass wondered how long she was expected to stay. A summer here would be no hardship. She could wander off into the hills and draw, maybe make a study of the wildflowers of the area. Possibly the birds too, if she could draw moving targets. Then, after a summer of comfort and fulfilment, she could go back to her mother's house in the Cotswolds and do the teaching course she had signed up for as a last resort.

What she really wanted to tell her father was that she didn't love photography as much as he did but far preferred to draw and paint. And she didn't want to be a teacher, either.

Cass hadn't been to university. She'd done well enough in school, but her family felt (and her thoughts went along with their opinions in this instance) that there was no point in racking up thousands of pounds' worth of debt studying something she would never use in real life when she could probably learn just as much getting jobs, working in the real world.

She would have liked to go to art school, but this had never seemed an option. There was no spare money to help support her at the time and, anyway, Cass kept her interest in drawing and painting fairly secret, knowing that even her mother felt there was no future in it.

Howard made tea and they took it into the sunroom, which looked out on to the Atlantic. Although the sun shone and the weather was calm, there was still a white lace frill of foam around the rocks which could be seen if you stood up and looked straight down. Ahead was the vastness of the Atlantic going on forever until it reached America, Cass knew. Seabirds swooped and dipped, and the sun sparkled on the wavelets like diamonds. This view would never be the same twice, Cass realised.

'This is the room I rented the house for,' said Howard. 'I plan to learn what all the seabirds are. You can see my telescope is in daily use.'

'I can understand why you fell in love with it. This view is amazing.' She stood watching the waves for a while, hypnotised by them. Eventually she said, 'But how did you hear about this place, this island, even? It's such a remote spot.'

'It was Ranulph. He and I met a few years ago. He heard through a mutual acquaintance that I wanted to finish a book and needed somewhere out of the way to do it. He got in touch and told me about it, sending some photos. I got in touch with Eleanor in my turn, and came along to see it. It was a filthy day, but it was still beautiful. I said yes immediately.'

'Ranulph lives here?'

'Most of the time. He's a hotshot journalist who happens to want to write a book about me. I think that was partly why he was so keen for me to move here.' Howard tried to look modest at the thought that anyone would want to write about him and failed. 'He was a bit of a wunderkind, won all sorts of prizes. But in spite of all that, he's a good chap.' He paused to pass the biscuit tin to Cass. 'I wanted to ask him to dinner tonight but Eleanor vetoed it. She said we had to spend some time together. Although she has agreed to stay herself.'

'I appreciate that. We should probably talk, Dad. What is it you want me to do for you, for example?'

Howard brushed away her question. 'I'll tell you later, darling. Is there anything you particularly want to say to me?'

Somehow Cass found she couldn't. It shouldn't be a big thing. It wasn't a big thing! All she wanted to tell him was that she wasn't interested in photography, not as an artistic pursuit, and didn't want to teach. She was far keener on drawing and painting, what her elder siblings referred to as 'colouring in'. Why did that seem so hard? She supposed it was that she felt rejecting photography in favour of drawing and painting was denying everything Howard stood for. She'd talk about it tomorrow; like her father, she wanted to put off the difficult conversation. 'Not now, Dad. I just want to enjoy having got here, and seeing you.'

* * *

After a long and delicious dinner, presided over by Eleanor, Cass had gone to bed, tired after her journey. As she lay in bed, appreciating the luxurious bedding, she was proud of herself for not asking questions about Ranulph. But the thought that she would see him tomorrow made her heart give a little flip of joy. She went to sleep thinking about him. It was such a shame that a high-flying journalist would never be interested in a girl like her.

She wasn't bad-looking, she reasoned. The hair her brothers had described as carroty was actually strawberry blonde and the rose-gold colour was unusual considering her eyes were dark. She was average height, average build and lots of people considered her pretty. But average wouldn't be enough for a man like Ranulph, she decided.

2

It was very early the following morning when Cass got up. Primed by Eleanor the previous evening, she found the stone steps down to a hidden cove. The sky promised another hot day, and the water was pale aquamarine, crystal clear. She pulled off her shorts and T-shirt and ran into the sparkling sea, naked, relishing the feel of the icy water on her body, confident that no one could see her.

Eleanor had told her how to find this tiny place, sheltered from the ocean by rocks that formed a natural harbour, making the water calm. There was a fingernail of pure white sand at the bottom of the steps. It was the perfect beach in miniature. According to Eleanor it was always sheltered, but in this spell of good weather, it was also warm. The water was still cold but not impossibly so. Cass felt she could have been anywhere in the world and not found a spot as lovely as this.

She was swimming on her back, luxuriating in the feeling of the water passing over her body when she heard a vehicle going up the track to the house.

The sound jolted her out of her dreamy state. She felt annoyed and excited at the same time. She recognised the engine of Ranulph's Land Rover, but why was he calling on her father so early? It wasn't even eight o'clock in the morning. She swam quickly to shore and found her clothes.

Cass rubbed her towel sketchily over her body and

pulled on her shorts, wondering if Ranulph had seen her swimming naked. But it wasn't so much that which bothered her; it was the timing of the visit. Howard wasn't a morning person. It was possible Ranulph didn't know that. She'd have to try and stall him.

She had nearly made it up the many shallow steps to the house, plaiting her hair as she walked, when she became aware that there were voices coming from the sunroom that looked over the sea. Just then, one of them laughed. It was Ranulph. There was obviously no emergency or there wouldn't be laughter, but why such an early visit?

Cass took the time to go into her room to find some more clothes and finish plaiting her hair. She didn't go as far as putting on full make-up — that would look strange so early in the morning when she didn't often wear it — but she did put a tiny bit of mascara at the end of her lashes and made sure her eyebrows all lay in the same direction.

Then she made herself a cappuccino and went to the sunroom to see why Ranulph had called at this time. She also wanted a chance to meet him properly.

He was standing with his back to the huge window and Cass realised that he was a man who had all the Scottish ruggedness that the house and weather currently lacked. Now she could get a proper look at him, she realised his hair was more grey than white; in the sunshine when she'd first seen him it had looked very light. His dark eyebrows and lashes drew attention to eyes the same bluey-green as the sea would have been on a less sunny day. He was a big man, and could, Cass decided, have stepped right out of the pages of a catalogue selling tough, vastly expensive outdoor clothing. He was, in an expression she'd read somewhere, 'a man to ride the water with'.

'Hi, Cass,' he said, his voice deep and slow. 'I don't suppose you expected to see me again so soon, and so early.'

'No,' she said, waiting for an explanation. 'Did you come for breakfast?'

'Not deliberately. Some of Howard's post came to my house while I was away and I brought it over in case he was held up without it. It has a publisher's label on it.'

'I think our usual postie is on holiday as post rarely goes astray,' said Howard. 'But I'm glad to get it, so thank you, Ran. And while you're here, what about breakfast?'

Ranulph looked at Cass. 'Would that be a lot of trouble?'

'Not at all,' she said.

One of her many jobs, one she'd done for several summers, was working at a small family-run hotel. When she wasn't being a chambermaid, she helped with breakfasts. On a couple of occasions, she'd had to do the entire breakfast shift on her own. Scrambled eggs were her speciality.

Cass set the big oval table in the dining room before calling in Howard and Ranulph. This room also had a view, almost as good as that from the sunroom.

There was butter, honey, a glass jar of muesli, and some marmalade on the table and a toaster on a side table. Cass added a plate of bacon and another of scrambled egg. As well as heating the plates they were to eat off, Cass found the electric hot plates so things would stay hot. This was definitely a 'we have guests' breakfast.

She was slightly worried in case it looked as if she had tried too hard and so went back to the kitchen for the tea. She would make coffee to order with the fancy machine.

Both men were filling their plates with eggs and bacon when she went back in. 'There are all sorts of other things in the kitchen if you want them. Marmite, peanut butter . . .' she said.

'We're fine,' said Ranulph. 'This is the most amazing spread.' And then came the smile that made Cass go weak at the knees.

I have to get over this, she told herself firmly as she took her place at the table. There was really no point in developing a crush on someone on the island when she was leaving Scotland at the end of the summer.

Eleanor arrived halfway through the meal. There were covered dishes and bowls in her basket. 'I'll just unload this lot and come and join you. Do you need more coffee? No, I see you have plenty. Cass, you've done an amazing job.'

Cass was aware she was sensitive, quick to feel patronised, even when she wasn't being, but Eleanor's praise seemed genuine.

'Thank you,' she said, pleased.

'So, Ran, we don't usually see you this early in the morning?' said Eleanor and then glanced at Cass, looking flustered.

'I had some of Howard's mail,' said Ranulph. 'I thought I ought to bring it straight over in case he's been waiting for it.'

'I think you have been waiting for something, haven't you, dar—Howard,' said Eleanor.

Cass smiled at her reassuringly, but Eleanor didn't see. She was fiddling with the things on the table. She was obviously embarrassed.

'There's a seat here,' said Cass. 'What can I pass you? Toast? The amazing Greek yoghurt I found in the fridge?'

'Oh. Just toast, please,' said Eleanor.

She and Cass exchanged smiles and then Cass noticed Howard smiling too.

He's obviously relieved I'm not giving Eleanor the evil eye, thought Cass. But it's interesting that he cares about my feelings. He never did before.

'So, Cass,' said Ranulph. 'Tell me a bit about yourself? Is it OK to ask 'What do you do?' these days?'

Cass laughed. 'I think it depends on what you do do. I don't do anything special, but if you're a rocket scientist, you'd long to be asked, wouldn't you? Imagine having to keep silent at a wedding when everyone else at the table are car salesmen or whatever?'

Ranulph joined in the laughter. 'But how do you tell which people it's OK to ask, and those who won't want to say?'

Howard interrupted. 'Cass is far too modest. Her half-siblings are all very successful, but she's the only one who can take a decent photograph.'

Cass was taken aback. 'How do you know? The only camera I ever use is my phone.'

He smiled fondly. 'Do you remember when you used to come and stay with me when you were little?'

Cass nodded. While her father was often working in some far-flung place, searching for rare birds' nests so he could photograph them, during the summer she would join him. She loved it. She only had to share him with a camera. And often, when he'd taken his picture, he would hand her the camera (provided it wasn't too heavy) and get her to line up the shot, focus, check the lighting, and press the button.

'You took good photographs when you were quite small.'

'Dad!' Cass said, secretly thrilled and openly worried. 'I'm delighted that you think I can take a decent photograph but I couldn't do what you do. And cameras aren't the same as the one you used back then. Really, I prefer —'

He interrupted her. 'That's true you can't do what I do yet, but I think you could.'

Cass felt herself go red. She was embarrassed by his praise and felt guilty because she didn't love photography as he did.

Howard went on. 'Do you remember that time I took you with me to Dominica?'

'Dominica?' said Ranulph. 'In the East Caribbean?'

'That's right,' said Howard. 'Do you know it?'

'I spent time there after university. But tell me about you and Cass first.'

'I was asked to do a last-minute job there,' said Howard. 'Photographing sites and locations where Jean Rhys had lived. I wasn't so much of a specialist then. I had Cass with me, so had to take her.'

'I was about twelve,' said Cass. 'Dad dumped me on the family of the man writing the book about Jean Rhys, but they were lovely and I really enjoyed myself. The mum took me and her daughters all over the place. The roads were terrible but the scenery was breathtaking. We weren't there for long, but I completely fell in love with the place.'

'I did too,' said Ranulph. 'I was on a dig there — I did archaeology at university — and stayed for a summer. It made a deep impression on me.'

Cass looked at him while he was spreading butter

on toast. He really was very attractive and this connection with a place she had loved made him even more so.

'It's quite a coincidence, all of you knowing about Dominica,' said Eleanor.

'But a very good one,' said Howard.

Cass wondered if he meant more than he was expressing.

Shortly afterwards, Eleanor got up and began to clear the plates. Everyone had finished eating and Ranulph and Howard had gone into the sunroom. Howard, who apparently had been dithering, implied he wanted to talk to Ranulph about the book he wanted to write about Howard's life.

Cass got up too and helped stack plates and screw tops back on the jars of honey and marmalade.

'You're good at this,' said Eleanor, seeing how efficiently Cass stacked the tray.

'I used to work in a small hotel. I picked up all kinds of skills. I can balance plates on my arm if I have to,' said Cass.

Once in the kitchen, Cass said, 'Eleanor?'

Eleanor looked up from stacking the dishwasher. 'Yes?'

'It's OK if you and Howard are together. I don't mind. I realise it must feel very awkward for you, but really, it's fine.'

Eleanor sighed and smiled. 'I begged Howard to tell you about me before you came, but he doesn't seem to like confrontation, so he didn't.'

'I'm the same!' said Cass, seeing an opportunity to unburden herself a bit. 'I've got something to say to Dad that I haven't said.'

'What is it? Is it bad?'

Cass shrugged. 'I'm signed up to do a teacher-training course in September. I really don't want to do it. I don't want to be a teacher.'

'I wouldn't want to be one either,' said Eleanor. 'I love kids but being a teacher involves a bit more than that.'

'Exactly!' Cass was delighted to find such a sympathetic ear. 'I think my family all think I have to have a proper profession and I'm sure they're right, but being a teacher isn't it.'

'What is it then, Cass?'

Cass regarded Eleanor, who was listening properly, and seemed to really care, but somehow she couldn't explain she wanted to do art, even if she couldn't go to art school. 'I need to psych myself up a bit more before I can confess that,' she said. 'But I will, very soon. Having you on my side is really helpful.'

'But you'll tell Howard about not wanting to be a teacher?'

'Yes.' The thought was daunting but it had to be done. She'd have to officially give up her place at university. The sooner the better.

'He won't mind, you know,' said Eleanor. 'Like most parents, he just wants you to be happy. And he thinks very highly of you, Cass.'

Cass laughed lightly. 'I've no idea why!'

'Go off and do something you want to do,' said Eleanor. 'I'll finish up here.'

Cass thought of her sketchbook and pencils at the bottom of her rucksack. 'Thank you. I will!'

3

Cass took her sketchbook and pencils to a sheltered spot outside. She was very private about her drawing. Her siblings would mock her, her mother would praise her to the skies, which would make Cass feel patronised and her father . . . who knew how he would react? Cass had no idea if she was any good although she knew she could get a likeness of almost anything. She was sure there was more to it than that though.

As she drew the delicate leaves of a plant she had yet to identify, she realised how happy she was, drawing simple things from nature. She would have to look up what she'd drawn when she got back later, but at this moment she didn't need to know what things were called. It was all to do with her eye and her hand, mostly her eye.

Cass was so absorbed by what she was doing it was only when she realised she'd reached the end of her sketchbook that she thought about going back.

Eleanor was in the kitchen. 'Cass! Are you OK? We were about to send out a search party. By that I mean we were going to ask Ran to keep a lookout for you on his way over. He's coming to dinner.'

'Great!' said Cass. 'Has Dad had tea? Shall I take some into him?'

'The sun is over the yardarm,' said Eleanor. 'He's on to whisky. Which would you like?'

'Tea, if it includes some of your wonderful shortbread. I didn't have lunch. No wonder I'm starving.'

Eleanor smiled. 'I'll bring you in a tray. You talk to your dad. He's been wanting to have a chat with you.'

'Hi, love!' said Howard as Cass came in and kissed him. 'What have you been up to?'

'This and that,' said Cass. 'But while I've got you alone, I have got something to tell you.'

'Oh? Nothing wrong, I hope.'

'Not wrong, exactly. But I don't want to be a teacher. I want to give up my place at university.'

Howard looked rather taken aback, but said, 'Then don't be a teacher. You must follow your heart, darling. What does your heart tell you to do?'

In spite of Howard's very relaxed reaction to her confession about training to be a teacher, Cass didn't quite feel ready to talk about doing art instead. Not yet.

'Just at the moment it's telling me I need to eat. I forgot to take lunch with me.'

'Where have you been?'

'Just exploring, roaming around. It's so beautiful here, isn't it? I know it's because the weather is so amazing, but I just love it!' Cass hoped this would explain the length of time that she'd been gone.

'I've made you some sandwiches,' said Eleanor, coming in with a tray which she set down on the table. 'And of course there's shortbread. And tea. Ranulph is coming to dinner so we may not eat until about eight.'

Cass bit into homemade bread, butter, ham and salad and Howard cleared his throat. 'Right, now, Eleanor has told me off for not telling you about her and me, so I'm going to tell you why I asked you here.'

'It can't be anything that bad, can it, Dad?' said Cass when she was free to speak.

'It is a very big thing, that's for sure. I want you to go to Dominica for me.'

Cass swallowed, then took a sip of tea. 'Sorry?'

'I want you to go to Dominica for me. I want you to take something I've had for years and years, something I should have sent to Dominica ages ago.'

'What is it?'

'A map. It shows how to get to a petroglyph.'

'I'm sorry, I have no idea what that is.' Cass was used to her half-siblings making her feel stupid, but not her father.

Howard chuckled. 'It is fairly obscure. Basically it's where faces or figures have been scored on to rocks. They're usually prehistoric — in this case pre-Columbian.' He paused. 'I think I'd better start at the beginning.' He refilled his glass, presumably to fortify himself for the task.

Cass took a piece of shortbread and emptied the teapot into her mug.

'I had an email about a fortnight ago. It was from the son of an old friend. Bastian, that's the son, had tracked me down after seeing my name in his father's papers. He's hoping I can help him.' He took another sip of whisky. 'Edward, Bastian's father, and I went searching for the petroglyph years ago, before you and I went to Dominica together. We didn't find it. I knew Edward badly wanted a picture of it and I always meant to go back, find it and take a photo. But I never did. Finding the thing is hard enough. I hoped that Edward would have found someone else to record it for him. Apparently not.'

'That's sad,' said Cass.

Howard nodded. 'I feel terrible because there was a map of where to look. It was made by an old man who used to walk past the petroglyph every day on the way to his land. Edward thought he knew where it was but we just couldn't find it when we went together. Bastian needs to see and record the petroglyph for himself.'

'Can't you scan the map and send it to . . . Bastian?'

'I doubt it would come out clearly enough. It's in pencil and very faint. Anyway, Bastian really wants the original to follow. He's writing a paper — more of a thesis, really — about the history of the island and the petroglyph is part of it. He needs to find it. I feel I owe it to him. And you taking the map personally will be the absolute safest way of getting it to him.'

'Couldn't you use a courier?' asked Cass.

'I'm not sure Dominica is set up for couriers, and I'd worry. I'd much rather you took it in person. I'd go myself if it wasn't for my work. I can't take time away.' He smiled ruefully. 'I'm late with my deadline as it is.'

'Well, going to Dominica wouldn't be a hardship.' Cass smiled. 'Since you mentioned it earlier, all sorts of memories have come back.'

'For example?'

'They do all run into each other, but the waterfalls, rivers you could swim in — I mean comfortably!' She laughed. 'We brought eggs with us to one place and buried them in the hot mud.'

'Where the volcano bubbled up?'

Cass nodded. 'They were cooked in minutes.'

'What was your favourite place?'

'That's a hard one, but on the last day before you and I had to go home, I remember — what was her name? Patricia? She drove us up to a place right at the top of the mountain. The road was terrible and it took ages —'

'Syndicate. Where the parrots are.'

'That's right! We did see the parrots, but it's the trees I remember. Huge roots, almost like rooms.'

'That's one of the *Sloanea* species. *Sloanea caribaea*, I think,' said Howard. 'Sorry, I remember hearing it at the time. I can remember that, but can't remember if I've brushed my teeth or not.'

Cass smiled. Her father seemed as on the ball as he ever was, but she realised he was in his mid-seventies now. 'Is that what it's called? But the thing that most surprised me was that there was a visitors' centre at the top. We'd climbed so high, through tiny banana plantations, hardly seeing a soul. I felt we must be on top of the world and there was this very informative centre and a little stall. I bought a necklace with wooden beads. I think I've still got it.' She paused. 'When would you like me to go?'

'As soon as possible. Bastian has a deadline for this paper and he has to make it. There's a prize being offered, and if he wins it, it'll mean thousands of pounds that he has promised to use for the good of the island. And the kudos from winning will mean that the publisher administering the prize is likely to want him to turn his material into a book for them. But of course, he's not the only one after the prize. It's generous and there's competition for it. The money could easily go to someone else.'

'Has not having the map slowed him down? Getting the paper — or thesis — written, I mean.'

'Possibly. He's spent a lot of time looking for the petroglyph. He needs proof it exists. I'm his last hope of finding it. Or, actually, you are.'

Cass exhaled. 'It's a lot of responsibility.'

'I know. But I have faith in you. But you'll need

to make sure you have suitable clothes and I'll make sure Bastian can put you up. Probably in a couple of weeks' time?'

Cass was excited. 'It's a bit different from what I expected to be doing this summer. I had thought I'd be staying here. But I'd love to go back to Dominica!'

'I don't just want you to take the map though,' said Howard. 'I'd like you to take a picture of the petroglyph, too, when you find it.'

'But surely someone else has taken a picture, in all these years.' Cass was daunted. It was one thing delivering a map to someone, quite another to try to find something no one else had managed to find in over thirty years.

'Not according to Bastian's email. I'd really like you to do it. Please, Cass.'

Cass was tremendously flattered but equally terrified. 'Of course, I'd do my absolute best, but —'

'You can do it, Cass. I know you can.'

A little later, Cass went off to have a shower. She had a lot to think about and found hot water pouring over her body helped the process. Also, her hair was full of salt from her morning swim.

She put on a dress and a bit of make-up and then went to find her father. He and Eleanor were in the sunroom with Ranulph.

Ranulph, she noticed, looked a bit caught out when she entered; they had been talking about her.

'Darling!' said Howard. 'Ranulph's come early. He has news.'

'Yes, and it's not good news, I'm afraid. I have a hurricane alert on my phone — I still feel attached to the island although I've never been back — and there's a hurricane heading straight for Dominica.'

'Oh my God!' said Cass. 'That's awful.'

'If it's a small hurricane, a one or a two, they'll weather it just fine,' said Ranulph.

'But we've looked,' said Eleanor. 'And it's increasing in power by the hour.'

'Of course it could easily veer away from the island,' said Ranulph. 'It won't definitely hit Dominica. Howard? Would you mind if I had a look to see how it's going on your laptop?'

'Help yourself.'

It wasn't long before the weather map was up and visible to all of them.

'To think just a couple of hours ago — less — we were talking about me going to photograph a petroglyph and now we're worrying about a hurricane.' Cass perched on the arm of a sofa. Everything was happening so quickly.

'Has Bastian found a petroglyph? asked Ranulph. 'He is incredibly knowledgeable about the island. I've met him a couple of times. He's very impressive.'

'Unfortunately, he hasn't found it,' said Howard. 'If he could, it would justify all his father's work as a historian and anthropologist. It would prove that very early peoples — pre-Columbian — were on Dominica. This has been denied by other academics. The trust awarding the prize really wants this to be the case. But of course they can't grant the prize without proof. And as I said to Cass earlier, there are several people chasing that money.'

No one spoke for a few minutes. 'I can't bear the thought of that beautiful island being dashed to pieces by a hurricane,' Cass said.

'We won't know if it is until the morning,' said Ranulph. 'But people do have advance warning. They can take precautions. Dominica has suffered hurricanes before.' He spoke gently, which for some reason Cass found a bit patronising.

No one spoke for a few seconds. Everyone studied the computer screen.

'I think we should have dinner,' said Eleanor. 'It's all ready.'

Although the food was delicious and Howard provided excellent wine to drink with it, no one could quite forget what was possibly going on thousands of miles across the world, and the atmosphere was sombre.

Cass declined the drams her father offered after the meal. 'I think I'll go to bed,' she said. 'If we won't know about the hurricane until morning if it hits, I might as well.'

'I think I will too,' said Eleanor.

'Ran?' said Howard. 'One more dram before we follow suit?'

Ranulph nodded. 'Just as well I walked over.'

* * *

Cass didn't sleep well and woke early. She desperately wanted to know about the hurricane but didn't want to wake the household finding out, so she took her towel and went down to the cove for a swim. It was all so still and idyllic, she thought, but the very water she was swimming in, the Atlantic Ocean, was the same water that might now be full of huge waves thousands of miles away. She walked back up to the house afterwards full of trepidation. What had happened to Dominica overnight?

4

When Cass got in, Eleanor was pouring coffee for Howard and Ranulph. He must have walked over as he had done the previous evening, Cass thought, knowing that a glance down would have revealed her swimming naked in the cove. But there were more important things to think about now.

'So?' she said, on the threshold of the sunroom where everyone was. 'Did the hurricane hit?'

Howard nodded. 'I'm afraid so.'

'Badly?'

'As far as we can tell,' said Ranulph.

Cass sat down, utterly dejected. 'It's so awful, not being able to help. Although we can send money to the disaster funds.'

Eleanor handed her a mug of coffee. 'Toast?'

Cass nodded. 'Thank you. To think just yesterday we were planning a trip. I was going to go to Dominica and find a petroglyph.'

No one spoke for a few seconds, and then Howard said, 'I still think you should go.'

'What? Go to Dominica when it's just been hit by a hurricane?' Cass thought she must have misheard.

'Yes,' said Howard. He'd obviously been thinking about this. 'The island will need the prize money more than ever. There's a tight deadline. Bastian has to win it. We can't afford to hang around.'

'Surely they'd extend the deadline if there's been a hurricane?' said Cass.

'Bastian will be the only person submitting from Dominica. Why would they change it just for him?' said Howard.

Cass was aware she knew nothing about the academic world and decided to move on. 'Even so, could I even get there at the moment? Flights, everything will be affected.'

'Neighbouring islands haven't been as badly hit,' said Ranulph. 'There'd be ways of getting there by sea. It could be complicated though.' He paused. 'I spent most of last night on the internet.'

Although she was determined not to show it, Cass felt a bit daunted at the prospect of a complicated journey by sea. She hadn't done a lot of travelling. 'I can't think they'd want tourists at a time like this.'

'We wouldn't be tourists,' said Ranulph. 'We'd bring useful supplies. We'd help.'

'What do you mean, 'we'?' asked Cass.

'Yes, Ran,' said Eleanor, 'are you saying you want to go too?'

'Why?' asked Cass.

He shrugged. 'I love Dominica too. The archaeological project I was working on all those years ago is still ongoing. I hate the idea of staying here, sitting on my hands, when there's work to be done.'

Howard smiled broadly at him. 'I admit, I'd feel far happier about Cass going if you were going too.'

Cass regarded her father. She was outraged and yet not really surprised. To her father, she would always be his little girl. Wanting someone to go with her (a male, strong, fit someone) was probably natural. 'Dad,' she said firmly. 'I don't need anyone to go with me.' She turned to Ranulph and smiled. 'Of course, it's terribly kind of you to offer, but it's not necessary.

I'll be fine on my own.'

'I know you would,' Ranulph said. 'I'm not going as your escort. I've got my own reasons for going. But if we were both going, we should travel together.'

Cass's heart did a somersault. 'You really think that going there, at this time, is a good idea? We shouldn't just send money and help that way?'

'I think because we've been there before and have a bit of local knowledge we could be useful.'

Cass couldn't help laughing. 'I was about twelve when I was in Dominica. I don't have local knowledge.'

'Bastian will know what needs to be done,' said Howard. 'You could be guided by him. And when things are a bit more sorted out, you can search for the petroglyph.'

'But how would we get there?' she asked.

Eleanor cleared her throat. 'I'm afraid I didn't sleep much either, last night. I got up and researched possible routes. You can go to Dominica via France, and the French islands route. Fly to Paris, then to either Guadeloupe or Martinique and there's probably a ferry from there. We'll have to find out how everyone's been affected but there's an island off Dominica called Marie-Galante. From there I imagine it would be whatever small boat you could find to take you.'

'Oh my goodness,' said Cass softly.

'Are you all right, darling?' said Howard. 'Ranulph will look after you.'

Suddenly Cass was angry. 'Look, you're sending me on this mission. If you think I need someone to look after me, it would be far better if I didn't go. I'll be fine. I am just wondering if our reasons for going are justifiable.'

'Of course they are! The history of Dominica is at stake here!' Howard was getting angry now too. Possibly, Cass guessed, because he was beginning to wonder if this was really a good enough reason for the trip.

'I take your point, Cass, I really do,' said Ranulph. 'But if we bring stuff they're likely to need on the island — as I said before — first aid, tinned food, bottled water, we won't be a nuisance, we'll be useful.'

Somewhere in her heart Cass relished his use of 'we'. She felt more positive suddenly. 'Well, I got quite far up in my St John's Ambulance exams,' she said. She didn't mention that she and her friend Rosa had taken up first aid because they heard it was a good way to get into events for nothing. Neither did she mention that she'd done an off-road driving course — a Christmas present from her mother — which might not be useful at all. 'And I can cook for large numbers of people if I have to.'

'There!' said Howard triumphantly. 'I knew you were just the person to send.'

Cass rolled her eyes. He hadn't known those things about her at all.

'The thing is,' said Ranulph, 'this is going to be expensive. Tickets, a suitably large donation to the disaster fund, food, first aid, all those things —'

'I'll fund it!' said Howard. Then he became more reflective. 'I owe it to Dominica. It was there, the first time I went, that I realised I wanted to be a photographer.' He paused, and Cass saw he looked older suddenly. 'I just wish I'd taken more photographs when I had the chance.'

'You've devoted your life to taking wonderful photographs,' said Eleanor.

'But is that enough?'

Cass went to make more tea before her father could get too philosophical. Eleanor followed her out.

'This is going to cost Dad an absolute fortune,' said Cass, the moment they were alone. 'Is it a wild goose chase, do you think?'

Eleanor shook her head. 'I don't think it is. It's important to Howard that the petroglyph is found and recorded so it would be wonderful if you could do that for him.' She paused. 'I'm delighted that Ranulph wants to go too. Howard still hasn't quite decided if he should let Ranulph write his life story or whether he's going to write it himself. But he has so many projects on the go, I don't think he'd get round to it. Ranulph will get it done, and I think it will sell. This is earning Ranulph major brownie points!'

'I don't think that's why he's doing it,' said Cass. 'He loves Dominica too.'

'I know, but I also know Howard will be far happier about you going if you're with Ranulph.'

'Ha!' said Cass. 'If he's that worried about me, why is he sending me there?'

Eleanor shrugged. 'Good question. I think he feels sending you is almost the same as going himself.'

'Well, not really,' said Cass, but she knew if something stopped her from going now, she'd be extremely disappointed. 'Are there any injections I should have before we go?'

'How's your tetanus? Up to date?'

Unexpectedly, this made Cass laugh. 'Bang up to date. I hardly like to confess this, but my last boyfriend was so, well, muddy that my mother insisted I get my tetanus booster if I was going to have anything to do with him.'

Eleanor laughed too. 'That is funny! And, as it happens, very convenient.'

* * *

The following days were full of preparations and included a rather difficult phone call with Cass's mother, which ended with an angry 'Put your father on!'

Cass went for a walk to avoid overhearing this conversation. Of course it was perfectly normal for her parents to treat her like a child but she didn't want to listen to them doing it.

But then, as she walked further, taking in the rugged scenery that surrounded her — rocks, heather and, beyond that, the sea — she realised that up to now she had behaved rather childishly. Living in a squat with a boyfriend nobody liked, never following anything through: it had all been a bit ridiculous. Maybe this trip to Dominica was her chance to prove to her family — and, most importantly, to herself — that she was an adult and could behave like one. She went back to Eleanor's beautiful house on the headland full of determination to be more responsible.

Ranulph was in charge of ordering high-end first aid kits that included sutures, needles and syringes. When they had arrived, a few days later, he brought them up to show Cass and to discuss luggage.

Cass looked at the first aid kit with horror. 'So much more than sticking plaster and some sterile wipes!' she said. 'I hope I don't have to use them.'

'Oh, don't worry, you won't have to. We'll pass them on to experienced first aiders. Now, food we'll buy locally. Will you need a rucksack?'

Cass fetched the one she had packed her clothes to come to Scotland in.

'I think you will need something bigger,' said Ranulph, looking at it. 'Would you like a kit list? I suggest you travel in your walking boots.'

'These aren't really walking boots,' said Cass. 'More substantial trainers.'

'They're perfect. It'll be muddy, that's for sure, so don't take anything precious with you. Assume everything will be ruined.'

'That sounds like good advice. By the way, Dad said he wanted a word when he heard you were coming up.'

Ranulph nodded. 'I want a word with him too.'

They went together through the house to the glassed-in veranda that made a painting of the tumbling sea. Howard spent almost all his time here.

After he'd said hello, Ranulph said, 'It's weird to imagine that the sea we're looking at now is the one you'll see in Dominica.'

'I know that's true: Dad told me. But I thought Dominica was in the Caribbean,' said Cass.

'It's both,' said Ranulph. 'There's the Caribbean side and the Atlantic side. There's a place on the island where you can see both at the same time.'

Cass sighed, suddenly wistful for Dominica, wondering how much of the island she had seen and loved was left after the hurricane.

* * *

Ranulph had said he would drive them to Glasgow Airport. They would spend the night with friends of his who lived very near, leave the car there, and be ready to catch an early flight to Paris.

Suddenly, after a whirlwind of preparation, research, packing and repacking, it was time to go. Howard and Eleanor stood by Ranulph's old Land Rover, which was now packed. Cass and Ranulph stood awkwardly by. A part of Cass didn't want to leave. She wanted to stay in the comfort of the rugged Scottish island she had come to love. But most of her wanted to start the biggest adventure of her life.

Eleanor began the awkward process of saying goodbye. She put her arms round Cass. 'Now, take care, follow your instincts and enjoy it.'

Cass hugged her back. 'I will!'

Then Cass went to her father. He got an even longer hug. 'I'm asking a lot of you, Cass,' he said. 'But I know you won't let me down. Or Dominica.'

Cass wasn't quite as confident but she hugged him again and didn't speak. Suddenly, she was crying.

Ranulph hugged Eleanor and said goodbye, but shook hands with Howard.

'Good luck, Ran,' said Howard. 'Make sure you take a lot of notes. And you, Cass, short for Cassiopeia, you take lots of pictures.'

'I've got your camera safe,' she said. The day before he had given her his precious Leica M3, paired with a 300-mm Zeiss lens he had adapted himself to fit. Although he had tried to appear relaxed about letting it out of his sight, Cass knew exactly how important it was to him. 'But remember my photos won't be anything as good as yours.'

Howard opened his mouth to argue, but shut it again. Everyone laughed; then, the tension broken, Cass pulled herself up into the Land Rover.

* * *

After driving in silence for quite a way, Ranulph said, 'Penny for them.'

Cass wouldn't have sold her thoughts to him for millions, they were so confused. Part of her was in awe at the thought of travelling halfway across the world with a man who made her heart lurch at the least thing. The other part wondered if she was mad. She didn't know Ranulph. Her father trusted him, but was he a good judge of character? Although, having mulled over this thought, Cass realised that she did trust Ranulph. He wouldn't make her feel awkward or compromise her in any way. Why she was so sure of this, she couldn't say.

To answer him she said, 'My mother says that before you get together with anyone permanently you should find out what sort of traveller they are. Do you like to be at the airport too early for check-in, or do you leave it until the last moment and then stop off for a cup of coffee?'

'What sort of traveller are you?' said Ranulph.

'I haven't done much travelling but I think I'm the first kind,' said Cass. 'I know it makes me a very boring person' — her ex-boyfriend had told her this — 'but I just prefer it that way.' She paused. 'There was a hen do I went on a while ago — I was friends with the bride's younger sister — when we nearly missed the plane to Ibiza. Everyone else thought it was hilarious, but I was dying inside.' She smiled at the memory. 'Everyone else also seemed to think Prosecco for breakfast was one of your five a day. I didn't.'

'In which case, we won't breakfast on fizzy white wine, nor will we arrive for boarding ten minutes after everyone else has. Mind you, after the first bit of our journey, we won't always be able to control things.'

'Thank you,' said Cass.

She now definitely trusted him but when would she stop having the dizzy, crazy feeling that she was in love with him? It made no sense. She hardly knew him. If she could have taken a pill, or had an injection, to stop this totally irrational feeling, she'd have done it. Otherwise, she realised, she just had to wait for the feeling to go away.

A little later he said, 'Have you got the map? You know, the one your father and Bastian's father made telling us how to find the petroglyph?'

'Oh, that map!' said Cass, flippantly. 'Yes. It's sewn into my clothes,' she said.

'What? Really?'

This made Cass laugh. 'No! But Eleanor has put it in a waterproof envelope, inside another waterproof envelope, and it's with my valuable documents. She put it in a secret pocket in my day bag with an invisible zip. I'm sure I won't lose it.'

But the moment she had said that, she stopped being sure. She needed to check she had it. She turned round to get her daypack, finding it difficult to reach.

'Would you like me to stop the car?'

'Yes, please,' she said, and once the car had come to a halt, quickly unzipped the pocket. She was relieved to see the envelope stowed safely inside. 'Sorry,' she said a few moments later. 'I just had to check.' There was something else she had slipped into that pocket which, while not really a secret, wasn't something she wanted Ranulph to know about. It was her sketchbook. She was so used to keeping her hobby from her family, she didn't tell Ranulph about it either.

'That's fine.'

Looking at his profile, Cass couldn't quite decide if it was fine, or if he was irritated by her. It was going to be a very long journey.

5

A lifetime seemed to have passed since they'd set off but at last the plane landed in Guadeloupe. Cass had felt bonded to the plane, to her seat, to the people around her. Now, when the long journey was finally ending, she felt as if she was exchanging a safe place for the dangerous unknown. She knew it was because she was tired.

The warmth of the air and the unidentifiable smell of vegetation hit her like a blanket as she reached the top of the steps. But at least she had feeling in her legs and feet by the time she got to the bottom.

Guadeloupe was one of the French islands and they were to spend a night here before finding the ferry to Marie-Galante — provided there was one. From there it was a matter of finding a fishing boat to take them to Dominica. There would be dozens of boats, bringing aid to their fellow islanders; they just needed to find space on one of them.

Cass followed Ranulph in a daze. Everyone was talking at the tops of their voices, dragging their cases and bundles and boxes along to the first of many queues.

Eventually, duly processed, they emerged and found the queue outside the airport for taxis.

Possibly because of the hurricane, the little town was heaving with people, but Eleanor had managed to find them a small Airbnb. This was a very simple concrete building with wooden windows and doors and a tin roof. Inside there was a bedroom with twin beds, a small bathroom and a kitchenette.

'It has everything we need,' said Cass, looking around. But in her heart she wanted a bedroom in a building with a proper roof, and preferably a bedroom she didn't have to share. Although when she thought about it more, she realised that, since she used to share a squat, she should be fine with this clean, simple building.

She put her backpack on the bed. It was mostly full of a first aid kit — one of the ones that they had collected in Glasgow. Ranulph had the others. The afternoon sun cast shadows and Cass longed to stretch out on her bed and sleep.

'You must be tired,' said Ranulph, making her feel like a child and a hundred-year-old lady at the same time.

'I'm fine!' Cass said airily and then she jumped and gave a small scream as something small scuttled across the wall at speed.

'It's a lizard,' said Ranulph. 'There are lots of them in the Caribbean. They eat the flies.'

Her heart was still pounding. 'If that had been a spider or a mouse, I'd have screamed the place down. Somehow knowing it's a lizard makes it better.' She shuddered. 'A spider that size would be utterly terrifying!'

She sat on her bed. 'I probably shouldn't lie down but I'm longing to stretch out.'

'You can have a short rest but not for too long. We must get a good night's sleep tonight.'

'What are you going to do?' Cass was feeling fragile. She didn't really want to be left alone in this little cabin, even if she had discovered she didn't mind lizards.

'I'm going to organise collecting the emergency supplies to take with us. Eleanor arranged for them to be here for us to pick up. Obviously we couldn't bring much in our rucksacks.' He smiled down at her. 'She's a bit of a miracle worker.'

Cass nodded. She suddenly felt close to tears. She knew it was because she was exhausted and her body didn't know what time of day or night it was. She had to hold it together.

Ranulph frowned, possibly seeing her effort. 'We don't know what's ahead of us, Cass, but one thing is certain: it's going to be tough. There'll be challenges neither of us have ever faced before. We need to rest while we can.'

Cass cleared her throat. 'I just hope I can do it . . .'

'Do what?'

'Everything my dad has asked me to do. It seems so much. Back in Scotland, surrounded by luxury, not feeling tired, doing this — coming here — seemed hard, but not impossible. Now it seems a ridiculous thing to even try.' She bit her lip hard.

She was aware that Ranulph was standing there, looking at her, unsure of how to help.

'All you really have to do,' he said, 'the only thing that no one else can do, is to give the map of where to find the petroglyph to Bastian.'

'But we might not find Bastian. Bastian might be dead.' Her voice broke as she said it.

Ranulph shook his head decisively. 'That's very unlikely. He had warning that the hurricane was coming. He would have taken every sensible precaution. He might be cut off from the world but he'll be there on the island, I'm sure of it.'

Cass sniffed.

'I do wish I knew what to say or do to make you feel better,' said Ranulph, having realised she was crying.

Cass looked up, having found a tissue in her pocket, and blew her nose. 'A hug would help.'

He was sitting on the bed next to her in seconds, his strong arms wrapped around her making her feel safe. He smelt quite strongly, she realised. He'd said how badly he wanted a shower on the journey to the Airbnb; but somehow this was comforting.

'Thank you,' said Cass after a moment, letting him go. 'You could have your shower now. I'm going to nap.'

'Are you saying that I smell?' said Ranulph.

She gave him a weak smile. 'I probably smell too.'

'You don't. Now have some rest and I'll wake you when I get back. We need to eat.'

* * *

They found a little beach bar which gave them fresh fish, rice, lentils and salad. It was perfect with a bottle of local beer each. For a short time Cass allowed herself to imagine they were on holiday together. Although all anyone talked about was the hurricane, it was still a lovely spot. Cass thought how magical it would be if they were in a relationship, if Ranulph felt the same way about her as she felt about him. In spite of her anguish, Cass couldn't help smiling at the thought.

'Something funny?' asked Ranulph, although Cass's smile had been very small.

'I'm just thinking how odd it is that we, virtual strangers, are together in what would be considered a honeymoon destination in normal circumstances.'

She was pleased with her quick thinking.

Ranulph laughed. 'I see what you mean. Now, shall we have another beer? Rum punch?'

Cass shook her head. 'Better not,' she said.

Privately she didn't want to find herself needing the loo in the night because of one too many beers. It was going to be very weird sharing a room with Ranulph. Would she even be able to sleep with him breathing in the next bed?

At the door of the cabin, Ranulph said, 'I'm going to go and see if I can pick up any local news. I won't be long. Is there anything you need that I might be able to find?'

Cass shook her head. 'I'll be fine.'

Being alone in the cabin would make the process of getting ready for bed easier, she reasoned. But she felt certain she'd be edgy until Ranulph came back.

Actually, she fell asleep very quickly and didn't hear him come in, although she realised it couldn't have been all that long before it started to rain. There was no question of sleeping through it. The tin roof meant the noise was deafening and the rain seemed to be made of rocks. Having checked to make sure he was there, she lay still, wondering if Ranulph could possibly be asleep. Several times the rain lessened as the squall moved away and sleep seemed possible, but then it came back, seemingly harder than ever.

'Are you OK?' Ranulph had to shout to be heard above the noise of the rain on the tin roof.

'I suppose so!' Cass shouted back. 'But I can't sleep.'

'I'll make us a hot drink. I bought supplies for us, too.'

He went into the little kitchen and Cass was aware

of him fiddling about. Curious, she got up. He was boiling cocoa and evaporated milk together. He added a lot of sugar and then produced a bottle of rum and added a large quantity.

'If this doesn't get us off to sleep, nothing will,' he said, handing her a mug.

It was delicious and very alcoholic. 'Normally this would have me unconscious in seconds,' said Cass.

'Not now,' Ranulph replied. It wasn't a question. 'But if you let yourself relax you can turn the noise of the rain into something soothing. I learnt how to do it when I was here before. It's very loud white noise.'

Cass couldn't help laughing a little at the suggestion that the battering sound could help her sleep but she did find herself getting drowsy.

It seemed just moments later when Ranulph was murmuring her name. It was pitch dark outside.

'I heard last night that the ferry isn't operating at the moment,' he said. 'I was told about a fishing boat that's going, but we have to be at the port early. Put your head torch on when you're ready.'

Cass had the quickest shower ever, aware it might be a while before she had the chance of another one. She pulled on her clothes and ate the spicy, chicken-filled wrap that Ranulph handed to her. Then they were off into the dark, stars shining so brightly it was almost as if they were artificial.

'We're lucky to find a boat,' said Cass, having to jog to keep up with him.

'Everyone wants to help Dominica,' said Ranulph. 'And thanks to Howard, I was able to give the fishermen quite a lot of money, which will pay for the trip and then some. They should already have the supplies we bought on board.'

It was dark and the ground was muddy and Cass wondered how Ranulph knew where to go. Then she realised he was following someone. Eventually she could see lights as they came to a jetty with lots of boats bobbing high up and down. Getting on might be a problem, Cass realised, suddenly feeling sick.

They stopped and watched boxes and crates being thrown on board, caught with casual grace and then stowed. She could also see there was a big swell at sea, presumably caused by the hurricane. Eventually it was time to get on board and she watched Ranulph jump as the boat came up. She knew she would never be able to do this, and luckily other people realised the same thing. Before she knew what was happening, she was caught up in strong arms and placed into the boat next to Ranulph, who caught her before she could fall over.

She sat down quickly on the lockers which edged the front of the boat, already feeling sick. She was about to travel really quite a long way on a small boat. She wasn't very keen on boats and had never been tempted by sailing. Maybe the fact that it was dark was good, she told herself, so she couldn't see how small the boat was, or how unsafe it seemed.

'We're going to stop off at Marie-Galante,' Ranulph told her, 'and transfer to another boat. The ferry not going has saved us time. We don't need to go through the formalities of leaving France.'

'Sorry?'

'Guadeloupe is French even though it is thousands of miles from France.'

Cass tried to return his smile but failed. Why hadn't she realised how terrifying it all was? Eleanor could have wrapped up the hand-drawn map and given it to Ranulph, surely? But that wouldn't have assuaged her father's conscience and she would not have been able to prove herself in any way.

At last, the boat was loaded with provisions and with people. Box upon box, crate upon crate, and every space between was filled with sacks of vegetables and fruit. Cass felt in the way and useless — her place should be filled with someone who could really help, she thought. She also knew she was going to be seasick. She was glad when Ranulph sat down beside her. 'I have life jackets in my pack if it looks like we need them,' he said.

She couldn't decide if this news was reassuring or just added to her anxiety. Why did Ranulph think they needed life jackets? Then she realised that life jackets were perfectly normal items at home. Everyone wore them on the small boats people used up in Scotland. Looking around, she saw no one here had one. 'Can't we put them on now?'

He shook his head. 'The guys would be insulted. They don't have the same respect for health and safety as we do. Wearing life vests would make it look as if we don't trust them to get us there safely.'

Cass bit her lip. Did she trust them? Then she realised that it didn't matter if she trusted them or not; she was in the boat and she was on the journey to Dominica whether she liked it or not.

She closed her eyes and leant next to Ranulph, trying to gain strength from his solid presence. It wasn't long before she knew she was going be sick, however. She opened her eyes to see if that helped but shut them again quickly. It was bad enough feeling the boat going up and down so violently without seeing it as well. She wished she'd asked Ranulph how long the journey was but it was too late. Maybe it was better not knowing how long the torture would go on for.

Ranulph seemed to guess when she was about to be sick and held on to her as she heaved over the side. He handed her a tissue for afterwards and she realised she felt a little better, although she was freezing cold and shaking. How romantic, she thought as she closed her eyes again, the man I have a huge crush on has just helped me throw up. He's bound to fall in love with me now!

The sea seemed to calm a little as dawn broke, although Cass still kept her eyes shut. The sickness made her drowsy and being asleep seemed a better way of getting through it.

* * *

Although it felt as if the journey lasted yet another lifetime, it was still morning when they arrived at Marie-Galante. Cass's joy at being able to get off the boat was tempered by the thought that there was another journey to come, although the next one would be much shorter. Then she saw that the boat they were to travel on for the final leg made the one they'd just got off seem huge. And with all the supplies loaded it would sit far deeper in the water. The smallest slop of a wave would surely make it sink.

But at least this time she could embark on her own, although her legs were shaky and she was still shivery. She was aware she was wearing a fleece which presumably belonged to Ranulph. He must have put it on her when she was too out of it to notice. She wasn't going to give it back now.

6

The trip to Dominica was much shorter and the sea calmer than it had been before, although Cass still kept her eyes shut and thought constantly about the buoyancy aids in Ranulph's backpack. There would surely be time enough to put them on if things deteriorated. She managed to relax a bit into the rhythm of the waves and while she certainly wasn't enjoying herself, she wasn't hating it as much as she had earlier.

And then suddenly everyone was jumping out of the boat into the sea and the vessel was being dragged up the beach. Like the rest of the cargo, Cass was lifted and put bodily on to the sand. She promptly fell over.

'Are you all right?' said Ranulph politely.

'Fine,' said Cass, meaning she was anything but. She'd been in Dominica ten seconds and already she was a burden, not a help. 'Oh dear, my legs don't seem to be working.'

They were on a beach at the bottom of some red rocks. It wasn't far to the top where Cass could see trees and people moving about; she could feel hot sun on her shoulders. It made her dizzy.

'You'll be OK in a couple of minutes,' said Ranulph. 'Take this.' He handed her a bag of limes. She wondered what she was supposed to do with them.

As she regained her balance, she realised the beach was covered in fallen trees. She looked up to the mountains beyond and realised that none of the trees had leaves on them. Many of the trees had been blown over but the others had been stripped of all their foliage. It was shocking. This was what hurricanes did, she realised, they savaged everything in their path. She braced herself mentally and followed the trail of people making their way up the rocks.

'Bastian lives up there,' said Ranulph. 'Very handy that the boats come in just here.'

It took a while to clamber up the path, past the fallen trees that people had already hacked at with machetes to clear a route. Ranulph turned to give her a hand up, but she shook her head. She couldn't go on being someone who needed looking after now. She walked on to what would have been some sort of lawn in normal times. She had arrived.

She put down her bag of limes, took off her day-pack and then swung her backpack down. She looked around for someone she could identify as a suitable recipient for the first aid kit which was taking up most of the space in it. She had some quite sophisticated equipment that could be really useful. A few moments later she realised that this was a ridiculous thought. The people around her were fishermen whom she had travelled with, or local people. It was hard to tell of course but she realised the chances of a doctor or a nurse living next door to where they were heading were tiny.

She looked at Ranulph, who was already laughing with another man and sawing at some branches that still blocked the road. Getting the path clear was the priority.

Cass was aware that to prevent herself being a complete waste of space, she had to do something. There was no one to tell her what to do; she had to work it out for herself. After a moment's thought, she decided the boxes that had come up from the boat needed organising. She wasn't entirely sure this would be useful, but it was something she could do.

She had lined up the last box when Ranulph came over with a bunch of bananas.

'Have some breakfast. There's someone in the house making cornmeal porridge.' He handed her one of the bananas, which was small and fat.

'I feel I should be useful,' she said, taking the banana. 'And not sit around eating breakfast. Besides,' she added, 'I haven't met Bastian. I don't feel I should go into his house until I have.'

At that moment a tall man with dark hair and an emerging beard came over. 'Hello,' he said. 'Did I hear my name just now?' He gave a wide, welcoming grin.

'You're the famous Bastian I've heard so much about? I'm Howard's daughter, Cass,' she said. 'I've brought the map.'

She knew it was too early to be talking about the map but she felt she had so much to prove, she had to make Bastian feel her presence here was necessary.

Bastian laughed in a kindly way, obviously surprised by this, then gave her a big hug. 'Welcome to Dominica,' he said. 'We've got other things to sort out before we have time to think about maps and petroglyphs. Although we will need to worry about them soon.' He frowned. 'For now, we have the hurricane to deal with.'

A yellow dog, a bit smaller than a Labrador but with the same benign expression, came up and greeted the party with a smile. 'This is Friendly,' said Bastian.

'He certainly is.' Cass had crouched down and was

stroking and petting the dog. It was comforting to have an animal to interact with, and she liked Friendly immediately.

'In England dogs have names like George or Sparky,' Cass said. Friendly thrust his nose into her hand, demanded that she should go on stroking him. 'But Friendly is better.'

'He just turned up here one day and so I kept him,' Bastian said. 'We saw the hurricane out together.'

Cass took a moment to wonder what it would be like, shut in a small space with only a dog for company, listening to a hurricane tear the world apart outside.

'Cass needs breakfast,' said Ranulph after a moment. 'In fact we both do.'

Bastian held out a welcoming arm. 'Ranulph, great to see you. Come into the house and we'll sort you out.'

The house was full of people doing things. There was a cheerful woman in the kitchen stirring a pot with one hand and pinning up her hair with the other. She was wearing a bright headscarf and lots of jewellery with her jeans and T-shirt. She gave Cass a big smile.

'This is Delphine,' said Bastian. 'She keeps me in order. This is Cass.'

'Hello, darlin'!' Delphine said to Cass. 'You hungry?'

'I am actually,' said Cass.

'Sit down and I'll give you a proper Dominica breakfast — or the nearest thing we can get these days! Blasted hurricane, eh?'

Cass, who had been feeling very shy and out of place, found herself relaxing over tea with evaporated milk, cornmeal porridge and more bananas.

'We have plenty of bananas,' said Delphine. 'They grow all around here.'

The porridge was strange but tasty; after eating it, Cass was caught out by a huge yawn.

'Were you seasick?' asked Delphine.

Cass nodded.

'And you got up early?'

'Before dawn,' said Cass.

'You're tired. Get some rest. There are camp beds in that room,' said Delphine.

And with just the right amount of bossiness, she guided Cass to somewhere which seemed to have several functions: storeroom, bedroom, study. Here she found her and Ranulph's backpacks.

Guiltily, because she was only too aware of the bustle and business going on around her, Cass took off her jeans and got into her sleeping bag.

She was asleep almost immediately, tired after a short night, two uncomfortable sea crossings and a lot to absorb.

She awoke two hours later feeling restored. She stretched, got dressed, then tucked her backpack under a desk. The camera her father had given to photograph the petroglyph with would probably be safe there. It wasn't particularly valuable but it was very special to her father. She thought the map would be safe in the secret compartment of her day bag, so she just kept the waterproof envelope Eleanor had lent her under her T-shirt. After she had found the loo, washed her face and brushed her teeth, she went out to see what she could do.

Bastian was in the middle of a circle of people looking to him for guidance. Cass couldn't see Ranulph and so joined the circle.

'Can I help with anything?' she asked when she could get a word in.

'Not unless you can drive my pick-up,' he said, seeming stressed and obviously expecting her to say no.

Cass smiled in relief. Here was a challenge she was capable of meeting. 'No problem. I can do that. I'll need someone to show me where to go, though.'

Bastian seemed doubtful. 'The roads aren't clear yet and it isn't an easy vehicle to drive if you're not used to manual gears. These people here' — he gestured around him — 'need to get back to their homes. They've been off the island and want to see how their families have fared in the hurricane. I can't go because I'm needed here.'

'I can drive vehicles with gears,' Cass reiterated. Was this the time to mention her off-road driving course, which had been pretty challenging? No. She held out her hand for the keys.

Bastian shrugged. 'Have a go. Come back if it's too difficult. The guys will help you clear the road.'

'The guys' seemed amused at the thought of being driven by a young white girl but Cass was determined. She could do this.

She was a little alarmed, a few minutes later, by the number of people who piled into the cab, filled the box, and hung off the back. She remembered what Ranulph had said about health and safety and tried to feel insouciant. This was all fairly normal here, it seemed. No need for her to panic.

To Cass's relief, the young man sitting next to her in the cab, Jerome, spoke recognisable English. Everyone else spoke a mixture of French and English, very fast, with lots of slang, which she found very difficult to understand.

'Bastian is famous for his pick-up,' Jerome said. 'He'll give anyone a ride anywhere. His father was the same. I never knew him, but his textbooks taught us all in school. His father knew everything there was to know about Dominica and the Caribbean islands, and so does Bastian.'

'Impressive,' said Cass as the vehicle roared into action, her hands gripping the wheel as she realised the road ahead was completely blocked with fallen branches.

When she could go no further and stopped, everyone jumped off and started dealing with the branches with machetes, saws and even a chainsaw.

'That was quick!' said Cass when the pick-up was full again and the blockage cleared away.

'They want to get home. They have supplies for their families. It makes the work go fast.'

'Will their homes still be there?' Cass asked.

Jerome shrugged. 'Maybe. Traditionally built houses are better than the ones with glass and air conditioning. Bastian's house is still standing because it's built traditionally. This isn't the first hurricane it has survived. Many people have a room built to withstand a hurricane. What you find when you come out of the room again is anyone's guess. Although I heard that the hurricane wasn't quite as bad as it was forecast.'

'That's something,' Cass said. She paused but then asked the question that was filling her mind anyway. 'Was your house all right? Or have you been away too, and don't know?'

'We were OK. We had everyone, my wife, her mother, my kids, their kids. We were all in the shelter together. It was a very long night but we survived.'

'And were you frightened to come out?'

'I was mad to get out!' Jerome laughed. 'Too many people in a small space! But when I got out, I felt wonderment. The world had completely changed. Now we have to cope with what's left.'

'You speak very good English.'

Jerome nodded. 'I have family in England. I spent a year with them when I was a youngster. Now, we need to stop here.'

As the road was blocked with trees, Cass didn't need telling. As before, everyone jumped off and out and started chopping and sawing and slashing. A few people said goodbye and left the pick-up, finding their way up the hill to their homes. What they'd find wasn't known, but everyone was in good spirits. Cass hoped no one would find that their house had been devastated.

7

It took Cass a little while to turn the pick-up truck round when everyone had gone, so she could go back to Bastian's house. She was remembering now how mountainous Dominica was. The roads hadn't been good when she had been here before, and they weren't any better now. They were twisting and steep even without the detritus from the hurricane. One road had completely fallen away leaving only what felt like a very narrow ledge to drive along. She didn't like heights and, when the road improved, she realised she'd been gripping the steering wheel so hard her fingers were reluctant to uncurl.

Although she put on a smile for Bastian, who was at the house when she got back, her legs were very shaky.

'That must have been tough,' said Bastian. He paused. 'Ready for another trip? In the opposite direction this time.'

As she climbed back into the driving seat Cass wished that saying 'no thanks' was an option.

But soon she found she had got used to the roads, the drops, and the accent of the people around her, and was understanding so much more that sometimes she could do more than just smile and nod by way of conversation.

A few hours later, Cass and a young man called Kai, in the seat next to her, were about to head for home. The sun would set soon, he told her, and they agreed they didn't want to be on the roads in the dark.

They came across a knot of people at the side of the road and Kai got out to see what was going on.

He came back shortly afterwards. 'There is a pregnant woman. She needs —' He demonstrated a slice across his stomach which Cass realised meant she needed a caesarean. 'She needs to get to hospital.'

'In Roseau?' asked Cass.

He nodded. 'Other direction.'

'The roads —'

'Not open. We'll take them as far as we can on the road but then they'll have to walk.'

Somehow, Cass managed to turn the pick-up round in the very small space available. The pregnant woman sat next to Cass with her husband squashed in by the door.

Although the road was a lot clearer than it had been in the morning, it still seemed to take an age and then, inevitably, they could drive no more.

'What will happen now?' Cass asked Kai, who had come up to the cab to speak to her when her passengers had got out.

He shrugged. 'We'll walk and carry the mother to Roseau, to hospital. What else can we do?'

'You need some sort of stretcher,' said Cass. 'Let's see what we've got.'

A tarpaulin was found in the back of Bastian's pickup and tied to some branches with a coil of rope.

'But won't she have the baby before she gets to Roseau?' Cass said to no one in particular. The woman had been making sounds which implied to Cass the birth of the baby was imminent.

'We hope not,' said one of the men who was part of

the team which had formed to help her.

'Does she need me to come with her?' said Cass, who was very unhappy about letting this woman in labour be carried on a homemade stretcher for many miles.

The woman's husband smiled. 'You are needed here. You take Bastian's pick-up back to his house. There's more work for it waiting.'

Soon Cass was alone, and on the drive back to Bastian's house she wished she could have done more to help that poor woman. It might take days to get to Roseau, even if there were mountain tracks that would be shorter than the roads. She felt it would have been better for the woman to stay at home. But it had not been her decision, and the group supporting her seemed certain of their mission.

The house was empty when she arrived back and Cass was grateful. A bit of time to herself, a cup of tea and she would be restored, although she hoped she wouldn't need to go out again or she'd definitely be caught out in the dark.

She had just made the tea, grateful for Bastian for having a large supply of tea bags, when there was a knock on the door. Since she'd been there, everyone had just walked into the house, calling for Bastian. She went to the door and opened it.

There was a large white man standing there. He was about the same age as Ranulph and Bastian — mid-thirties — and was wearing a linen shirt and trousers; he was holding a Panama hat. 'Hi,' he said in a friendly way. 'I'm Austin Gilmour. Sorry to call unannounced!'

He had an American accent and a white-toothed smile. Cass smiled back, a little bewildered.

'Is this where Bastian lives? I gather he's the hot-shot on the island.'

Cass became even more bewildered. She could have found many ways of describing Bastian but 'hot-shot' wasn't one of them. 'He does live here, yes.'

'Thank goodness. I've just come across from Marie-Galante —'

'Did you bring supplies with you? Tinned tuna is what is popular right now. You can eat it without cooking it. Not everyone one has fuel.'

Austin Gilmour seemed surprised at this suggestion. 'No, I came in a hurry — no time for shopping.' He smiled again. It occurred to Cass that he had spent a lot of money on his smile and wanted to get value from it.

'Oh, well, I really hope you're a doctor. I have a very high-end first aid kit and I don't know how to use half the things in it. If I could hand it over to you —'

'I'm not a medical doctor, I'm afraid. Although I am a doctor. Anthropology and archaeology is my area.'

Cass nodded. Why couldn't he have been something useful? 'Would you like some tea?'

It felt awkward saying this: it implied they were in a vicarage in the Home Counties and she was the daughter of the house. What she longed to ask was why, as an anthropologist, or archaeologist, he'd thought it a good idea to visit Bastian just after a hurricane. But she felt obliged to rein this in, not least because her own reasons for being on the island didn't bear much inspection either. She wished Bastian or Ranulph would appear.

While she was boiling water on the Primus it

occurred to her she hadn't seen Ranulph for ages. Of course there were a million possible reasons for this but she found herself longing for him. If this was the crush she was so determined to get over, or a need for someone familiar in this strange environment, she couldn't tell.

She had given a mug a rudimentary wash, having no idea how much water there was available, when she realised her guest had disappeared. He had left the kitchen and gone into the large sitting room. Currently this was filled with boxes of provisions, camping stoves, crates of fruit and vegetables, bottled water and cases of baby food. But Austin Gilmour was ignoring the supplies and was peering at the bookshelves beyond.

'Here's the tea,' she said. 'Did you come all this way to borrow a book?'

Austin Gilmour laughed. 'That's your English sense of humour, right?'

'Do you take sugar?'

'Is that canned milk?' He said this with distaste.

Cass remembered having canned milk when she had visited before and had really got to like it. His fussiness annoyed her.

'It's all there is. It's fine when you get used to it.' For some reason she didn't like her guest. She didn't know why — he was friendly and good-looking. He wore nice clothes. So what was it that had made her take against him? The fact that he'd brought nothing with him was definitely part of it.

He reached over the piles of boxes for a book on a high shelf.

'Maybe you should wait until you meet Bastian before you start reading his books.' Cass kept her tone light and her expression friendly. She imagined someone behaving like this in her father's study and knew he would hate it. Bastian might well be the same.

Austin Gilmour laughed. 'Oh, I'm sure he won't mind. My father was a great friend of his father's.'

Cass nodded. If she had liked him, she would probably have said that hers had known Bastian's father too. 'But you haven't met Bastian, have you?'

At this moment Friendly the dog came bustling in, greeting Austin and Cass with the same bonhomie he showed to everyone. Bastian was close behind and didn't seem unduly surprised to find a man he had never met in his sitting room.

'I've made tea,' Cass said. 'I'll take it on to the veranda.'

Cass picked up the tray and left the room. Austin Gilmour made her feel uncomfortable and she wanted to find Ranulph even more urgently.

Ranulph was in the parking area at the side of the house, which was currently acting as a builder's yard. Fallen branches had been stacked and a large tree had had the larger limbs removed to make a bit more space. He was wearing a tool belt and was looking hot but purposeful and engaged.

'What are you up to?' Cass asked.

'We're putting some roofs back on and making some houses safe.'

'Can I help? I've got nothing else useful to do.'

'To be honest, unless you're very good at building, you might be a bit in the way.' Ranulph seemed in a hurry and felt the need to be frank.

'OK!' said Cass blithely, hoping to hide the hurt his reply had caused her. She wanted to tell him about the trips she had made in Bastian's pick-up, driving in very difficult circumstances and managing just fine.

She went back into the house and delved into her backpack. Among the more essential things she had slipped in a small pad of drawing paper and a few pencils. She found a space on the veranda and started sketching.

Instantly she began to feel calmer. Focusing on the lines of the plants, the way the light fell, meant other worries evaporated.

She was engrossed in the way a bright pink flower emerged from the leaves when she became aware of someone behind her. It made her jump.

'Let me know if you want some larger paper,' said a deep voice. 'I can give you some.'

Cass looked up, embarrassed. Bastian was standing behind her, looking at her drawing. Behind the vivid flowers was a fallen branch and the bright optimism of the flower contrasted with the devastation behind.

'I'm just filling in time.' Cass stuffed everything back into her backpack. 'You don't want the map just yet, do you?'

Bastian shook his head. 'You keep it safe for me. It's important. Now, Delphine tells me she's put you and Ranulph in the spare bedroom.'

'Yes. It's so kind of you to give us a bedroom when you must have lots of people who need to stay.' She didn't mention Austin, hoping that Bastian would say something that would explain his presence.

Bastian shrugged. '"First up, best dressed,' as my father used to say. And as Howard's daughter, you will always be welcome here.'

Simple words, but they meant a lot to Cass.

8

Later, as Cass and Delphine were preparing pumpkins for the evening meal, Cass said, 'Are you worrying about your family?'

Delphine shook her head. 'They live in a good house and we had warning. They will be safe, and my brother lives nearby. I'd have had a message by now if all was not well. I'll go and visit when the roads are clearer.' She paused. 'Come, let's look at the sunset. See if we can see the Emerald Drop, or the Green Flash, as they call it.'

'What's that?' asked Cass, following Delphine on to the veranda.

Austin prepared to speak. He was sitting in a wooden chair designed for lounging in. He had a drink in a glass resting on the arm and had the air of someone on holiday.

'It's when the sun sets and the blue and violet lights are scattered by the atmosphere, and the red, orange and yellow lights are absorbed. During the last few seconds before the sun goes, the green light is the most visible,' he said to no one in particular.

Delphine shrugged off this scientific description. 'That's it. I have seen it, but only once. I don't usually have time to look for it. It's over so soon.'

But although she watched intently, Cass saw nothing except the sun dropping into the sea.

The darkness followed very quickly and soon they were bathed in warm, soft air full of the sound of crickets and frogs and other unidentifiable creatures, all intent on making their nocturnal music. How had they fared during the hurricane?, Cass wondered.

'Oh my goodness,' she said moments later, looking up. 'Look at the stars!' She watched the stars appear, one at a time at first and then in clusters. 'They are so bright! It's amazing!'

'They are pretty,' said Delphine, who reappeared at that moment, carrying some dishes. She was obviously more accustomed to a night sky dotted with diamonds than Cass was.

'I must try and take a picture for my father,' said Cass. But she wondered how well the picture would turn out and so didn't fetch the camera.

The two women went back into the kitchen. 'I didn't know that one was staying,' said Delphine, leaving Cass in no doubt who she was talking about. 'Bastian is too kind. Takes everyone in! It's fine if they need shelter, but that one has been ordering me about, treating me like a servant.' She laughed. 'I keep the house running, but I'm not running around after Bastian's guests too!'

Shortly afterwards Bastian came in, Ranulph and a couple of other men following. Ranulph came straight over to Cass and gave her a one-armed hug. 'How have you been?'

Cass found her heart lift as she felt his warmth around her. They'd hardly been on touching terms — a peck on the cheek had been as far as it had gone — but this embrace was very welcome.

'Fine. Busy. Getting in Delphine's way.'

'Not at all!' said Delphine. 'You're useful. You can chop and peel. Now, let's get the food out. People are hungry!'

'I certainly am,' said Ranulph. 'I'll just wash a bit of the soil off me.'

Cass was glad to see Delphine sitting at the table with everyone else although it was she who got up and fetched hot sauce or water, or sliced bananas.

'This is delicious,' said Ranulph. 'I wasn't expecting freshly cooked food after a hurricane.'

'We had stores handy,' explained Delphine. 'We've been through hurricanes before.'

'I never thought kidney beans could be so tasty,' Ranulph went on. Then he coughed and took a sip of water. 'The sauce is hot though, isn't it?'

'Simple, peasant fare,' said Austin. 'Nourishing if not exactly gourmet.'

While Cass couldn't quite decide if he'd been massively insulting or not, she found she was taking offence anyway.

'What's the plan for tomorrow?' said Ranulph.

'I'm anxious to get on and look for this petroglyph,' said Austin. 'I don't personally believe it's there, but I feel obliged to search for it.'

Cass was astonished by this. It seemed that Austin was there on the same mission as she and Ranulph were.

Bastian didn't seem surprised. They must have been talking about it when Cass was in the kitchen. 'My father was convinced of it,' said Bastian. 'So it's there.'

'But surely there's just been a hurricane,' said Cass to Austin. 'Surely you don't want to be doing . . .' She paused as she tried to remember how he'd described himself, '. . . anthropology and archaeology in the middle of an emergency.'

'I was on my way here anyway,' said Austin. 'I

decided not to let the hurricane stop me.'
There was an awkward pause.
'Have some more plantain,' said Delphine, holding out a dish. Cass helped herself, glad Austin hadn't questioned her in exchange.
'I'll be very busy for the next few days, Austin,' said Bastian. 'Helping people on the island. I won't be able to help you find it.'
'I gather there's a map,' said Austin. 'Do you have it?'
'No, I don't,' said Bastian firmly. Which was the truth, Cass realised, currently.
'I bet you don't know half of what you have in your study,' said Austin. 'If we both looked, we'd find it.'
'I did say I was busy,' said Bastian, polite but firm.
'But it's important for you too,' Austin insisted. 'If it's there, your father's work is validated. My thesis supports the theory that the Kalinago people were never on Dominica at that time. I'm convinced they didn't come until much later. We need to know one way or another. If there really is a petroglyph here, it will be proof that they were here.'
'It's not the right time,' said Bastian.
'Will you at least let me search for the map?' Austin insisted.
'The man said no,' said Delphine firmly.
'I'd rather hear it from him,' said Austin.
Cass suddenly started coughing. When people had stopped banging her back and offering her water, the subject seemed to have been forgotten.
'Are you all right?' said Ranulph, concerned.
'I'm fine. The hot sauce was hotter than I expected it to be.'
Nothing more was said about the map after that

and Cass and Ranulph retired to their room.

'It's been a very long day,' said Ranulph. 'It seems a lifetime since we set off from Glasgow.'

'Two lifetimes, and another planet, really,' said Cass. 'And in spite of the devastation, it's still the beautiful island I remember from when I was twelve.'

'And you can see why I wanted to come back. I'm so glad you understand. Not everyone does. Dominica is so different from other Caribbean islands, even when it hasn't just had a hurricane tearing through it.'

'I've loved working with everyone here,' said Cass, partly because she wanted Ranulph to know what she'd done. 'Driving Bastian's pick-up with a full load of people, taking them as near to their homes as we could get, made me feel I was helping.'

'Of course you were! And I'm impressed. The roads aren't easy at the best of times.'

'I did do an off-road driving course once and, of course, I learnt to drive in my father's old car with manual gears.' She paused, feeling she'd spent enough time showing off. 'What did you do?'

'Mostly put sheets of 'galvanise', as they call it, on houses.' Cass knew that 'galvanise' was what the locals called the corrugated iron that was used to roof almost every building in the countryside. 'It was fun in a way, and also it turns out the hurricane wasn't quite as bad as we feared. There are some areas that have hardly been touched. Others will take a long time to recover, of course, but no loss of life that I've heard of so far.'

'That's amazing! I won't feel so guilty for being here.'

'Guilty? Why do you feel guilty?'

Cass regarded Ranulph. 'We've come because of the petroglyph. We're no better than Austin.'

Ranulph didn't answer immediately. 'Should we take a look at the map? See if it's survived the journey?'

Cass retrieved it from her daypack and slid it out of its protective covering. Ranulph shone the head torch on to it.

'For a map, it's really, really faint,' he said. 'Was it like this before?'

'Pretty much,' said Cass. 'Don't you remember?'

'I thought it was a bit clearer, I must say.'

'It'll look better in daylight of course, but maybe I should trace it, to get a clearer copy?'

Cass and Ranulph looked at each other for a few moments. 'Could you do that without Austin seeing or finding out?' he asked. 'And do you know how to do it?'

'Luckily, when I was a Brownie, our Brown Owl was very into teaching us low-tech stuff. Tracing with paper, turning it over, scribbling on the back, all that stuff, was something I got a badge for.'

Ranulph looked a little nonplussed for a moment. 'Who'd have thought you'd ever need that skill in real life?'

'I know! But could you lure Austin away from the house, do you think? Were you a Boy Scout, and did you get a badge for luring skills?'

Ranulph laughed. 'I'm a journalist and my luring skills are first rate, even if I haven't got a badge.'

'But seriously, Austin doesn't seem keen to help with the clear-up, so we'll need to send him on an errand, and Bastian doesn't look as if he'll throw him out.'

'I'll see what I can do to get Austin out of the way,' said Ranulph slowly.

Later, when they were both tucked up in their sleeping bags, it occurred to Cass that when they'd set out — was it only two days ago? — she had felt so shy of Ranulph. Now they were chatting like friends. Except, of course, he made her heart beat faster in a way no friend had ever done.

9

Several days went by with everyone doing what they could to help. Ranulph and Cass continued to help rebuild homes, reunite families and deliver supplies. Austin was somehow still at Bastian's house, pacing around, peering in the bookcases and muttering. When Bastian came in after long days co-ordinating people and supporting his neighbours, Austin asked him about the map.

When Cass wasn't helping Delphine in the kitchen, with meals and soup for people without camping gas to cook on, she wondered how Bastian managed not to punch Austin — or at least ask him to leave. Delphine was very vocal on the subject and she and Cass spent a merry time in the kitchen making rude remarks about him.

Gradually, the news filtered through that what Ranulph had heard was right. The hurricane had veered off, away from the island at the last minute, reducing its destruction somewhat.

Cass was getting anxious about the map. With the emergency ebbing, the subject of finding the petroglyph would become more pressing for them all.

She had looked at it in daylight (in the bedroom, with a lot of boxes pushed up against the door, knowing this was probably a bit paranoid) and the map definitely needed to be traced so it could be read. But Ranulph still hadn't managed to draw Austin out of the house.

Finally she managed to get Bastian on his own, following him to an outbuilding. 'I need your help,' Cass said.

'Anything I can do, I will,' said Bastian. He was preparing Friendly's dinner, a process that included cooking rice, and, surprisingly to Cass, chicken carcasses.

'I need to trace the map. It's illegible. Do you have tracing paper, or anything like that?' Cass had already searched the kitchen for greaseproof paper but had found nothing.

Bastian nodded. 'I often make maps. I'm no good at drawing but I can produce a map.'

This was good news. 'If I could trace it, I could ink in the tracing, but I don't want Austin to know I'm doing it. I don't trust him.'

Bastian put a dollop of cooked rice into a large dog bowl. 'I don't trust him either, but I don't think I can contrive to keep the map from him. However, if you traced it, and we gave him a copy, I'm sure he still wouldn't find the petroglyph. My father didn't find it and he had the map when it was freshly drawn.'

'Dad said your father didn't draw it?'

Bastian shook his head. 'No. It was drawn by an old man who used to pass the petroglyph every day. That was many years ago now, and the bush has really grown up since then. That's why the map is so precious. It couldn't be drawn again unless we found the petroglyph.'

Cass felt stubborn. 'I still don't want Austin to know I've got it,' she said. 'He'll ask how I came by it and why I've been keeping it a secret. And frankly I don't know why he hasn't already asked why Ranulph and I are here.'

Bastian laughed. 'Oh, he has asked. You know there's a site that's been uncovered by the hurricane — on the beach?'

'Ranulph did say something last night.'

'We found very old delft pottery, possibly belonging to pirates, alongside ancient artefacts of the Kalinago people. Which indicates they co-habited. It hasn't been seen before. Of course these people were here later than the ones who would have created the petroglyph so it wouldn't affect Austin's theory.' He paused. 'I told Austin that Ranulph was an archaeologist who had heard about it and come to check it out.' He laughed. 'Luckily Austin didn't ask how Ranulph could have heard of it when we're cut off from the world, with no internet or anything.'

'Goodness!'

'Although Ranulph did study archaeology at university and worked on a project here years ago,' Bastian went on. 'So what I told Austin is almost true.'

'I did know that Ranulph studied archaeology. Has he seen the site?'

'I've told him about it. Of course he is very interested. But if you want to trace the map, I'll take Austin out of the way for a few hours.' He paused. 'Of course he doesn't want there to be a petroglyph. It suits his argument that there were no Kalinago here before Columbus. Better for him for there not to be one.'

'So there's a sort of scholarly rivalry between you?'

Bastian nodded. 'And there is money at stake. If the petroglyph isn't found, Austin's work is likely to win the prize, rather than mine. If it *is*, the money may come here. There's a lot of good that can be done with that money.'

'Then we must find it!' said Cass and left Bastian

to his rice and chicken carcasses. Friendly seemed to thrive on what anyone in England would think of as lethal for dogs.

Having Bastian ready to help was one thing, Cass discovered, but there was still so much to do, she didn't have a minute for map tracing. Supplies were still coming in from other islands and had to be organised and delivered. She loved driving Bastian's pick-up and was learning her way around the local roads as they were cleared. She was also getting to know the locals, and while she couldn't always understand them the first time they spoke, she got it the second time. She felt part of the rescue team now. She had also learnt how to be useful in the kitchen even when Delphine wasn't there.

She hardly saw Ranulph and although they shared a room at night, they both fell into bed exhausted so they didn't really talk. He was involved in rebuilding local houses. It turned out he'd had a job on a building site as a student. Cass still felt a bit tongue-tied around him and longed to just feel normal again.

A couple of days after Cass had spoken to Bastian, things became a bit less busy. Neither Bastian nor Austin were at home and Cass had delivered a lot of provisions to people in the morning, so she decided to devote the afternoon to the map.

She had just got herself set up in Bastian's study, with everything laid out on the desk, including tracing paper, when Ranulph came in, panting hard. 'There's been a landslip. Some kids were playing and the ground just disappeared from under them. I've come to get rope. Could you bring one of the first aid kits and follow me?'

Cass rushed after him, hardly able to keep up. He

got into a green pick-up truck she hadn't seen before and she hurled herself into the passenger seat beside him. 'Do we have to go far?' she asked.

'It's quite close by, thank goodness. The land slipped, sending one lad to the bottom of the valley pretty quickly. He's making a lot of noise so I think he must be fairly OK. I need you to patch him up. I have to get the other two who are still at the top of the slip but who might come crashing down at any moment.'

'Oh God, Ranulph. Will you be able to do that?'

'I hope so,' said Ranulph. 'I've done a bit of climbing and have been out a couple of times with the Mountain Rescue team at home. Only practice runs, but it all helps.'

They arrived at the mudslide where there was a small crowd of anxious adults waiting. To Cass's huge relief, the slide wasn't particularly high, but she realised there must be a huge weight of earth waiting to collapse still further.

'I have first aid!' she said gaily, approaching the adults as if a well-applied sticking plaster might cure the problem.

The boy, who looked about fifteen, was with the adults and did have a cut on his leg, but it wasn't bad and now he'd had a chance to recover a bit from his fall, he was calm as she opened sachets of saline solution and cleaned the wound before applying some butterfly closures.

While she was concentrating on doing this, she was aware that behind her, Ranulph was climbing carefully up the edge of the landslip where the other boys were crouching. She gathered from the people around her he had to go that way as it would take hours to approach the boys from behind the landslip and there might not be much time before more mud and rocks came rocketing downwards.

She had complete confidence in Ranulph, of course she had, but she was glad of an excuse not to watch him climb a wall of soil that could collapse at any moment.

She decided she should still go on chatting and joking with her patient even after she'd heard roars of delight which indicated Ranulph had got to the top.

But eventually she had to turn and watch. Someone had fashioned short wooden stakes which Ranulph had hammered into the earth and put rope round so he could travel across towards the two remaining teenagers. Obviously accustomed to climbing, he made the crossing quite quickly and persuaded one to come to him. Then, holding on to the rope, the boy was able to traverse across to safety. Encouraged by seeing his friend reach the other side, the second boy made the same journey. Then, just at the end, when Ranulph was coming back, one of the stakes pulled out of the soil sending him crashing down.

Cass suppressed a scream. Both boys were safe, clinging to some tree roots, but Ranulph had ended up at the bottom of the mud slip. She realised that the loose soil could tumble down on top of him, burying him, at any moment.

Cass shut her eyes. The crowd around her were gasping and exclaiming in horror.

'Is he alive?' she asked no one in particular.

Someone put their hand on her arm. 'He's alive. He's hurt, bleeding, but alive. You might need some of those fancy plasters for his leg though.' Cass looked up to see the mother of the boy she had patched up. She looked concerned but not horror-stricken.

Then a man came to her. 'Hurry! Bring your kit. We've pulled him out of danger but Ranulph is bleeding.'

A few minutes later, Cass found herself at Ranulph's side without knowing how she got there.

He was lying on a bit of plastic tarpaulin and one glance at his leg told Cass that butterfly closures would not be enough. He smiled weakly.

'What a nuisance. I sliced my leg open on some galvanise. There must have been a banana shed caught in the landslip.' He gave a rallying look, as if she was the one in need of support. 'Just clean me up and get me back to the house. Someone there will be able to fix me up.'

A quick glance at Ranulph's leg gave Cass a glimpse of subcutaneous fat and something that might have been bone. It didn't take her long to take a mental register of who might be able to 'fix Ranulph up' and conclude that it was her.

'I think I'm probably your best bet for now,' she said. She glanced down at his leg. 'Let's get you back to the house. I can't clean this here.'

She bandaged his leg as well as she could and then turned to the many people around them. 'Can we get him to Bastian's?'

It didn't take long before a stretcher was made and Ranulph was lifted on to it. He seemed in good spirits, for which Cass was extremely grateful. She might be able to deal with a bad cut if she had to, but if an infection set in, it would be beyond her capabilities.

They loaded Ranulph into the back of the pick-up he and Cass had arrived in, and Cass got into the driver's seat.

A welcoming party had assembled at the house and could be seen long before they reached their destination. Delphine was at the front of the group there to unload him. 'You rescued my little cousin,' she said, referring to one of the boys in the landslip, taking hold of part of the stretcher and waving people away. Ranulph was a king to her now and would receive proper respect and attention.

While Delphine was making Ranulph comfortable on the sofa Cass wondered if Delphine would turn out to have first aid skills as well as the many others she possessed.

'It needs stitches,' Cass said to her, gesturing towards the wound on Ranulph. 'Have you done that, ever?' She knew it was a vain hope but she wanted the best person to sew up Ranulph.

'Sewn up a person?' Delphine looked at her in horror. 'My mother says I can hardly sew a patch on a pair of trousers.'

'OK!' said Cass, determinedly upbeat, on the surface at least. 'I'll do it. But we must get the wound clean first.'

Delphine may not have been able to sew but she produced cooled boiled water remarkably quickly as well as clean bed linen for Cass to use as cloths.

'This may hurt a lot,' she said to Ranulph. 'I'm sorry.'

'That's OK. You do what you need to do. I'll just have to be a brave little soldier.'

They exchanged the briefest of smiles; his attempt at humour did give Cass courage.

'I'm going to wash my hands,' said Cass. 'I'll be back as soon as I can.'

As she scrubbed and scrubbed she knew she

mustn't delay. Only when she was convinced that her hands were as clean as they could be did she go back to Ranulph.

When she rejoined the others she found that Delphine had extracted everything they might need from the first aid kit and laid it out on a side table.

'There's a needle and thread for the stitches,' she murmured to Cass. 'But I don't see any local anaesthetic.'

'You'd better be quick then, Cass,' said Ranulph, who'd obviously heard Delphine perfectly well. 'Or it will really hurt.'

'I'll get the rum,' said Delphine.

Cass put on the gloves that Delphine had laid out. When she had cleaned the wound as well as she could, she picked up the needle. 'Maybe think about something else for a while,' she said.

'It's OK,' said Ranulph. 'I've been stitched up before and the local anaesthetic hurt worse than the stitches. And yes, I know that rum isn't a good idea.'

Cass gave him the briefest smile and then set to work.

* * *

It seemed to take hours. Cass was sweating, occasionally wiping her forehead with her arm. She knew when she was hurting Ranulph because of the way he caught his breath and cleared his throat. At last, she felt she could stop stitching.

'I think that's done,' she said.

'Thank you,' said Ranulph softly.

Just for a moment it was as if they were alone. The expression in his eyes said so much more than his simple words had. And Cass's silent reply was relief although she knew she really wanted to burst into tears.

'I'm not sure this will be OK permanently,' she said briskly, looking at the line of stitches. 'It might get infected. I might not have cleaned the wound sufficiently. I think you should go to hospital as soon as possible. But I realise that probably won't be very soon.'

'Maybe we should give you some antibiotics?' suggested Bastian, who had appeared while Cass was focusing entirely on Ranulph's leg. 'But it looks as if you've done a very good job, Cass.'

Cass felt extremely tired. She got up, stiff from having been in the same position for so long. 'Could somebody —'

Delphine caught her as she swayed. 'You go and get cleaned up, honey. I'll take care of Ranulph now.'

Cass was suddenly desperate for the loo and while she was there, she washed her face. Then she went on to the veranda, sat on the step and looked out to sea. It was so calm — very hard to imagine that only a week earlier things had been so different. The sea looked benign and gentle as if it could never have had anything to do with a hurricane.

But although the view was serene Cass was shaking. It was shock; she'd had to do something difficult and important that she'd never done before. Friendly, the dog, came and sat next to her. Gratefully, Cass put her arms around him. He was warm and furry and utterly non-judgemental.

Not that anyone was judging Cass for her efforts, she knew that. But she was judging herself. Supposing she'd done something wrong that could make

Ranulph ill? Supposing she hadn't cleaned the wound sufficiently? Suppose it went septic?

Bastian came and sat down beside her, handing her a glass. 'In Martinique they call this a 'pet't punch'. It's rum, sugar and lime juice. We might put ice in it if we had ice. But better without.'

She took a sip. It was as he described, very strong and very sweet. It felt good as it went down.

'Nearly sunset,' said Bastian.

'I haven't got used to the sun just dropping out of the sky at seven o'clock,' said Cass. 'At home we have twilight and the day ends slowly, especially in summer.' She gave a little laugh. 'But I think I'd swap twilight for the stars.'

'Ranulph will be fine, I'm sure. You made a very good job of sewing him up.'

'Do you think so? I've never done it before. Butterfly closures are the nearest thing I've come to anything like that.' She laughed again. 'And that was very shortly before I had to sew up Ranulph.'

Bastian laughed too. 'You're a good woman,' he said. 'Delphine says so, which means it must be true.'

'Did she say that? I'm very touched.'

'She's also looking after Ranulph. The boy he rescued was one of her cousins. Did you know that?'

'She told us.'

'You just stay here as long as you need to. Although I think Ranulph would really like to see you.'

She instantly started to get up. Bastian put a hand on her shoulder, keeping her sitting. 'In a while will do.'

* * *

The moment Bastian left, Cass finished her drink and went to find Ranulph.

'Did I say thank you?' he said, the moment he saw her. He was in their bedroom, lying on his bed.

'Yes. Did I say sorry for hurting you?' She sat down on her bed.

'You didn't hurt me. At least, no more than you had to. I'm going to be fine. I'm just worrying about you?'

This was a surprise. 'Me? Why?'

'Because when we set out on this mad trip you weren't supposed to become a nurse. You were just going to take the pictures we needed and then we would go home.'

'But we knew it wouldn't be that simple. We knew we'd have to help people here as well.'

'And you have,' he said.

'We both have. And you rescued Delphine's cousin. I couldn't have done that.'

'I don't think I could have sewn you up afterwards if you had!'

She laughed properly now. 'Of course you could have!' A sudden yawn overtook her and she remembered how tired she was.

'You need to go to bed, but have something to eat first,' he said.

'I was going to say that you sound like my mum, but the thought of Mum in these surroundings is just so weird!'

'I think I sounded a bit like Eleanor. Concerned but businesslike.'

Cass got up. 'That is exactly how you sounded. And I am now going to see if I can find some rice and peas and then I'll go to bed, even if it is only eight o'clock.'

10

The moonlight shining on to her face awoke Cass. It took her a moment to remember where she was and all that had happened, she'd been so deeply asleep. Now she was completely awake.

She got up to go to the loo. Now the moon was up the house was full of light. Passing Bastian's study she saw how light it was and realised that now was the perfect time to trace the map, when everyone else was asleep.

She pulled on some clothes, took the map out of its hiding place and went to Bastian's study. Everything except the map was waiting for her on the desk.

She put on her head torch and taped the tracing paper to the map, glad that Bastian had all the right equipment, including fine-nibbed pens.

It was strange, she realised, to be doing this more or less by moonlight, but she found it calming. She was good at this sort of thing, something everyone, including her, tended to forget.

Something made her look up. It was Austin.

'What are you doing?' he asked.

'Drawing.' Cass couldn't very well pretend she wasn't drawing, after all.

'What are you drawing?'

'Why are you up?' she said, trying to buy herself some time to think of an answer.

'I went to the bathroom, saw you in here. Why are you up?'

'Well, I went to bed ridiculously early,' Cass said. 'When I woke up and knew I'd never get back to sleep I decided to use the time to finish something I had been working on before.' This all sounded very plausible. Some of it was even true.

'What are you drawing?' He came into the room and looked at her work.

'I'm redrawing the map,' she said, feeling she couldn't pretend otherwise. 'The one showing how to find the petroglyph. It's very fragile and difficult to read in places.' She couldn't think of a single thing she could have said instead of the simple truth.

He nodded. 'Well, don't make any mistakes.' Then, abruptly, he left the room.

Cass stared after him. Of course it was weird that she was drawing the map in the middle of the night but his manner as he left had been as if she was a draughtsperson employed by him to do a job.

Making mistakes was never part of her plan, she realised. But things could change.

* * *

She awoke late the following morning and her first thought was to see how Ranulph was. He wasn't in his bed so she hurried with her dressing and went to the table on the veranda where everyone seemed to be.

'How are you, Ranulph?' she asked, having given the table the most cursory nod. She went to him and put her hand on his leg, which was propped on a chair. 'It doesn't seem hot. That's good.'

'Everyone has done that already,' said Austin. 'No one thought it was hot.'

'He's my patient,' said Cass. 'I have to make sure for myself.'

'He's doin' well,' said Delphine. 'Now eat some breakfast.'

'Did you finish redrawing the map last night, Cass?' said Austin.

Cass nodded.

'So when are we going to look for this petroglyph?' Austin went on.

'We should wait until Ranulph can walk,' said Bastian. 'It's quite a trek.'

'Ranulph doesn't need to come,' said Austin.

Ranulph cleared his throat as if to speak. Cass interrupted him. 'We need Ranulph to be there,' she said firmly.

'If you say so,' said Austin, looking at her. 'But we definitely don't need you. You'd slow us down.'

Cass studied him. Austin really didn't like her, but that was fine, she didn't like him either. 'I am quite fit,' she said. 'I'll keep up.'

'She's certainly fitter than I am,' said Ranulph. 'Currently.'

'Let Bastian decide when to go,' said Delphine. 'He's the one with local knowledge.'

Bastian laughed this off but Cass knew that Delphine was right.

'OK,' said Bastian slowly. 'Let's wait a day or two to see how Ranulph gets on and then decide. We could always take one of the guys with us. I don't want to climb all the way down the side of a mountain without enough people if something goes wrong. We don't know how the hurricane will have affected the landscape.'

'Oh, we shouldn't take anyone local!' said Austin.

'We need to keep it secret.'

Cass agreed with him. Austin would have been the person she felt the existence of the petroglyph should be kept secret from, but that ship had sailed.

'I know who I can trust,' said Bastian firmly.

'What the big secret is about some old thing no one knows is there, I don't know,' said Delphine with a shrug, resigned and accepting. She got to her feet. 'Working for 'de history boy'' — Cass could hear the inverted commas in her voice — 'is strange, but I like it.' She gave Bastian the fond smile of a parent who didn't really understand her child but was very proud of him anyway. She got up. 'I'll make more coffee.'

'I think we should go to this place as soon as possible,' said Austin. 'I have to get my book finished. Once I know there is no petroglyph — or at least not one we can prove is there — I can go for the prize.'

'It's hard to prove a negative,' said Bastian.

'My father is convinced the petroglyph is there,' said Cass, on impulse, knowing she should really be keeping her connection with the petroglyph vague, or non-existent.

'He may *want* one to be there, but has he got proof?' demanded Austin.

'He and Bastian's father met a man who used to see it every day,' said Cass. 'Of course it's there.'

Austin frowned. 'My research makes it clear that the Kalinago people didn't get to Dominica until after Columbus did. And even if they did, they wouldn't have made petroglyphs. They did that to honour spirits who sent water. But here, there is no shortage of water.'

'There are parts of the island that aren't so blessed,' said Bastian. 'But I suggest we go and look as soon as is practical.'

'I'll be able to walk in a couple of days,' said Ranulph.

Cass inhaled sharply. She wasn't having him risk her handiwork before he was completely ready.

Bastian shook his head. 'The hurricane may well have changed everything, but the valley we'll be searching in is very steep. You won't manage on even a slightly damaged leg.'

'I promised Cass's father —' Ranulph went on.

'I'll be fine without you,' said Cass quickly, hating to think she was someone to be looked after. 'I'm not going on my own. I'll have Bastian, and Austin.'

'And my friend Toussaint,' said Bastian.

'Do you really need to bring him?' asked Austin.

'Yes,' said Bastian firmly. 'He knows the area as well as I do.'

'OK, everyone,' said Delphine. 'If you've eaten enough I have things to do.'

Cass got up to help clear the dishes. She wanted Delphine's view on the matter of the petroglyph.

'No point in going while we're cut off from the world,' she said after Cass had asked her. 'But people are saying the roads are being cleared and it'll soon be possible to get to Roseau. The internet will come back there first.'

'But you don't think Ranulph will be able to go?'

Delphine shrugged, bringing a saucepan out of the washing water. 'It might strain the stitches you put in so carefully.'

Cass shuddered, remembering how difficult it had been for her and painful for Ranulph, although he had hardly made a sound. It would be better if he stayed behind. 'How do you know about the roads?'

Delphine shrugged. 'People walk, people talk, news travels.'

* * *

As far as Cass was concerned it was annoying that the news about the roads travelled to Austin first, especially as she knew Bastian was in no hurry to go on a long trek when there was still so much work clearing up after the hurricane.

'We need to do this thing, guys!' Austin said the next morning. 'We can drive to Roseau now, although it will take a while. And they have the internet there, or will have very soon. Then we can be in touch with the world.'

'Do you have a car, Austin?' said Bastian. 'I wouldn't be willing to let my pick-up be used on a trip that would take several days when there's still so much that needs doing here.'

'Come on, Bastian! What are you afraid of? That we won't find your precious petroglyph?'

Bastian sighed. 'OK. We'll look for the petroglyph. But you realise the part of the forest it's thought to be in could have been utterly destroyed by the hurricane? We may just find trees tossed about as if they were spillikins.' He took a breath. 'But we'll look for the petroglyph and then we'll see about getting you to Roseau.'

Cass realised she had been so focused on the map and reproducing it that she hadn't taken the hurricane into account. They were almost definitely going on a wild goose chase. But Bastian was willing to give it a go and Cass could tell he was torn between the desire to get rid of Austin and his reluctance to let his pick-up out of his sight for long.

* * *

'Bastian,' said Delphine slowly, surveying the expedition members lining up the following morning, 'does not like an entourage. He'd rather go on his own with a bottle of water, some crackers and a tin of tuna.'

Cass, who was part of the entourage, shrugged. 'I'm taking photographs. I need to go.'

'You're fine, honey. Bastian likes you.'

'Does he? How can you tell? He's always so good-natured with everyone.'

'I can just tell. Now, off you go. And let's hope that the forest is still there.'

Cass climbed into the pick-up. Toussaint, Bastian's chosen assistant, was there, as well as three other young men who were getting a lift somewhere. It seemed to Cass that Bastian's pick-up never went anywhere without a full box. Its cargo was people, getting where they needed to be.

After the passengers had been dropped off, Bastian drove a little further up the road and then parked. Cass got down from the back and Bastian took the map and they looked at it together. They were looking at the tracing, far sturdier than the original.

'Is this the copy you made the other night?' Austin asked suspiciously.

'Yes,' said Cass. 'The original was almost unreadable and was falling apart at the creases. As you know. You saw it.'

'You didn't make any mistakes when you traced it?' Austin asked.

Cass looked him straight in the eye. 'Absolutely none,' she said.

11

To everyone's relief the area of forest they had driven to was not the heap of trees and destruction they were dreading. There were fallen trees, of course, but the hurricane seemed to have mostly passed over this particular valley.

The party set off, in single file and in silence. The path they were following was narrow and there was a fair amount of climbing over fallen branches to be done. Often, Toussaint would need to use his machete to clear the path, but they were able to keep moving.

Eventually, somewhat to Cass's relief, Bastian called a halt. People found spots to perch in while they drank water and ate bananas.

Toussaint said something to Bastian, and Bastian nodded. 'We're just going on ahead for a few yards to check we are where we think we are. You two stay here.'

Austin and Cass sat in an awkward silence for a few minutes. As a way of passing the time, Cass took her father's camera out of her bag to check she remembered how to work it.

'Are you all right carrying that camera?' asked Austin. 'It looks quite heavy and old-fashioned.'

'It was my father's,' said Cass, forgetting for a moment that she'd resolved not to tell Austin anything about her father. It was quite heavy and old-fashioned.

'Oh! Interesting!' said Austin. Then, without asking permission, he took it from her. He spent a long time inspecting it before making to hand it back to her but just as Cass was about to take it, he gave a little flick and it flew off into the undergrowth.

'No!' screamed Cass watching it bounce from tree to tree. 'Dad's camera!'

She turned to Austin, hardly believing what had just happened. It took him a moment to react. 'I'm so sorry! I don't know what happened. Here, let me look for it.'

Speechless, Cass watched as Austin got to his feet and walked off, rummaging through the greenery that was below them on the hill. She was absolutely certain that her father's camera crashing down through the undergrowth had been no accident.

Eventually Austin came back. 'I'm really sorry, Cass!' he said gently, as if he was an adult explaining that a beloved teddy bear had been lost. 'I can't find it. I'm afraid it's gone for ever. But don't worry, I can claim on my insurance when I get back to the States. And it's not that valuable anyway. You can pick up those old Leicas quite easily.' He paused. 'But you could get a far better one with the money.'

Cass stared at him. She was so convinced that he'd deliberately lost her camera she almost accused him. But what would be the point? The camera was gone and her throat was clogged with sudden tears. She cleared her throat. 'There's not much I can say, is there?'

'I guess not.'

Before Cass could either cry or kill him, Bastian and Toussaint came back.

'We're fairly sure we're going in the right direction,' said Bastian. 'According to the map the petroglyph should be down the hill a bit, and across a river.

Unfortunately we can't find a river.'

'Rivers move,' said Toussaint. 'The map was drawn a long time ago.'

Suddenly both men became aware that something had happened.

'Everything all right?' said Bastian.

'I dropped Cass's camera,' said Austin. 'I feel terrible.'

'The camera your father gave you to use?' said Bastian.

Cass nodded.

Bastian turned to Austin, not speaking but managing to seem threatening anyway. Austin stepped back. 'I looked for it and I'll claim on my insurance —'

Toussaint shrugged. 'It's gone, it's gone. Let's go.'

Cass followed them down the path, trying to adopt Toussaint's matter-of-fact attitude. Losing the camera might have been a disaster for her, and for Howard, but the petroglyph could still be found. And she was certain that either Bastian or Toussaint would have their own cameras. One of them could take the picture of the petroglyph if they found it. Usually, of course, she'd have her phone but as there was no signal after the hurricane, she'd left it behind.

She stopped suddenly. 'Actually,' she said, loud enough to make Bastian and Austin turn round. 'I am quite tired. I may just wait here and let you go on to the petroglyph.' She wanted to sound certain that they'd find it. 'I won't be able to photograph it now, anyway,' she added, looking at Austin.

'Are you sure? We'll be at least a couple of hours,' said Bastian. 'Possibly longer. You'd be on your own for a long time.'

'I'll be fine. I have water and a snack. I can doze if

I want to.' She yawned widely. 'A siesta might be just the thing.'

Austin too expressed concern but it was only cursory. Cass could see that actually he was delighted she was no longer with the party.

The moment they were out of earshot (they were out of sight quite a bit sooner), Cass made her way further down the path until she arrived at some large stones. She could make herself comfortable here if nothing else. But there was another reason she chose this spot. Here, she was convinced, was the actual site of the petroglyph.

The trouble with the map was, although it had large rocks, rivers and valleys marked on it, it was very old. Now they were deep in the forest, geography changed. There was no river here for instance, although Cass knew there should be one and that, at one time at least, it had been quite wide.

Of course, she didn't have the map with her and she was relying on her memory of it. But she had traced the lines of the map several times by the time the image was reproduced on to a fresh bit of paper, so she knew it fairly well.

She looked around and studied the stones where she was but there were more, further down. The map would have led the others off to the right — she knew this because that was what she had drawn — but the original stopped nearer to where she was now. She had deliberately led Austin away from the petroglyph.

She looked around her, but could see no sign of anything resembling a petroglyph. Frustrated, Cass sat and leant her back against a rock and closed her eyes. She was genuinely tired after their trek though the valley and she could have remembered the map wrong. She tried to visualise it in her mind. And then she heard it: the trickle of running water. It was barely audible but there.

She opened her eyes and straightened up. What had been a river years ago could now be the tiniest stream. Petroglyphs were always near water, but Bastian, Toussaint and Austin couldn't have heard it; they had walked right past the spot.

She followed the sound of the water as best she could, hanging off branches to give her support as she plunged down into the valley. She could now see the rocks more closely; they were quite clear and recognisable. Whether they were the ones with faces carved into them she had no way of knowing: she couldn't get any nearer to them without a rope or some other help.

Cheered by finding the necessary water and genuinely tired now, she settled with her back against a tree. Then she burrowed in her bag and brought out her drawing things. She had slipped her pad and a couple of soft pencils into the secret compartment that Eleanor had made for the map. When she put them there that morning and not in the main bag she had wondered if she was being paranoid, but after Austin seemed to have deliberately lost her camera, she felt she had been justified.

Soon she was immersed in drawing the rocks and the surrounding trees and greenery, putting in as much detail as she could. It was a beautiful spot and, if nothing else, she'd have something to remember it by. Once she was sure she'd recorded every detail as accurately as she could, she closed her eyes.

She might have actually been asleep for a few moments when a breeze caressed her cheek. She opened her eyes as the sun came out from behind a cloud, sending a shaft of light on to the stones in front of her. At first she couldn't believe what she was seeing, but there — if not as clear as day, at least discernible — was a face.

Cass's pencil flew. Now she had seen it, she realised that without the light at the right angle it was hidden in plain sight. Centuries of rain had worn away at the shallow engraving making it almost invisible. She had believed it was here and, now she had seen it, she couldn't quite believe that she'd missed it. As she drew it now, she thought of the old man who had told Bastian's father about it, who had seen it daily and had helped with the map. Did he know he was looking at pre-history too, she wondered?

Once she was happy with the drawings and had several of them, from different angles, she knew she had to mark the place more definitely. This spot was deep in the forest and coming back to it would not be easy.

Eventually, Cass relaced one of her trainers that she was wearing, so she had a spare piece of shoelace. She cut this off with the tiny Swiss Army Knife she carried and tied it to the foot of a plant.

Then she walked back up to the spot where the others had left her, put her back against a tree and closed her eyes. But she couldn't help smiling with happiness and satisfaction. There was indeed a petroglyph and she had recorded where it was. Bastian's father had been right, and Bastian's faith in him was fully justified.

She called out when she heard Bastian and party approaching, although she knew the answer. 'Did you find it?'

'No,' said Austin. 'Because it isn't there.' He seemed pleased. 'What did you do while we were gone?'

'Oh, I slept. I knew I would. It's jet lag, I think.'

This seemed to satisfy Austin and no one else spoke until Bastian said, 'Let's go home.'

Cass followed the group up the steep valley. Part of her was bursting with excitement because she'd found the petroglyph, but the other part wondered if a drawing would count as proof that it actually existed? She could have just made up the image, out of her imagination. But if she'd seen it, Bastian could see it. She'd just have to be able to find the spot again.

Then Toussaint, who'd gone in the opposite direction for a little while, came up to her. 'I think this is yours,' he said, and handed Cass her father's camera.

She was amazed. 'It doesn't even seem broken,' she said.

'It was snagged on a branch. It caught my eye, so I went back for it,' said Toussaint. 'It's good as new.'

Cass laughed. 'It's not new. It wasn't even new when my father first had it.'

Austin turned. 'Well, I'm really glad it's been found and not damaged. It'll save me a bunch of money. But why would your father have an old camera?'

'I think it's the camera he brought when he came to Dominica when he was a young man,' said Cass. 'I'm so thrilled that you found it, Toussaint. Thank you so much.'

Toussaint brushed off her gratitude with a grunt but Cass could tell he was pleased.

'We should be getting on,' said Bastian. 'We don't want to be out in the forest when it gets dark.'

Austin nodded. 'And I could use a rum punch.

Let's get going!'

But with every step Cass wondered if she should have found a reason to go back, to photograph the petroglyph, now she had the camera. Although the thought of being alone in the forest in the dark was not appealing; she didn't think there was anything in there that could harm her, but she could easily break an ankle. And of course she'd be terrified. She hurried on. The important thing was that she'd found the petroglyph. She couldn't wait to tell Bastian; he'd be even more delighted.

12

They were back on the veranda of Bastian's house in time to watch the sun drop into the sea, albeit with no Green Flash. Ranulph wasn't there for Cass to check how he was, so she went to her room to freshen up a bit. By the time she came out, there was a group of people waiting for Bastian. He barely had time to have a quick drink of water and a cracker with tuna on it before he was off again, with a full pick-up of people.

Just for a second, when Cass realised she would have to wait to tell him her news about the petroglyph, she wanted to cry. Then she realised she was tired. Was it possible, she wondered, to still be suffering from the jet lag she'd used as an excuse before?

Austin was soon drinking rum punch made by Delphine. She put a pet't punch, with a squeezed lime and sugar, into Cass's hand.

Ranulph came up, limping, supported by a homemade crutch, but looking well.

'Hey!' he said to the group.

'No petroglyph,' said Austin, sounding annoyingly pleased about this.

'But it was interesting,' said Cass.

'Really?' said Austin. 'Personally I found trudging through the bush, knowing we weren't going to find what we were supposed to be looking for, to be tedious.' He put down his empty glass. 'Where's Delphine? I need a refill here.'

'You know where the rum is, Austin,' said Ranulph. 'We haven't run out yet.'

Grumbling, Austin got up and went to find himself another drink.

'I want to check your wound, Ranulph,' said Cass. 'In private.'

He looked a little bit surprised. 'Of course. Let's walk along the veranda a bit, that should be private enough. We can pretend we're looking at the ocean. Or the stars.'

Cass was aware of blushing but hoped Ranulph wouldn't notice in the dusk. The thought of looking at the stars with him in a romantic way made her stomach flip over. She coughed to cover any emotion that may have escaped.

'Sit down,' she said to him when they reached a bench. 'Put your leg up so I can feel it.' She helped him raise it. Then she put her hand on his leg to check for heat and looked at his dressing.

'So?' he asked.

'It seems OK.'

Ranulph made to put his leg down but Cass stopped him. She couldn't wait another moment to give him the good news.

'I found the petroglyph! I had drawn the map I gave Bastian and the others a little bit wrong but I remembered the original pretty accurately. I knew where the petroglyph should be, although I couldn't find the river it would have been on.'

'You drew the map wrong?' Ranulph sounded amazed.

Cass flicked a hand. 'You know I don't trust Austin. I didn't want him to find the petroglyph. I thought he'd find a way of making out it wasn't real or something. Anyway, I found somewhere to rest and I heard running water. The river had reduced to a little stream over the years. Then, by some miracle, a gust of wind parted the tops of the trees and sunlight shone on the rocks — and I saw it.'

'My goodness! Cass!'

'I tied a bit of shoelace near the spot. I didn't say anything to the others because I wanted to get Bastian on his own. The thing was, Austin had pretty much flung my camera into the trees earlier on, pretending it was an accident.'

'So you didn't manage to get a picture of the petroglyph?'

'No, but I did draw it, so hopefully Bastian will be able to find it again fairly easily.'

'Can I see the drawing?'

'Of course.'

They went into the house and back into the light. 'I'll get it,' said Cass. 'Wait here in the library. Rest your leg.'

She was back with her drawing in seconds and Ranulph looked at it. 'But, Cass, this drawing is amazing! I didn't know you could draw like this.'

'Not many people do know, to be fair,' she said. 'Photography is more respected in my family. Although, according to my dad, I do have a good eye for that, too.'

Before Ranulph could answer they heard the sound of the pick-up returning.

'I'll put it back in the bedroom,' said Cass quickly. 'We'll eat now Bastian is home.'

'No rush. Let him get in the door first,' said Ranulph. 'I'm so impressed, Cass. You're — so much more than I was led to expect.'

Just for a moment their eyes met. Cass had always felt that Ranulph looked on her with a sort of kind tolerance. But now there was something else — an expression she didn't quite recognise.

* * *

After dinner, while Cass and Delphine were still clearing the table, Austin, Bastian and Ranulph took drinks on to the veranda. Cass hurried to join them. As she got there, Austin was talking.

'I understand that you're disappointed your father was wrong about the petroglyph, Bastian,' he said, apparently sympathetic. 'But it's obvious he was, and we academics have to accept the facts and not get emotional about it.'

Bastian sighed. 'Is drinking rum, sitting watching the stars being emotional?' he asked.

'No, but you must be disappointed —'

Austin obviously wasn't going to stop baiting Bastian until he did get emotional. Cass, who didn't want to watch the process, said, 'Actually, Bastian, if I could disturb you for a minute?'

'Something you need, Cass?' he said.

Cass thought rapidly. 'I just thought we should think about our journey back to the UK —'

Bastian sighed. He sounded tired. 'Can we leave it until tomorrow, Cass? It's late and currently there's no way anyone can get off the island anytime soon.'

Deflated, Cass went to bed.

* * *

She tried again in the morning, following Bastian to the outhouse where he cooked the dog food. Annoyingly, Austin hurried to catch her up, probably guessing she wanted to get Bastian on his own.

'Sorry to go on about it, but our journey home —'

'Ranulph isn't fit to leave yet,' said Bastian.

'I know! But I was awfully sick on the boat —' It didn't sound the sort of problem that she'd need to talk about to Bastian while he was cooking chicken carcasses but it was the best she could do.

'Oh, me too!' said Austin. 'But don't worry, kid. We'll get on a plane. There'll be one quite shortly, I'm sure. There are important people here who want to get off Dominica.'

Bastian looked from Cass to Austin, his expression inscrutable.

Just then, Ranulph appeared. 'Oh, Austin! There you are! Just the man I need. Can I borrow you?'

Austin seemed reluctant to move.

'I really need an archaeologist,' said Ranulph.

Cass knew that Ranulph was one — or at least had studied it at university — but hoped Austin wouldn't remember that fact, if he'd ever known.

'It's hard to find someone with the right experience. Having you here is a real stroke of luck,' Ranulph went on.

Cass was beginning to see the funny side. At last, after a couple more compliments from Ranulph, he managed to draw Austin away.

Bastian smiled. 'That was well done of Ranulph. I'm glad I told him about the archaeological site that the hurricane uncovered on the beach. Signs of Dutch pirates co-operating with early indigenous people have never been recorded before. It's important.'

'Good,' said Cass. 'But now we're alone, I have something to tell you.' She took a breath. 'I saw the petroglyph.'

'What? When?' Bastian was extremely excited. 'Yesterday?'

'Yes!' Cass's enthusiasm returned. 'I'd deliberately drawn the map wrong — I really didn't want Austin knowing where the petroglyph was — but there was a river —'

'But we had the map with us — even if it was wrong. How did you know where to look?'

'When you trace something you copy it several times, so I had it in my head. I sat down and was still for a bit. I closed my eyes and pictured the map and then I heard running water.'

Bastian nodded. 'The river had become a stream.'

'Then there was a little gust of wind which parted the trees. The sun was suddenly shining down on the rocks. I opened my eyes and there they were. I saw the faces.'

'That's amazing, Cass! But you didn't have your camera, did you? How will we ever prove that the petroglyph is there?'

'I marked the place with a shoelace, and I did a drawing,' Cass offered tentatively. 'Shall I get it, while Austin is out of the way?'

Bastian indicated his patient dog. 'I'll just finish up here,' he said. 'I can't keep Friendly waiting any longer. I'll come in when I'm done here and make some coffee. I'll call you when it's ready.'

'But hurry! We don't know how long Ranulph will be able to keep Austin out of the way.'

'Oh, Austin will be fascinated by the site, have no fear. He may be . . . not our favourite person but he is a serious archaeologist.' Bastian smiled. 'Meet you on the veranda.'

* * *

'But this drawing is amazing!' said Bastian, looking intently at it. 'Can I keep it?'

'Of course.' Cass was utterly delighted at his reaction. 'I did it for you. But will it work as proof the petroglyph exists?'

'Probably not, but you've put in so much background detail, even without the shoelace, we could probably easily find it. I can't tell you how grateful I am.'

'I did it for my dad, really. He felt he let your father down and wanted to make amends. He's genuinely too busy to do it himself now so he sent me.'

'And you've done a terrific job.' He paused. 'But you realise you won't be able to come with me to find the petroglyph, although you'd be so useful.'

Cass nodded. 'Austin would know something was up. I'm disappointed but I knew I wouldn't be able to go again.' She smiled at the memory. 'I'll never forget seeing it though. The sun shone down like a torch, showing it to me. I felt I was looking at it for my father, and yours. A glimpse of history.'

They sipped the rest of their coffee in companionable silence.

13

Ranulph still couldn't walk without difficulty and so spent his time recording and investigating the site on the beach. The evidence showed that the indigenous people had very early Dutch delft vessels which could only have come from pirates or some such. This indicated that the two groups must have co-operated, which had never been known of before.

'I'd feel bad spending so much time there,' Ranulph said at supper one night, 'only I still can't walk well enough to do anything useful.'

Cass also spent time helping Ranulph when she wasn't doing things for Bastian or Delphine. She was there the following morning sketching the site with Austin. Ranulph was halfway up the beach with a camera, when suddenly Austin said, 'Oh, who's this?'

Coming along the beach was a group of people led by a woman a little older than Cass. Ranulph looked up and suddenly the woman started running towards him, hampered by the soft sand.

'Ran!' she called.

Ranulph held out his arms.

Cass felt as if she was seeing the end of a romantic film and looked away before the couple met. She didn't want to witness their meeting. But Austin, next to her, said, 'Boy, is he pleased to see her!'

Cass didn't wait to be introduced to the little group, but instead fled back to the house as quickly as she could. Now it was she who was floundering in the soft sand, only she wasn't running towards Ranulph, she was going in the opposite direction.

Only very briefly did she wonder if Austin had told her how pleased Ranulph had been to see that woman in order simply to hurt her. Could he have guessed how she felt about Ranulph? She'd always been so careful to be 'casual, just friends, no one special' around him. She didn't want anyone to know and if Delphine had guessed it was because she had got to know Cass well as they cooked together. That said, Austin also had a knack of knowing things no one had told him, of finding out things that others had intended to keep hidden.

She found Delphine in the kitchen. 'There may be extra people for supper tonight,' she said. 'Ranulph has met an old friend.'

'A woman?' Delphine also had a knack for knowing things.

'Yes.'

There was only the tiniest crack in Cass's voice as she said this, but Delphine enveloped her in a hug anyway. 'Oh, honey,' she said.

Cass stayed there for a few moments and then freed herself. 'I knew he had friends here. And word of an archaeological site like that is bound to get around, even when there's no internet or telephones.'

'Quite right,' said Delphine. 'And everyone who gets to hear about it will turn up at Bastian's house expecting a meal.' Delphine didn't seem put out by this. Cass reckoned it must be a fairly frequent occurrence. 'Peel me some yams? Just as well Bastian has plenty of provisions.'

Cass knew that 'provisions' also meant the starchy vegetables, including yams, sweet potatoes and dasheen. Amongst similar things, these were the backbone of Caribbean food. With them at hand, meals could be made to stretch.

* * *

Becca was the life and soul of the party, thought Cass a little later, although there were four archaeologists in all. Of course she and Bastian knew each other and chattered away about mutual friends and how they had fared in the hurricane.

Becca was also very attractive, thought Cass, with short, dark hair, elegantly cut, making her look a little French. And while she had been outdoors, grubbing in the earth, doing whatever archaeologists did, she still managed to look professional and quite smart. She was supremely knowledgeable about everything, it seemed to Cass, with interesting things to say about every subject likely to fascinate Bastian, Austin and of course Ranulph.

She and 'Ran', as she called him, had obviously known each other very well. Cass found this so upsetting that she could barely look at Ranulph, dreading to see love in his eyes when he looked at her.

'He wouldn't have gone away if he loved her so much,' said Delphine, reading Cass's mind as they scraped plates in the kitchen before getting out the fruit course. 'Don't worry about her, girl.'

'I don't care about Ranulph; he and I are just travelling companions,' she wanted to say but couldn't. Delphine would know she was lying anyway.

Cass was desperate not to engage in conversation and wouldn't have joined everyone at the table if Delphine hadn't said 'Sit down and eat your dinner' in a very strict way. It was all she could do to look pleasant and not pick at her food like a heartsick teenager.

'So, Cass,' said Becca pleasantly, 'how do you come to be in Dominica so soon after a hurricane? I would have known if you'd been here before.' She laughed. 'The grapevine works well in Dominica!'

'Well,' said Cass. 'It's a bit of a complicated story —' She might have imagined that she saw Becca's eyes glaze over. 'To cut it short, my father was friends with Bastian's father and so when we heard there'd been a hurricane, we came out to help.'

'Great!' Becca paused, obviously framing her question in her mind. 'And what did — I mean — what special skills did you bring with you?' She smiled warmly and her teeth looked very white against her tan.

'Cass has been invaluable,' said Bastian quickly. 'I don't know what we'd have done without her. She can throw my pick-up around our roads like a local —'

'And she can cook,' said Delphine.

'And she sewed my leg up,' said Ranulph, giving Cass a look which made her heart leap and then subside again.

'She's also very good at map-drawing,' said Austin, 'although she does sometimes make mistakes.'

'I didn't make any mistakes, Austin,' Cass said firmly. She hoped she sounded convincing. She hadn't made a mistake; she had deliberately altered the map.

'I never did get to see the original,' Austin went on.

'I'm afraid it completely disintegrated,' said Cass.

'I threw it away,' said Delphine. 'There's enough paper in this house that you can read without keeping the scraps.'

None of this was true. Cass still had the original

map, hidden in the secret pocket in her daypack, along with a copy of the new map and her drawing of that particular part of the forest.

Becca was looking intrigued. Ranulph told her the story of the petroglyph.

'The map was of where Bastian's father thought it was,' he finished.

'He never saw it himself,' said Bastian after shooting a cross look at Austin. 'But he met a man who used to pass it every day on his way to his garden which was a little bit of land he'd cleared. He tended it every day. This man drew a map which he gave to my father when he heard he was interested in the petroglyph.' He paused. 'Years ago, my father and Cass's father went to look for it.'

Cass broke in. 'Somehow the map ended up with my father's things. He was horrified when he realised he had it, and asked me to bring it to Bastian. Then there was the hurricane.'

'And before you ask,' said Austin, 'we took the map and looked for the petroglyph and it wasn't there. Probably never had been.'

'What a shame,' said Becca, who, thought Cass, was looking at everyone as if trying to work out what was going on.

'Not from my point of view,' said Austin, happy to take centre stage. 'I have a book due to be delivered to my publisher soon. I just needed to clear up a couple of details. Which I have now done, but of course I can't get off this bloody island!' He laughed, as if he was joking, but no one was convinced. Cass noticed that he had also failed to mention that there was a large prize going for research writings about early Caribbean peoples, and that Bastian's own extended paper was also eligible.

'So now we've established the facts,' Austin continued, 'I'm trying to find out when there'll be flights off the island. I need to get home to the States.'

'Possibly not for months,' said Delphine.

'I can't wait months!' Austin protested. 'I'm on a deadline.'

'So leave the way you arrived,' said Delphine with a shrug. 'On a fishing boat.'

Austin shook his head. 'No way! I was so sick I wanted to die.'

'Well, if you can't fly and you won't go on a boat, what are you going to do?' asked Bastian.

Austin shrugged. 'I plan to get to Roseau. There might be someone with a private plane who could give me a lift.'

'But the airport is on this end of the island,' said Ranulph. 'Roseau is over a mountain and on the other side.'

'I reckon the money — and so the private jets and helicopters — are where the capital is,' said Austin.

'He's right,' said Delphine. 'There are places where helicopters land or take off. They take rich people to see the Boiling Lake.'

'We walked to the Boiling Lake,' said Becca. 'Do you remember, Ran? All those years ago. It was some hike! Took all day but it ended with that amazing swim in Titou Gorge.'

'It was one of the highlights of my visit,' said Ranulph. Cass couldn't avoid seeing the warmth in his eyes as he reminisced.

'It is such an amazing place,' Becca went on. 'All that bubbling sulphurous mud.'

'So there are helicopters on the island at the

moment?' asked Austin.

Delphine shrugged dramatically. 'How can we possibly know? All the rich people may have got into their choppers and fled when they heard a hurricane was on its way.'

'But they might have come back,' suggested Bastian, possibly horrified at the thought of being trapped with Austin for months. 'Without any regular flights, there would be money to be made getting people off the island.'

'That would be fine by me,' said Austin. 'It would be expensive, but worth it.'

'You know,' said Becca thoughtfully, 'I did hear of someone with a small plane taking people who can afford to pay. He only goes with a full load though. That might be another possibility.'

'Hallelujah! There is a way out of this godforsaken place!' said Austin. Then, obviously realising just how rude he had been, he said, 'Dominica is beautiful, of course, but I need a bit more civilisation.'

There was a short pause and then Ranulph started talking about the archaeological site and Cass tuned out.

While before her feelings for Ranulph were painful but bearable, now she felt she was about to witness him falling in love — or back in love — with a woman who was genuinely suitable for him. Could she tolerate it? Should she leave as soon as she could? With Austin, possibly?

It's just a crush, she told herself. You've fallen for a good-looking, slightly older man. It was bound to happen. It doesn't mean anything and my feelings won't last. She took a breath that was almost a sob and hastily sipped some water to disguise the sound.

He wouldn't have fallen in love with you, anyway, she told herself, even if this Becca from his past hadn't turned up.

⋆ ⋆ ⋆

After dinner, everyone drifted on to the veranda apart from Delphine and Cass, who cleared up. Then Delphine cut up some limes, filled a jug of water, and put glasses on a tray. Then she got out a bottle of rum and a bowl of sugar.

'I'm off home now,' she said. 'I'll be back, but after breakfast. Will you be able to cope? Everyone can make their own breakfast if you can't.'

Cass took out the drinks tray and then the glasses. Bastian had disappeared into his study and Austin was sitting a little way away. When everyone had what they wanted, she took her drink and sat next to Austin. She had made a decision.

'Keep me up to date about your plans to leave, won't you? I want to leave too. I realise it will be expensive, but if I could borrow the money from you, I can get it back from my father as soon as we're near an internet connection.'

Austin sipped his drink and looked at her, making her feel very uncomfortable. 'Why is that? I thought you liked it here.'

Cass realised she should have anticipated this response and had a reply ready. Friendly came up to her and she was able to gain some time while she fondled his ears. 'I don't think I'm needed here.'

'What about your boyfriend?'

'He's not my boyfriend!' Cass replied, more vehemently than she meant to. 'We're just travelling companions. He's a friend of my father's. And it will be easier for just two of us to leave than three — if we're to try to get a lift on a private plane.'

'That's true, and maybe it will be easier for me to do that if I have a pretty girl with me.' Austin looked at her, his eyes roving over her in a calculating way.

She wasn't dressed remotely provocatively. She'd hardly looked in a mirror since she'd arrived, and although she had washed her hair in cold water, she'd just let it dry in the sun. It would be sticking out at all sorts of stray angles. She didn't know if she could even find the small amount of make-up she'd brought with her and she was wearing combat shorts which were incredibly grubby. With a pair of very battered trainers on her feet she looked like a Boy Scout at the end of a long jamboree. She certainly didn't feel pretty.

His words made Cass feel uncomfortable and the thought of travelling with him made her shiver. She also found the thought of being Austin's 'pretty girl' demeaning.

'Yes,' said Austin. 'I think us teaming up is a very good idea.'

'I haven't definitely decided —'

'There's nothing for you here, Cass. Don't make yourself look like an idiot.' Then he walked to the drinks table and helped himself to more rum.

Cass went back to the kitchen and poured herself some water, grateful it was in plentiful supply because of the huge tanks to collect rainwater, put there when the house was built. Now, as she sipped from her glass, she heard Bastian's pick-up drive off. He never seemed to rest, Cass thought.

She went back to the end of the long veranda. She

didn't want to join Ranulph, Becca and the others up the other end but was reluctant to go to bed. The air was warm and the gentle swish of the waves was soothing. And the stars shone like a million torches, bright, illuminating.

From there, one could only see the sea, and in the distance the island of Marie-Galante. There was no trace of the destruction the hurricane had left behind it. Everything was calm. But surely it was time for Bastian's guests to go home?

Ranulph came up behind where Cass was sitting. He made her jump. 'Bastian kindly took the other archaeologists to where they're living but Becca is going to stay the night. I was wondering if you could lend her some things?'

Cass forced herself to swallow the great lump of resentment this request caused. 'Won't the people she's staying with be worried about her if she doesn't go home?' She hoped her grumpiness didn't show. It was bad enough feeling so devastated — she didn't want Ranulph to guess how she felt.

Ranulph seemed confused. 'Of course not. The others will let them know where she is.'

'Oh, yes.' Cass forced a smile. 'You've had a good evening?'

Way to go, Cass, she thought. She sounded as if she was delighted for Ranulph and Becca.

He smiled, obviously pleased. 'It's been great to catch up. So much has happened since Becca and I were last together.'

His obvious happiness showed he was completely unaware that his words made Cass feel they were tearing into her flesh.

'Of course,' she said. 'It's great Becca found you.'

'Ah! She was more interested in the archaeological site. I just happened to be there.'

'Oh, she seems pretty glad to see you too. And why not? Come and let's see what she needs.'

Ranulph followed her into their shared bedroom, which for now, was also a storeroom. Cass got out her rucksack. 'What do you think she wants?'

'Something to sleep in. Toiletries. Nothing much.'

'I have a spare T-shirt. Some shorts. My soap and toothpaste are already in the bathroom. I'm not prepared to share my toothbrush.' She smiled to prove she was perfectly happy to give Becca anything else she required.

'One other thing — I've told Becca she can sleep in here with you. I'll sleep on the veranda. She said she'd feel nervous sleeping more or less in the open.'

Cass's irritation turned into rashness. 'Tell her that I'll sleep on the veranda. You stay here. It's better for your leg and I'll be fine.' She paused. 'You can have more time to 'catch up'.'

Ranulph frowned and took the bundle Cass handed to him. 'Are you sure you won't be nervous?'

Cass tossed her head. 'What is there to be nervous about? Anyway, I'm sure Friendly will keep me company.'

14

Cass didn't feel generous enough to lend Becca her sleeping bag. If she was going to sleep under the stars — or more accurately under the roof of the veranda — she'd need the very high-end pure down sleeping bag that her mother had bought her years ago and which she loved.

In spite of her bold statements, Cass knew that she might well feel anxious about strange noises when she was sleeping outdoors, and she decided rum was the answer. She went into the kitchen and found the bottle that Delphine kept there for anyone who was cooking. She poured herself a large measure, added the lime slices left over from earlier, and a large spoon of sugar.

She leant against the wide teak rail as she looked out to sea and sipped her drink. Austin came up to her. 'So, it must be tough for you having Becca here.'

Instantly she was on the defensive. 'Not really.'

'No? She and Ranulph obviously have a real connection.'

'Maybe, but it's nothing to do with me.'

'You don't need to pretend with me, kid.'

Neither of them spoke for a minute or two.

'So were you serious when you said you'd come with me when I leave Dominica?'

Cass shrugged. The island was so beautiful, in spite of the hurricane. There was still work to do, and while Ranulph would never be hers, not now Becca was on the scene, was being near him enough? Or should she take her pride and her backpack and leave as soon as she could?

'I need to think about it some more,' she said at last.

'Well, don't take too much time over it. I'm off as soon as I get the chance. I want to get my book in; the deadline is very close. That's why I came here the moment the hurricane was over.'

Bastian had the same deadline as Austin, Cass realised. How near was he to completing his work? Austin would have been working on his project until he'd set off for Dominica and would carry on with it the moment he was back, but Bastian would have put his community before his work so his deadline would be even tighter than Austin's, even if they were roughly at the same stage when the hurricane struck. If she could help Bastian, she definitely should.

'I'll sleep on it,' Cass said. 'I'll tell you my decision tomorrow.'

She watched him go back to the group and then took her drink to the part of the veranda where she would be sleeping.

Cass didn't want to waste the powerful effect of her drink and the moment she started to get sleepy she settled herself in her spot on the veranda. It was a little way away from where the others were still talking. Their voices would be a calming background noise and she would sleep soundly, she told herself sternly. It would be lovely waking up with the birds. She would feel happy and in tune with nature and the world around her. She wouldn't care about Ranulph and Becca and she certainly wouldn't wonder what they might be getting up to in the storeroom.

The more logical part of her brain said that Ranulph had a bad leg, the beds were extremely narrow and he and Becca hadn't seen each other for years.

Delighted to find someone else sleeping where he usually slept, Friendly took advantage of Cass's good nature and snuggled up next to her. Cass, soothed by low voices, the sound of the sea and strong drink, did manage to drop off to sleep quite quickly. She awoke shortly afterwards, aware of Friendly sitting bolt upright, listening. Then a few moments later, she heard a vehicle. It was Bastian's pick-up. Friendly jumped off the wide seat and went to welcome his master home.

'What are you doing here?' Bastian said quietly, seeing her on the veranda. 'Is Ranulph snoring?'

Cass shook her head. 'No — at least I don't think so. He does snore a bit but that's not why I'm here.'

'So why?'

Caught off-guard by this question, Cass suddenly felt tears pricking her eyes. 'Becca is staying. She didn't want to sleep on the veranda so I offered her my space.'

'That's very generous of you!'

'It's not a problem — really. In fact, this seat is wider than the camp beds we're sleeping on.'

'Well, it was designed to be able to accommodate guests should they need it.' Bastian laughed. 'The rum punches can be powerful.'

'Especially the kind Delphine makes. I made a sort of pet't punch for myself.'

Bastian seemed in no hurry to get to his own bed.

'Can I make you a hot drink? Or a snack?' said Cass.

'No thank you to a snack, I had one with Toussaint's family. We were planning a visit to the petroglyph.'

'Oh, that is exciting!' Cass was delighted at the thought that he might find the petroglyph while she was still there. 'Some cocoa then?'

'I'd love that. Do you know how to make it? I don't want cocoa-tea. I want cocoa like my father used to make it.'

'With condensed milk, like my father likes his?'

He nodded.

'Will you have a drop of rum in it?'

'It's part of the tradition!' said Bastian. 'I've never met anyone who understood that before.'

'Our dads obviously shared more than just the petroglyph,' said Cass.

She took trouble over Bastian's cocoa and enjoyed making it. He always did so much for others, now especially, that it was nice to have the opportunity to do something — even such a small thing — for him. She made enough for two.

When she got back out, Bastian was sitting gazing out to sea. Moonlight filled the veranda, dimming the stars and adding mystery to the night.

He sat up and smiled. But in spite of his apparent good spirits when he arrived home, Cass was aware that now, he wasn't his usual positive self.

'What's up?'

'It's proving hard to find an opportunity to go on our search. I don't want to take anyone other than Toussaint because I know I can trust him. He isn't so fond of gossip as some of the locals. But he has lots of calls on his time, especially now.'

'And you still need a photo? Proof the petroglyph exists.'

'Yes. I need to see it with my own eyes, too.'

Cass sipped her cocoa. 'I wish there was some way

I could help.'

'There is.' Bastian paused. 'I wondered whether you could help me with my paper — well, it's a book really. It's almost long enough for a book.'

'But how?'

'With drawings? I can draw up to a point but I'm very short of time. My research carries on from my father's and he did stick men, more or less, to illustrate his work. But if you could turn them into flesh and blood people, with plants and trees we recognise, that would be a huge help.' He paused. 'If — when — I get a publisher, I wouldn't be expected to illustrate the book myself so there'd be no problem with you doing them.'

Cass felt overwhelmed for a few moments. 'You want me to illustrate your paper?'

'Yes. Why are you so surprised? Your drawing abilities are superb.'

Cass didn't reply immediately. 'No one has ever had that sort of faith in me before.'

'What do you mean?'

'My family see me as a bit of a failure, the family joke, the one who gets into trouble, does silly things and won't amount to anything.'

'That sounds very unfair.'

'I was very loved, but no one ever expected me to be successful. They're all very academic, you see. I was considered good at art at school, but compared to Latin and Greek, art didn't amount to much. Drawing wasn't considered useful. Dad is only interested in photography, although he does think I have a good eye.'

'It's a shame. And I'd be thrilled if you'd illustrate my work. You have just the right blend of accuracy and artistic interpretation. All the plants you drew —'

'I had no idea of what any of them were.'

'But I knew what they were. You are really good at drawing, Cass, no matter what anyone else has made you believe.'

'It would be an honour to help.'

'It would make the whole difference to the project. My father's drawings are very . . . dull really. At the moment they look as if they were copied from an old-fashioned museum exhibit — they look wooden.'

'I'm not sure I could do any better.'

'I know you can. But if you want to go home, we can forget it.'

'Not at all!' Cass was excited. It would be a challenge, obviously, but she loved the thought of being able to do something for Bastian, who did so much for others. It would be great to have something important to occupy her time. 'I can give it a go tomorrow, see how I get on?'

'That would be perfect! It would bring the whole paper to life.' The moonlight caught his smile. 'I am glad you came, Cass. You're making this difficult situation a lot easier.'

He went to bed shortly after that, but Cass stayed awake for a while. In her heart she knew she didn't want to go home, she just wanted to be doing something that didn't involve mooning after Ranulph and his old flame — or whatever Becca was.

Just before she drifted back to sleep she remembered she'd have to tell Austin she didn't want to leave with him after all. She'd have to find an excuse for changing her mind.

* * *

'How was it, sleeping on the veranda?' Ranulph was standing there with a cup of something that steamed. He handed it to her. 'You weren't nervous?'

Cass sat up indignantly and took the mug. 'Of course not!' she said, forgetting the couple of times when she'd been startled awake by something loud cracking and how frightened she'd been, until she realised it was the branch of a tree falling and was nothing to worry about.

She sipped the cocoa-tea. 'It's lovely out here. The sea breeze keeps off the midges,' she said. 'How did you and Becca sleep?' Then she wished she hadn't asked. Her question seemed to imply that Ranulph and Becca were sharing a bed.

'Fine. My leg hardly hurts any more. Becca changed the dressing. It's healing well.'

Of course it was fine for someone else to change Ranulph's dressing, but Cass still felt possessive about it. She forced a smile. 'Let me know when you've finished with the room and I'll go and get dressed.'

Cass realised she'd have to stop feeling so jealous when she discovered Becca in the kitchen, helping Delphine, and doing it far more efficiently than she had been doing up to now.

'Hi, Cass!' said Becca brightly. 'It was so kind of you to give up your bed last night. I would have been fine sleeping on the veranda but Ranulph insisted.'

As Ranulph wasn't there to deny this, Cass just smiled. 'Did you manage without a sleeping bag?'

'Ranulph gave me his and he found another old one. Now, what do you want to eat? I'm making banana fritters, although we haven't got eggs.'

Cass found herself sitting at the table being treated like a guest by Ranulph's old — and possibly revived — flame.

Austin came in. He looked pink and damp, full of beans and ready for the day. 'Hi there!' he said.

'Hi,' said Cass, far less enthusiastically, although his greeting had been directed at Becca.

'For an archaeologist you look as if you're handy in the kitchen!' said Austin to Becca.

Becca laughed. 'Well, officially I'm an archaeologist, yes, but currently I'm a short-order breakfast chef. What can I get you?'

'Are there eggs? Over easy with bacon?' said Austin.

'No eggs,' said Becca, still in a friendly tone, although she probably realised Austin hadn't been joking. Surely he must know there were no eggs or bacon available at present? 'Banana pancakes?'

'That's what's on the menu,' said Cass, liking Becca a little bit more.

'I'm getting mighty fed up with bananas,' Austin said irritably.

Ranulph joined the group, and later, Bastian, yawning a little. Delphine made coffee. Becca came and sat down.

'So, Cass, you going to leave with me?' said Austin after a little while.

Cass, who hadn't been focusing on the conversation, sat up. 'Er —'

'You never said anything to me,' said Ranulph, looking startled.

'Why don't we talk about it after breakfast?' said Cass to Austin. 'Ranulph and I need to chat first.' She gave a little smile, implying that Ranulph had some say over her actions.

Cass was hoping she'd be able to tell Austin that Ranulph had made some irrefutable argument about why she couldn't go. She didn't want to tell Austin she was staying so she could do drawings for Bastian's paper. Apart from drawing the map, Austin didn't know her skills went way beyond that. And she knew, as sure as night follows day, that he would try to stop her if he found out.

* * *

The washing up didn't take long with Becca efficiently drying up and finding where things went. Cass realised that Becca had been in Dominica a long time and knew far more about it than she ever would.

'So,' said Becca, addressing Delphine, who'd just come in. 'Does Bastian have a partner?'

Delphine laughed. 'Everyone always wants to know that. But don't get your hopes up. He has a lady friend in Barbados, and they visit. She won't come and live here, and he won't go and live there, but it works fine.'

Becca laughed back. 'I was only asking. A girl likes to know these things.'

Cass had wanted to know those things too but hadn't liked to ask. Maybe Becca had her uses, she thought. It was only a bit later that she wondered why Becca wanted to know about Bastian if she and Ranulph were more than just old friends.

15

Ranulph and Becca had gone down to the archaeological site on the beach, so Cass was alone when Austin found her sweeping the veranda later that morning.

'Can we get this clear, Cass?' he said. 'Do you want to come with me or not? We need to set off soon as we don't know how long it will take us to get to Roseau. Or even how to get there.'

'Actually, I've changed my mind.' She smiled apologetically. 'I realise there are still things I can do here.'

Austin frowned. 'To be honest, I have never been quite sure what you were doing here.'

Cass realised she should have worked out an answer to this obvious question before. 'Oh,' she said, flapping her hand. 'It's all to do with my father. He's a quite well-known photographer.'

As Cass had hoped, this mention of fame distracted Austin.

'Oh?' he said. 'Should I have heard of him?'

'I don't know about 'should',' said Cass. 'He's Howard Blakely?'

Austin shook his head. 'Never heard of him. Probably because he's English.'

'Oh, well, it's because of him that I'm here, and it's because of him I've decided to stay.' She paused. 'I don't want to disappoint him.'

'Why would he be disappointed?'

Cass wished she'd thought of something else to say,

but having started down this route she had to continue. 'Because I'm his daughter?'

'Yes?'

'Well, he asked me to do something.'

'What?'

Austin knew about the petroglyph and the map but not that Bastian had asked her to illustrate his academic paper, the one that was in direct competition with Austin's own entry for the prize. She had to keep this secret.

'There's been a hurricane, Austin! My father would think I should take what pictures I can of the devastation and, generally, stay to help.'

'I'm just wondering how useful you are, actually.'

'That's a bit unfair. I've driven Bastian's pick-up everywhere locally which has been really useful. Not to mention sewing up Ranulph's leg. I've achieved a lot.' She suspected she sounded like a teenager being questioned on how much revision she'd done. Then, more truthfully, she said, 'I want my father to be proud of me!'

She looked up at Austin briefly. It was true that she didn't want to disappoint Howard, but staying to help Bastian was a more powerful reason. Her father would definitely want her to do that.

* * *

Austin brought the subject up again at lunch. Bastian wasn't there but Ranulph and Becca were, as well as another couple of the archaeologists she knew. As Cass helped Delphine get things on the table, Delphine told her that the new member of the archaeology team had brought a box of solar lanterns and paraffin for local people.

'So they're not freeloadin' on Bastian, like some people I could mention.' She looked pointedly at Austin.

Cass could easily understand why Delphine hadn't taken to Austin. He tended to treat everyone like staff, as if they were there to look after him. Although Delphine had put him right on this matter early on, he still persisted on treating Bastian's house like a hotel.

When everyone was seated and the bottle of hot sauce was going round the table, Austin turned to Ranulph. 'Do you know why Cass has changed her mind about leaving the island with me?'

Ranulph put down his fork. 'You're staying, Cass? That's great news.'

'I thought you two were going to discuss it,' Austin persisted, obviously trying to make trouble between Cass and Ranulph. 'I'd have thought you'd be pleased to think she was returning to civilisation sooner than you thought.'

There was an awkward pause and then Becca said, 'She's a free agent. She doesn't have to discuss all her decisions with either of you.'

'Did your father — this Howard someone — ask Ranulph to look after you, Cass?' said Austin. 'Is that why you've changed your mind about leaving?'

'No!' said Cass, although Howard had more or less placed Cass in Ranulph's care. 'I don't need a man to look after me. Which century are we living in?'

'Victorian times, obviously,' said Becca. 'But don't worry! Think of all those intrepid female travellers there were then.'

Austin narrowed his eyes in thought, making Cass wonder what he was up to.

* * *

Cass spent that night on the veranda again, thinking about how she was going to illustrate Bastian's paper and wondering why Austin was so keen for her to travel with him. He'd had another little go at her about it in the evening. Was it really because he thought she'd be able to make it easier for him to get a lift in a plane?

Or, and this she felt was much more likely, was it that he wanted to get her away from Bastian's house because he suspected her of helping him? She'd thought for a while that he had a horrible way of knowing what no one had told him.

He would probably abandon her in Roseau if he could, and get on the first plane that had room for him. A space for one was far more likely than for two and he wasn't the sort of man who would step aside and say, 'You first.'

* * *

The next morning, Becca was coming out of the bathroom as Cass was on her way in.

'Hi, Cass!' she said brightly. 'It was so kind of you to lend me things so I could stay these couple of nights but you'll be glad to hear that the whole group are coming over to help with the dig and we've found a house to rent. It's had a bit of damage from the hurricane, but our lads will fix it up in no time.'

She then handed Cass her moisturiser, which Cass hadn't realised she had. 'I hope I haven't used too much. But I'm about ten years older than you — a year younger than Ranulph in fact. My need is greater than yours!'

Cass entered the bathroom, which smelt of Ranulph's deodorant, wondering if Becca was giving her a message. If she was, its meaning was clear: she was too young for Ranulph.

* * *

After breakfast, Cass had hoped to catch Ranulph before he set off with Becca but Austin waylaid her. Cass watched Ranulph and Becca setting off down the beach together, talking intently. Ranulph was hardly limping now, and although Cass mentally took the credit for this, just now she was taking no pleasure in it.

'I think you're making a big mistake, Cass,' said Austin, holding her arm. 'I get that you want to make your dad proud and all, but really? Do you want to watch Becca and Ran making sheep's eyes at each other?'

'They haven't been doing that,' said Cass.

'It won't be long before they do,' said Austin.

For once, Cass found herself agreeing with him. She sighed.

'You don't have to decide right away. But as soon as I find a way to leave — and no, I'm not going to walk to Roseau like the locals — I'm out of here. You'd do well to be with me.' He paused. 'I'm going to join them at the dig now. There might be something there that could add a finishing touch to my work.' He gave her smile, cold but determined. 'I'm going to win that prize. You may as well get used to the idea.'

* * *

As she hadn't heard Bastian's pick-up drive off, Cass had hopes of finding him in the outhouse. And there he was, mixing up food for Friendly, who was thumping his tail against the floor from time to time. Friendly got up when he saw Cass.

After a suitable amount of time fussing the dog, Cass said, 'We have a bit of a problem.'

'We have many. Which one do you want to talk about?' Bastian gave the waiting dog a biscuit and regarded Cass.

She cleared her throat. 'I think maybe I should leave with Austin . . .' She didn't want to tell him that part of the reason was because of Ranulph and Becca getting together, and trusted that he wouldn't ask. 'But not until I've done the drawings. I'll work as quickly as I can but of course we don't know when Austin will leave. That's the first problem.'

'I didn't know there was a list . . .'

Cass smiled briefly. 'Sorry, I didn't know either, until I started. But there are only two items on it.' Bastian didn't say anything so Cass went on. 'Where can I do the work? If Austin finds out what I'm up to he'll make it difficult, or impossible. You must be aware how fixated he is on this prize. He'll do anything to sabotage your chances.'

Bastian nodded. 'You can use my study. There's a lock on the door.'

Cass shook her head. 'It wouldn't be hard for Austin to find out I was in there, even if I locked the door. And if I did lock the door I'd be forever worrying that Austin was going to start banging on it.'

Bastian didn't speak but nodded.

'But the harder problem is how are we going to keep Austin here so I've got time to finish? If he finds a way out, he won't wait for me.'

'And why are you so keen to go with him? Don't you like it here?' Bastian smiled to indicate he wasn't really offended.

'I love it here,' said Cass seriously. 'There's always going to be a big place in my heart for Dominica, no matter what happens.'

Bastian smiled. 'I guessed you felt like that about it. I wish everyone felt like you. So why do you want to leave?'

'Bastian! Haven't you thought about this? When Austin leaves, he'll take his completed — or nearly completed — work with him and get it to the judges of the prize before the deadline.'

Bastian sighed. 'I have been thinking about how to get my entry in on time. But with the hurricane and all I couldn't make it a priority.'

'But you have to! Otherwise Austin, or some other entrant, will win the money. If I leave with Austin I can take your paper with me. Get it to the judges!'

Bastian didn't speak immediately. 'That would be a very big thing to do for Dominica, Cass. I would be very grateful.'

'And?' For once Bastian's relaxed, thoughtful manner was driving Cass mad.

'I think we should take a walk along to Delphine's house.'

'I wouldn't want to intrude on her free time —'

'She'll be happy to see us. Come, Friendly,' he said, and they set off.

'Where does Delphine live?' said Cass after they seemed to have been walking quite a way. She was keen to get going on the drawings while she knew Austin was occupied at the dig.

'Not far now.' He stopped and pointed to a collection of small buildings just above a small cove.

'Oh, wow,' said Cass, when she had taken in what a wonderful position the property was in. 'The views must be outstanding!'

'They are. The property was left to them by the family who had once owned them.'

Cass swallowed. She knew, in theory, about slavery, but it was a shock to hear it mentioned openly.

'Although then the property wouldn't have been worth much. Now, it's prime real estate. Delphine and her family rent out little cabins that look out to sea —'

'Oh!' said Cass. 'I see! They won't have guests, so, if the buildings are still standing, there might be one I could work in.'

'Exactly that. Delphine's brother has a garage on the site. He keeps my pick-up on the road. But he's been busy putting the house back together recently.'

They walked on for a couple of moments and then arrived at a courtyard with buildings around it. Some were stone but a couple of them were traditional wooden buildings on stilts.

Delphine came out to meet them. 'Hey, Baz!' she said. 'What you doin' here?' Her lazy tone belied her smile of welcome.

'I've brought Cass with me. We have a big favour to ask.'

'I bet it involves that Austin!'

Cass nodded. 'He's such a nosy parker. I have work to do for — er, Baz, without Austin knowing about it.'

'You want to borrow a cabin?'

'Rent one,' said Cass, aware that the cabins were how the family earned their money.

Delphine shook her head. 'There are no cabins to rent,' she said firmly. 'But you can certainly borrow one.' She threw up her hands. 'Don't even think about arguin' with me!'

Cass laughed. 'OK!'

A young man emerged from a building. He was wearing a boiler suit up to his waist, the top tied with the sleeves. 'This is me brother Errol,' said Delphine.

Errol nodded at Cass and then said, 'Hey, Baz. Pickup need something? I've got another one waiting to be repaired.'

'Who does that belong to?' asked Bastian, looking interested suddenly.

'Me,' said the young man. 'I'll do it up and sell it on.'

Something suddenly struck Cass. 'How long will it take you to do up?'

'I won't be getting round to it for a while, till this place is fixed up.' He indicated the buildings around him.

'But when you start? How long then?' asked Cass.

Errol shrugged. 'About a week.'

'That could be perfect!' said Cass.

Bastian looked at Cass. 'Are you thinking what I'm thinking?'

'You're both thinking that Austin will buy Errol's car to get to Roseau, aren't you?' said Delphine. 'But you don't want him going immediately?'

Cass nodded. 'That's right.' Bastian then explained about the drawings.

'How much will you want for the pick-up, Errol?' asked Delphine.

Errol named a sum. 'I know it's a lot but it'll be a good vehicle and pick-ups are scarce as hen's teeth now.'

'I'm sure Austin could afford to pay that much,' said Bastian.

'But will he have that much cash?' asked Cass.

'Well, if he doesn't we'll just rent it to him. He doesn't want to take it off the island,' said Delphine. 'We can pick it up from Roseau later.'

'Genius, Sis!' said Errol with a broad grin. 'Let's get him round here and convince him he wants to buy it.'

'But not when I'm here somewhere drawing!' said Cass, wondering if her good idea was already a bust.

'The cabin I have in mind is a little way away from here,' said Delphine.

'Where is this Austin now?' asked Errol.

'He was with Becca and Ranulph at the site on the beach. I think he wants to add details about Dutch pirates and the Kalinago people to his book,' said Cass. Bastian grimaced.

'Aren't you tempted to add that in yourself, Bastian?' she asked.

He shook his head. 'My paper is pretty much written. My focus is on the Kalinago who came earlier than the ones who left traces on the beach. I just need to do the last section, where I left off before the hurricane hit.'

As they walked back to Bastian's house Cass said, 'Austin seems very keen that I should leave when he does.'

'I think I can guess why,' said Bastian. 'He's muttered things to me about having help. I don't think he was referring to Delphine.'

Cass took a few moments to digest this. 'He doesn't know I can draw, does he?'

'I don't think so, but he's very good at truffling out

anything and everything. He could have got Becca to tell him things. Ranulph might have mentioned it to her. But the thing is, we — you — need to get the drawings done as soon as possible. Could you do it in a week, do you think?'

'I don't know how many drawings you need me to do.'

'I can reduce the number if I have to.'

Cass grinned suddenly. She was being given a responsible job at last and she would love the challenge!

16

Neither of them were surprised to see Austin on the veranda waiting for them when they got back.

'Where have you been?' he asked as they joined him.

'Visiting Delphine's family,' said Bastian.

'She's been asking me to visit for a while,' said Cass, untruthfully, 'but I waited until Bastian was able to come with me. I would never have found it otherwise.'

'So where's Delphine now?' asked Austin.

'At home,' said Cass. 'It's her day off.'

Austin's face fell. 'Oh. What about lunch?'

Cass took a breath, about to tell him off for being so demanding and entitled but was spared because Ranulph and Becca appeared. They seemed to take in the situation.

'Hey, Cass,' said Becca. 'Shall we get some lunch on the table? I know we should leave it to the guys, but I'm hungry!'

In the kitchen, Becca apologised. 'Sorry for roping you in but I reckon if you feed Austin, and let him get at the rum, he's less of a pain.'

As they found bread, vegetables they could make salad with, and fish, Cass realised that Becca was a nice woman. If Ranulph fell back in love with her, she couldn't blame him. And she, Cass, probably was too young for him. It was a pity her heart didn't agree with her head: her head had all the answers.

* * *

'What have you been up to this morning, Cass?' asked Ranulph. 'Surely not cooking?'

Cass shook her head. 'I made the salad, but Becca did most of everything else.'

'We went to see Delphine's place,' said Bastian. 'And while we were there, we saw her brother. He's the guy who keeps my pick-up on the road.'

'There's nothing wrong with it, is there?' asked Becca.

'No,' said Bastian. 'But he told us he's got a pick-up there he's doing up.'

Austin was suddenly listening. 'Oh?'

'Yes,' said Bastian. 'I thought that might interest you, Austin.'

'Is he willing to sell it?' Austin asked.

'He is,' said Bastian. 'But he'll want a lot of money. Pick-ups like mine are scarce, and particularly useful just now.'

'How much?'

Bastian quoted the figure. 'And he'll want cash.'

Austin shrugged in a way that made Cass think he'd arrived, not with useful supplies, aid to a hurricane-torn country, but with wads of bank notes, probably dollars. And he must have had a lot of cash if he was planning to hire a private plane — potentially for only two seats.

An hour later, Cass was calmly sipping her herbal tea, looking out to sea, wondering when she could get to work on the illustrations, when Austin's voice cut through to her.

'What have you got planned for this afternoon, Cass?'

Why did the bloody man always have to catch her out? What would be a good answer? Nothing came to mind. 'I might just chill out here.' The moment the words were out of her mouth Cass realised they made her sound as if she was here on holiday, not on a rescue mission.

'That's unlike you. You're usually such a busy little bee.'

Cass smiled to conceal her grinding teeth. He was so patronising! 'I know,' she said, annoyed, 'that's why I think I need a bit of downtime.'

Bastian, possibly hearing Austin's voice, appeared on the veranda just then.

'Do you want to come and meet Errol, Austin? See how long the pick-up will take to repair? Negotiate a price?'

'Maybe I should,' Austin replied. 'You could come with us, Cass. You said you didn't have anything to do.'

'Actually, Cass,' said Bastian. 'If you're not busy it would be really handy if you could take an inventory of the stores.'

Cass was a little confused. 'Which stores?'

'The ones in my study,' he said. 'I'm having to keep the door locked in case of looters, but it would be good to know what we've got.'

Cass smiled at Bastian, but then hoped it wasn't too warm a smile; he had given her the perfect excuse. 'I'll be on to it,' she said. 'I'll just give Ranulph and Becca a hand in the kitchen. With the washing up,' she added, with a look at Austin that was almost a glare.

With Bastian and Austin off the premises, Cass rushed through the washing up. Ranulph came into the kitchen to dry up while Becca put everything away.

'I hardly see you these days, Cass,' he complained. 'Are you OK?'

Cass usually avoided looking at Ranulph as she was worried she might blush or look awkward but this time she didn't. 'I'm getting on with things, Ranulph. I'm absolutely fine.'

Ranulph nodded. 'Good.'

'Right!' said Becca. 'That's the kitchen sorted. Let's go down to the dig, Ran. I won't be here too much longer.'

'I'm going to miss you, Becca!' said Cass, and realised it was true.

Once certain that everyone was out of the house, Cass took out the key that Bastian had given her. She planned to see how many drawings he needed, and to calculate roughly how long it would take her to do them. She just hoped it would be the same time as it took Errol to repair a pick-up.

She had found the file and looked at the pictures that Bastian wanted redrawn, the ones in the early section of the work that his father had done. She had made a start on the first when she heard a noise. She didn't want to be caught in Bastian's study as she hadn't actually done anything about starting an inventory of the supplies. While she knew it wasn't an urgent task, it was her cover for her drawing, which meant she'd have to do it.

She looked around carefully before leaving the study and was just relocking the door when Austin came up behind her.

'Hello!' he said. 'Finished already?'

'Er, no,' she said, flustered. 'I haven't really started. I was just getting a rough idea of how much was there.'

'Well, why don't we do it together? That sort of job is much easier if one person says what's there and the other writes it down.'

Of course he was right. Cass looked at him, holding her breath, mentally trying to remember if she'd put away every sign of Bastian's work. She couldn't be sure. 'That's OK,' she said slowly. 'There's no rush. How did you get on with Errol's pick-up truck? You were very quick negotiating. Are you sure you got the best deal you could?'

Austin made a dismissive gesture. 'He could name his price and knew it. But Bastian told me there was an old ham radio set in one of the outbuildings. I thought I'd fire it up and see if I could get any connection to the outside world.'

'Now that could be useful!'

'If I had a connection, I might be able to arrange a plane to come and pick me up.' He paused. 'Although I would need help with costs, which is where you'd come in.'

'Oh — er — I don't know — I'd have to talk to Ranulph —' It was an excuse and Austin recognised it as one.

'Don't you think it's time you stopped talking to Ranulph and started organising your own life?'

'Maybe!' She tried to sound lighthearted. Austin had a point but she and Ranulph had come here as a team and if she planned to leave without him, he needed to be informed. She decided to go on the offensive. 'Supposing you hear of a plane before the pick-up is ready?'

'That's when I'll negotiate with Errol how much he'd need to pull an all-nighter to get the truck done.'

'Although if the plane was coming specifically to collect you, presumably it could wait until you could get to an airfield?'

'I know Europeans tend to think all Americans are

loaded, but it's not actually true. I wouldn't be chartering a plane, I'd be hoping for a space on one that's returning from an island with a functioning airfield, or has a couple of passengers already and wants a full load.' He looked at her intently. 'It will affect you, Cass. We can get out of here if we co-operate.'

Cass smiled, certain she must look like an idiot. 'I still need to think about it. Now, if you don't mind, I'm going to have a shower quickly before the archaeologists come back and want one.' Too late she remembered that the archaeologists had their own house now.

* * *

While she was in the shower, Cass contemplated going down to the archaeological site to talk to Ranulph, and get him to tell her what she should do for the best. But by the time she was wrapped in a towel, rubbing at her hair with another one, she'd decided against this. She had to sort this out herself. When Austin had said she should think for herself he had hit a nerve. How could she ever expect anyone to think of her as an adult if she was constantly asking other people what she should do?

She went to look for Austin after her shower.

She managed to locate him but didn't have to ask how he was getting on. He was in one of Bastian's outhouses, looking at a very old piece of equipment.

'This thing is out of the ark! Pre the ark! Pre Amerindians!' he said.

Cass bit back the 'what did you expect?' remark that was her initial response and changed it to, 'I'm sure you can work it out, Austin.'

He snorted in derision. 'You'd have to be an archaeologist to work this out, this set is so old.'

She was about to say that surely he *was* an archaeologist, and suggested tea instead. 'Or I could make coffee?'

Austin regarded her. 'That would be great. And I'm glad you're starting to be a bit friendlier, Cass. Up to now you seem to have been seeing me as the enemy.' He smiled. 'I really like you. I think we could get along just fine.'

They walked back to the house in silence. Cass's mind was whirring; would it be a good thing if she appeared to like Austin?

She made him coffee, longing for Ranulph, after which she and Austin sat on the veranda together in silence.

'Why don't you ask Ranulph to sort out the radio for you?' Cass suggested, choosing her words carefully. 'He's very practical. He's not an academic like the rest of you guys. He might be able to fix it.'

'What does he do?' I mean in real life?' asked Austin.

'He's a journalist,' said Cass.

'I might have guessed,' said Austin. 'Happy to hang on the coat-tails of work others have done.'

'I wouldn't say that, exactly.' Cass was put out by Austin's disparaging attitude but didn't know if sticking up for Ranulph would be good or bad. She still hadn't worked out if she should pretend to like Austin or not.

'You wouldn't, but I've had my work taken apart by journalists in the past. It's so easy to find holes in what others have done. It's so much harder to do the work from scratch.'

Cass smiled again. She could actually agree with this statement although she longed to shout, 'Ranulph's not like that!' In truth, she didn't have much of an idea of what Ranulph's journalism was like. She hadn't spent any time reading it when she had the opportunity. Now she wished she had. 'It's weird not having the internet, isn't it?' she said.

'Why did you say that suddenly?'

Cass shrugged. 'I was just thinking. I've always had it, I suppose, and now I don't.'

'You're young.'

She sighed. 'I'm going to go to the dig and ask Ranulph if he's up to fixing a radio set.' She gave Austin a fake beam. 'That would be cool, wouldn't it? If he could fix it?'

'Sure would,' said Austin with the sort of patronising look that normally would have made Cass want to throw something at him. As it was, she just smiled again and set off down the beach at a run.

A few minutes later, she arrived in front of Ranulph panting slightly.

'Hey!' said Ranulph, putting his hands on her arms. 'What's the rush? Is everything all right?'

'I think so. But I wanted to talk to you without Austin being around.'

'Where is he?'

'I left him on the veranda. He knows I'm coming to talk to you.' She paused for breath. 'Do you know anything about ham radio?'

'A little bit. I've had to use it a couple of times when I've been somewhere that's cut off from the world.'

'Bastian told Austin there was a set and he's keen to get it going. But he can't! I suggested you might be able to fix it.' She paused and took a breath. 'He thinks he might be able to pick up details of when a private plane is coming over to pick people up.' She licked her dry lips. 'He wants us to travel together.'

Ranulph frowned. 'How do you feel about that?'

'Not great, but I will if I have to.'

'But why would you have to, Cass? It doesn't sound like a good idea to me.'

She didn't reply immediately.

'Why would you do that, Cass?' Ranulph persisted.

'I'd forgotten I hadn't told you. I'm going to do illustrations for Bastian's entry for this prize. Bastian can draw but his father couldn't. He wants me to redo those illustrations, or as many of them as I can. His work must be the best it can be if it's going to win. Him winning would help the whole island. If Austin wins, he'll just keep the money.'

'So . . .?'

'If the paper is finished, with illustrations, I can take it with me to somewhere it can be emailed to the competition before the deadline.'

'Ah, now I understand —'

'But the paper won't be done unless you can do something to keep Austin out of my way, so I can get on and do the drawings. Austin will find a way to stop me if he thinks I'm helping Bastian.'

'I don't like that helping Bastian means you should travel with a man I think is a jerk —'

'I know he's a jerk. But he's a jerk I have to keep onside! If you did the radio thing, at least we'd have control. Although if you fixed it, I'm sure he'd be able to operate it.'

Ranulph considered. 'Come on then. If I fix the radio, I can unfix it afterwards, so Austin won't have control of it.'

* * *

The next couple of days were busy. Cass was constantly finding excuses to leave the house and go and visit Delphine's holiday cabin so she could draw. Ranulph was struggling with the radio set — it had been left unused for so long and everything was rusty. Austin paced between Ranulph's radio shack, the beach and Errol's garage. But, at last, Ranulph got a connection.

Cass was there at the time and Austin instantly came into the little building and leant over Ranulph's shoulder.

'Who've you got there, Ran?' he said. 'Can he put us in touch with a small plane company?'

Ranulph got up. 'Tell you what, Austin, why don't you communicate with him? The system works now and it's all yours. I'm going down to the dig. We have to secure it soon so it can be properly investigated.'

When everyone, including Becca, who had been invited, finally sat down for dinner that evening, there was not much in the way of conversation. Everyone seemed tired and preoccupied. Cass was thinking about her drawings. She had done some but not as many as she would have liked. She was copying some of the plants from an old book with botanical plates, but she wanted to add grasses and fallen foliage. Putting in the amount of detail she liked took time. But should she concentrate on a few, really good pictures? Or try and get them all done, even in a sketchy way? She hadn't managed to ask Bastian and wasn't sure he'd give her a useful answer anyway. He'd just say, 'Do the best you can.'

Becca and Ranulph began to talk in low voices

about something apparently urgent concerned with pottery that had been broken possibly (Cass had no idea!) thousands of years ago. Eventually they got up and carried on their conversation on the veranda.

Cass had tuned out of what was going on to the extent that when Austin spoke to her it made her jump. 'Sorry, what was that you said?' she asked him.

'I said, what have you been up to today? I haven't seen you at all. I know you weren't delivering supplies because Bastian's been out with the pick-up.'

'Oh, I've been helping Delphine over at her place,' she said breezily.

'But Delphine's been here all day. I've been here too, trying to get some sense out that darn radio set,' said Austin.

'I don't have to be there for Cass to help me,' said Delphine, coming on to the veranda just then. 'I can't be in two places at once. The cabin I used to rent out before the hurricane is in a mess. Cass is helping me sort it out.'

It was a wonderfully logical answer and Delphine said it with such conviction that Cass relaxed.

'I can't wait to see the end result,' said Austin. 'Maybe I can take a peek when I visit Errol tomorrow.' He sounded about as sceptical as he could without being rude.

'I'd rather you saw the cabin when it was finished,' said Delphine. 'Are you thinking of renting it? I'll give you a good deal.'

'Well,' said Austin. 'I'm not planning to stay here much longer, but if I need to come back to Dominica it would be good to have a place to stay.' He gave Bastian a smile of fake gratitude. 'I can't sponge off this guy here forever.'

'No,' said Delphine. 'You've done that for quite a while already.'

'You've been very welcome,' said Bastian, getting up and giving Austin a small bow. 'But feel free to leave at any time.' He then went off to his study.

'This woman!' said Austin, smiling, pretending he was paying Delphine a compliment. 'What would we do without her?'

'I suggest you don't do anything, with me or without me, Mr Austin,' said Delphine.

'Sorry, Delphine,' said Austin. 'I didn't mean anything by that. I'm just impressed by you. Cass, are you ready to show off your handiwork — whatever you've been doing in Delphine's rental?'

'No,' said Cass, emboldened by Delphine's feistiness. 'I'll show you when it's ready, not before.'

'But I may not still be here,' said Austin. 'I may have a plane to collect me and get me out of here. And don't forget, I'm planning on taking you too!'

'Only if she wants to go,' said Delphine, very much in charge.

17

Later that evening Bastian found Cass at her usual spot, staring out to sea, admiring the stars. 'Take a walk with me?' he asked. He was carrying a head torch like a lantern.

Cass followed his torch that shone down the path to the opposite side of the house which led to the other side of the beach, away from where the archaeological dig was going on.

'Did you want to say something? Something private?'

Bastian had stopped at what was obviously a favourite spot, and he and Cass found a couple of rocks to lean on.

'I have a problem.' Bastian got to the point. 'I have very nearly finished my work. I have lots of notes, but they are in longhand.'

'Oh?'

'Toussaint and I only actually saw and photographed the petroglyph the other day. And thank you for making it comparatively easy to find, by the way.'

'You found it? Oh, Bastian! I'm so thrilled! That's so exciting!' Cass could hardly contain herself. 'All the difficulties we've been through have been worth it. The petroglyph was why I came, after all.'

Bastian smiled, pleased by Cass's excitement. 'But I need to write up that last bit.'

'And you have no computer because of not having electricity,' said Cass. 'What a shame they haven't invented a solar laptop.' She paused. 'They probably have, only obviously you don't have one.'

He laughed. 'You don't need electricity and fancy equipment if you have a typewriter.'

'And have you got one?'

Bastian nodded. 'My father wrote all his books on it.'

'So did mine, years ago! So, how can I help? I'm quite good at typing. I taught myself to touch type when I was bored one summer holidays. I practised on a manual typewriter I found in Dad's shed.'

'Oh!' Bastian seemed taken aback. 'I wasn't going to ask you to type it for me. I was going to ask if I could share your space at Delphine's. I don't want to type at the house as Austin will hear me. I told him my paper was finished. He doesn't know we found the petroglyph, so he doesn't know I had more to write.'

'OK,' said Cass slowly. 'I just hope we're going to have time to do it.'

'Errol is a very obliging fellow,' said Bastian with a laugh.

'What do you mean?'

Bastian laughed again. 'We've known each other since we were kids. He'll contrive to give me all the time that I — and you — need.'

The typewriter, which weighed, in Cass's opinion, an absolute ton, was transported to Delphine's cabin very early the next morning. No one else was up. Cass, hurrying along behind Bastian with the pages of longhand notes, realised that even if Bastian was used to a manual typewriter it would be much harder work than using a computer. Not only did depressing the keys require much more effort, but any mistakes would have to be rubbed out with a special eraser.

'I hope your final section isn't too long,' she said as Bastian finally dumped the typewriter on a table next to the desk Cass had been using for the illustrations. 'A picture paints a thousand words and all that.'

'Luckily there is a maximum word count — a generous one but there is a limit! The book, when I write it, will be longer. We'll need another chair, if we're both working in here at the same time,' he said.

'This one is fine with a few cushions on it and I know Delphine will produce another if we ask.' She paused. 'I just thought, how will we keep a copy of your work? What did your father do?'

'He used carbon paper. I haven't got any, sadly.' He glanced at Cass. 'I don't suppose you've ever used carbon paper? You put a sheet in between two plain pieces in the typewriter and you get a copy? You can put several bits of carbon paper in. It worked well.'

Cass shook her head. 'I suppose my generation has become totally dependent on computers.'

'Not only your generation! We do have power cuts from time to time so we're better prepared, but frankly, if I couldn't use my computer I'd just wait until I could. If the matter wasn't urgent, of course.'

'But it's urgent now,' said Cass. 'I just hope Austin can be stopped from sticking his nose in.'

Bastian nodded. 'He knows you're doing something for me, which is why he's so determined to get you away from here.'

Cass nodded. 'Well, we'd better get on! Having got up before the birds, I don't want to waste my time. I have lots more drawings to do.'

'I should have taken more photos as I went along, and now, with no internet, it's too late.' He smiled. 'The hurricane has a lot to answer for.'

'It certainly does!' Cass agreed.

'Did Ranulph notice you leaving, do you think?'

Cass shook her head. 'I told him I liked sleeping on the veranda. And I do. He won't notice we're missing until breakfast.'

Delphine produced the second chair and soon both Bastian and Cass were working. Cass soon took her table out on to the veranda as it was hard to concentrate with the bang bang — pause — bang of Bastian's typing going on in the background.

She found the thought of there being only one copy of the final section terrifying, but she knew Bastian wouldn't have time to type it twice. She resolved to make a copy herself if she had time. She knew Bastian would protest, but she'd be doing it for her own peace of mind.

Partly because she felt she couldn't disappear all day without being noticed, Cass went back to Bastian's house for lunch. Everyone was used to Bastian being out and about, but she was different.

She was tired. She hadn't realised quite how exhausting listening to someone using an old-fashioned typewriter would be. She really wished Bastian had let her do it, but he had refused, and this way she could focus entirely on the drawings. Too late, Cass realised that she and Bastian should have staggered the times they used the cabin.

'So what have you two been up to?' asked Austin, the moment she arrived on the veranda. He was already on the rum.

Cass had had the walk back from Delphine's to think of an answer. 'I've been sanding down some planks. I need a quick shower before lunch. I'm covered in dust.'

She ducked into the shower before anyone could spot this wasn't true.

When she joined the lunch table she noticed that Bastian wasn't there, Ranulph was looking very serious and possibly grumpy and Austin was, as usual, bumptious and smug.

'I nearly forgot to tell you, Cass,' Austin said. 'Someone called Howard is trying to get in touch with you on the radio.'

'Howard? He's my dad!'

Cass was suddenly overwhelmed with homesickness. She longed to be in the comfortable Scottish house with electricity and hot water, and all the things she had got used to not having here. She also wanted a more simple life where there were no secrets, no underhand dealings, no tricky personalities to handle.

'When can I speak to him? Could we call him back?' she asked.

Austin shook his head. 'It's not as simple as that. He must have been contacting me in the early hours. There's a time difference, you know.'

Cass took a moment before replying. 'I know there's a time difference, but he spoke to you, so it must be possible.'

'He was lucky to get me. I won't be there next time,' said Austin.

'But Cass is anxious to speak to her father,' said Ranulph. 'Can't we work out the best time to be waiting for his call?'

Austin shook his head in the same patronising way he had shaken it at Cass. 'Everyone wants to contact everyone at the same time, Ran; it clogs up the lines. You can't necessarily get in touch at a busy time.'

'In which case we'll have to try to call Howard at

a less busy time. Maybe I'll take over the radio from now on.'

'Nuh-huh,' said Austin. 'It'll be confusing if we change over now. I'll take care of it.'

Cass, who realised she knew less about ham radio than could be written on the back of an old-fashioned postage stamp, didn't speak. She was filled with a longing for home, for her dad, for normality.

* * *

After lunch she went into the room she shared with Ranulph and slept. When she awoke, she decided not to go back to Delphine's — it was quite a long walk — but to stay and, if she could, do some drawing while she was here.

There seemed to be no one about when she emerged, so she found her sketch pad and pencil and went off to find somewhere she could be on her own. If anyone came across her — and by this she meant Austin — she was just drawing local vegetation. He wouldn't know they were sketches for Bastian's paper that she would work up into proper illustrations.

18

A week later, Cass pulled the last typewritten sheet — the extra copy she had made for safety — out of the machine and added it to the pile. She had already finished her drawings. Bastian had everything he needed for his paper. It could be submitted, just as soon as it could be got off the island to somewhere with an internet connection.

She packed the typed sheets, her illustrations and Bastian's notes into her day bag and set off for Bastian's house. She was weary. She'd started work at 6.30 a.m. — everyone started the day early in Dominica — and it was now after two. She was also starving hungry and her shoulders felt as though they were in steel clamps but she had finished. The paper was complete.

To her surprise, everyone was still sitting round the lunch table when she got back.'

'Hey!' said Becca. 'Come and join us!'

'I'll just go and wash my hands,' said Cass, 'and then I will.'

She threw her day bag in the bedroom and had a quick wash, then she went back to the big table that was in the centre of the house.

'Sit by me,' said Becca.

Bastian got up. 'You look tired. Come, let us wait on you.'

While Becca passed dishes, some sort of vegetable stew, salad, some freshly made juice made from a local plant called sorrel, Bastian rubbed her shoulders.

'You're very knotted up, my dear,' he said. 'You should ask Delphine to give you a proper massage sometime. She's excellent at them.'

Delphine, who had been passing and filling Cass's plate, nodded. 'I do it for the tourists,' she said. 'They go on these long-distance hikes and come back broken. They're not used to walking.'

'Well, I'm not used to using an old-fashioned typewriter,' said Cass and then realised she shouldn't have said that. Her extra copy of Bastian's last section that she had banged out was a secret, currently even from Bastian.

'So what have you been typing?' asked Austin, who never missed a trick.

'I've been writing my impressions of the island and how it's surviving the hurricane,' she said smoothly. 'My father asked me to keep a diary and, of course, I haven't done that.' She laughed. 'I've been too busy and now I'm making up for it.'

'So is Howard planning to use your account of the island after the hurricane in his own work?' asked Ranulph, who seemed even more tight-lipped than ever.

'Oh, I doubt it,' said Cass, 'I think he just wants to know my impressions. You know he loves Dominica — he spent a lot of time here with Bastian's father — and he wants me to love it too.' She smiled at everyone at the table. 'Of course I do already. I spent a formative ten days here when I was twelve. Loved it then, love it now! This curry is amazing!' she changed the subject, digging into it with her fork, hoping she'd satisfied everyone as to what she'd been up to on Bastian's old typewriter.

'Well, you've been doin' a great job on my little cabin,' said Delphine. 'I owe you a massage in return for all that hard work.'

'I'm longing to see that cabin,' said Austin. 'Perhaps when I go to check on the pick-up Errol is working on, I could take a look-see.'

* * *

When Cass awoke from her siesta at about four, she looked briefly for Ranulph but quickly realised he must have gone back to the dig. She had wanted to ask him about the radio situation but as he wasn't there, she went into the little building herself.

Austin was sitting in there with headphones on fiddling with dusty knobs and dials.

'Hey! Austin, I was wondering if you could help me get in touch with my dad,' Cass said cheerfully.

'Oh, honey, I thought I'd explained. We can't do that.'

Austin was very firm about this but Cass didn't believe him. 'Surely we can work out a time when he is more likely to be sitting by his radio set?'

Austin shook his head. 'He knows you're OK. What else would he need to know?'

As she looked at Austin, established in the seat at the radio, Cass realised that he was never going to help her get in touch with her father. She'd either have to ask Ranulph or do it herself. She looked at the array of knobs and switches and added a third option: go without talking to her dad.

'I would be so grateful if you could help me speak to him,' she said, smiling in a way she hoped was appealing.

'Oh?' said Austin. 'And just how grateful would that be?'

For a horrible moment Cass wondered if Austin was asking for sexual favours. Surely not! She had intended to be ingratiating, maybe to give the impression they were friends, but her attempt seemed to have gone badly wrong. She decided to seek clarification before she ran from the room. Although she felt sick, she managed to laugh. 'What exactly do you mean, Austin?'

'Oh, I'm sure you know.'

'No,' said Cass, being deliberately obtuse.

'I just mean if you could be a bit more helpful to people other than Bastian, who you seem obsessed with, in my opinion.'

'I'm not obsessed with Bastian,' said Cass. 'But his father was a friend of my father, which gives us a connection.'

'Really?' said Austin.

'Yes, really. And what do you want me to do for you anyway?'

Austin paused; he appeared to be thinking what was in his best interests to say. 'I want you to help me get off this island.'

Cass sighed. 'That again. But what can I do? Errol is fixing up a pick-up for you so you can drive to the airport. I can't book you a flight on a plane. I really don't see how I can help!'

'If I did manage to hook you up with your old dad for a phone call, he might be in a position to arrange a flight out of here. For us both.'

Cass thought for a few moments.

'I'd really need to speak to him myself,' she said at last. 'And of course I'll do anything reasonable to help you get off the island.'

She left the little building wondering what game Austin was playing. Of course he wanted to leave Dominica so he could submit his book in time for the deadline. He'd get to another island where they had the internet and it would be done.

But Bastian's paper was also ready for submission, most of it on a memory stick, and the last bit, and the illustrations, ready to be put in her backpack. And surely, having come to Dominica to help Bastian find the petroglyph, getting his paper to the judges in time was just as important, if not more so?

How could she make this happen? It would not be easy.

Back on the veranda, in her favourite spot, Friendly came up to her. 'You're the only one, aren't you?' she said to him, fondling his ears. 'You understand without having to have everything explained to you.'

* * *

At supper that evening Bastian had some worrying news. 'There's a rumour there's going to be another hurricane.'

'What?' said Cass. 'But surely there's just been one. There can't be another.'

'It's not like Christmas, honey,' said Delphine. 'You don't get it over and then relax until the following year. It's hurricane season: you can have several.'

'But it's not likely, is it?' said Austin, oddly relaxed at the prospect. 'And with no internet, how would you know there was going to be one?'

Bastian regarded him. 'It's only a rumour but a Kalinago friend told me there are signs.'

'When might it hit?' asked Ranulph.

'Very hard to be precise even with modern technology,' said Bastian.

'Have the Kalinago people always been able to predict hurricanes?' asked Ranulph.

'There is a record of them warning early settlers when one was about to hit, but as the sky was blue and there was no wind, the settlers took no notice. When it did come, they accused the locals of witchcraft.' Bastian also seemed surprisingly calm about the prospect of another hurricane.

'Well, if there is going to be another hurricane, shouldn't you organise a generator?' said Austin. 'It seems bizarre not to have one.'

'I prefer to rely on the solar panels, but if I was going to change my mind, I've left it a bit late,' Bastian said.

'So how can we prepare?' said Cass, not sure if she was worried or a bit excited.

'We'll board up the windows and make sure nothing is outside that isn't secured. Fill up water containers and assemble food that doesn't need to be cooked, just basic things.'

'You seem very relaxed about it, Bastian,' said Ranulph.

'Not so much relaxed as calm,' Bastian replied.

'Bastian knows what needs to be done. You guys just trust him and stop fretting,' said Delphine.

'I'm not fretting,' said Austin, who seemed edgier suddenly. 'How is your brother getting on with the pick-up, Delphine?'

Delphine shrugged. 'It'll be finished when it's finished.'

'I'll go over and see if I can hurry up the process,' he said.

* * *

Austin found Cass while she was finishing clearing up dinner a little while later.

'I've been to see Errol and the pick-up is ready. We'll leave at dawn tomorrow for the airport. All the small planes are coming in there. We'll get a place on one, easy, I'm sure. Sleep on the veranda so I can wake you.'

'But the hurricane, Austin! We can't set off in a hurricane!'

'The hurricane is just a rumour. One of Bastian's weird friends might think there's one on its way but we've no real evidence.'

'I still think —'

Austin suddenly slammed his hand down on the table. 'Enough arguing! You have to come with me, Cass. If you don't I will personally ruin your boyfriend's academic career. I will tell the academic world that there are parts of his thesis that are not supported.'

'But it's only your word against his!'

'Mud sticks! I have some standing in those circles. I can ruin Bastian, make no mistake!'

Then he picked up the rum bottle and took it to his room.

Cass didn't know what to do. Ranulph had gone down to the dig for the evening with Becca, so she couldn't consult him. She had no idea where Bastian was but she knew if she told him, Bastian would say she shouldn't go with Austin. It wouldn't be fair to ask him, even if she could.

Ultimately, she knew she had to leave as she had to prevent Austin from ruining Bastian's reputation. But more importantly, she had to get Bastian's work sent off in time for him to be in with a chance of the prize that he and Austin were competing for. That was the only way she could be sure that Bastian would have an equal chance.

As she couldn't talk to anyone, she wrote some goodbye notes. *Dear Ranulph, sorry to go without saying goodbye but Austin is taking us to a plane that will get us away. I really need to go. Bastian will explain why. Thank you for everything.* Then she paused for a very long time before writing *love, Cass.*

Signing off a letter wasn't usually something that had to be thought about, but the simple words she'd end almost any email with seemed loaded with meaning.

Bastian's letter was easier to write. *I'm going with Austin. I have everything I need. Thank you for having me to stay for so long. Lots of love, Cass.*

If Austin found the note (and Cass was almost sure he would find it) it didn't say anything revealing (she hoped). But with luck, Bastian would realise it meant she was taking his work with her.

* * *

That night, Cass packed very carefully. Although she really didn't have a lot to bring in her rucksack and her day bag, her packing was very precise. It included her travel documents, a large box of tampons and the small pot of moisturiser that Becca had used. She had her father's camera wrapped in her clothes for added protection. She couldn't help thinking of the day she had found the petroglyph as she tucked her jeans around it.

Ranulph came back up just as Cass was saying goodnight to Bastian. She had wanted to whisper to him about what she was about to do. Of course, Ranulph appeared just as she had her lips near Bastian's ear and Bastian had his hand on her arm to keep her close, so she wasn't able to tell Bastian anything.

She realised this must have looked a little odd — intimate even — but it was too late, she couldn't explain to Ranulph what was going on. She just nodded to him and then went to get ready for bed.

She hadn't really slept by the time Austin woke her. She had her rucksack and her day bag under the bench she used for sleeping on and was wearing her clothes.

'I'm ready,' she said. He nodded and she followed him to his pick-up truck which was parked a little way away.

'You're obviously a woman to travel with. I'm sure you've got useful things in that pack of yours.'

Cass clambered into the passenger seat of the pickup. 'Apart from my passport, I've got water, sticking plasters and some bananas, if that's what you mean. I never travel without them.' She didn't mention the more personal items. He didn't need to know about them.

19

Even before they'd set off Cass had realised this was a huge mistake. The talk round the dinner table had been all about when the hurricane might hit. The answer was dawn, just as Austin and Cass set off in Austin's pick-up for a little airstrip he'd heard about near the main airport.

At first it was the tops of the trees that were being tossed about but then the gusts of wind became more intense, buffeting the vehicle. Austin was struggling to keep it on the road and Cass held on to the door and the dashboard in front of her, gripping so hard her fingers went white. She knew if a tree fell on them, they'd be finished.

When they had to slow right down to negotiate a huge pothole, she put her hand on Austin's arm. She had to shout to make herself heard over the wind and the rain. 'We have to go back! This is utter madness. We could be killed at any moment.'

Austin didn't even look at her. 'No way. We're going to get on that flight.'

'But the plane won't be able to take off.'

'But I'll be there the moment it can.'

Then he set off again, battling with the steering wheel, the wheels of the truck spinning in the mud. Now she couldn't make herself heard while they were moving. But the state of the road meant she had another opportunity as yet again they were stopped by a tree which had to be driven round.

'Seriously! Austin! We're risking our lives.'
He looked at her. 'You want to get out?'
'No! I want us to turn round. Go back to where we can be safe!'
He shook his head. 'Not happening.'
Cass looked about her. The rain had turned the road into a river of mud. 'We can't go on!' she shouted.
'OK,' said Austin, putting the pick-up into gear again and moving forward. 'You can get out. But I'll say when.'
'I don't want to get out!' she shouted, but he appeared not to hear her.
They slithered and slipped, sometimes forward, sometimes sideways, often backwards. Cass was in a state of anxiety that was just short of terror. She thought only of the next inch to travel. She had no idea when death would come but she was fairly sure it would in the next couple of hours.
At last, Austin stopped. For a few moments Cass thought he'd come to his senses. They were only a couple of miles from a small town and she thought maybe he would go there and get out of the torrential rain and gusts of wind that could easily have swept them off the road, had it not been for the trees which gave them a little protection.
'OK, get out. I'm going to the airstrip on my own.'
Cass couldn't believe what he'd said. 'I can't get out in this!'
'Do you want to carry on with the journey?' Austin demanded.
'No —'
'Then get out.' He leant across and opened her door. Then he gave her a great shove.
Cass barely had time to grab her day bag which

fortunately was on her knee, then she was sprawling on the road, slipping and sliding in the mud, unable to get to her feet.

Austin didn't wait for her to stand up or to get her rucksack, with all her things in it, out of the back of the pick-up. He set off into the weather, skidding madly, sending a cascade of mud over her.

Cass was drenched in seconds. Stunned and disbelieving, she sat there on the ground, in a small river, clutching her bag to her chest. Somehow she got to her feet, then put the strap of her bag round her neck and secured the main part with the belt of her shorts, so it wouldn't flap around. She'd risked her life for the contents — she couldn't lose them now.

She had no idea what to do. She staggered to the nearest tree and clung to it so she could keep herself upright; this seemed like a positive action. But she had no clue about her next move. It was hard to think clearly when cold water was pouring down on to your head.

She heard a huge crack and, just a few feet in front of her, saw a huge tree break and fall. She gazed at it for several seconds, her heart beating like a tiny bird's. Then she realised that the tree had formed a sort of bridge. If she could get to it, it would give her at least a bit of shelter.

She wasn't sure how long it took her to get from where she had been thrown out of the pick-up to the tree, but it was slow progress as she struggled through the river of mud. Eventually, however, she got there. It was so wonderful to be out of the cold shower the heavens were throwing down that it felt like safety. But she knew it wasn't. She had to make a better plan. But what? There were no options. She would surely die here.

Gloomy thoughts went through her mind and, of all of them, it was the idea that she'd never see Ranulph again that made her the saddest. They'd shared so much, been through such a lot together. She was sure that if some years passed, the age gap would shrink. Whether he would ever love her as much as she loved him, she couldn't know. But surely she loved him enough for both of them?

She wasn't sure if she was crying, it was hard to tell when the rain was so strong and she was so wet, but she had closed her eyes when someone laid a hand on her arm and it made her jump.

'Hey, girl, you shouldn't be here,' said the owner of the hand, a tall man of indecipherable age. 'Follow me.'

Cass didn't hesitate. He gave her a walking stick and, aided by this, she slipped and slid through the mud behind him until they got into the forest where it wasn't quite so wet. Then she followed him through the forest into a clearing. In the clearing, surprisingly, was quite a large house. Although she didn't stop to look, she had the impression that the house was half-way up a mountain. She caught a glimpse of the forest over a ravine. It was shelter.

He opened a door and she followed him inside. In front of them were some steps. At the bottom of the steps, it seemed, was a party: music, people, light, and an atmosphere that did not seem suitable for break-fast time in the middle of a storm.

An older man got up as she arrived. 'Welcome to the hurricane bunker. Take the weight off. Garvin?' he shouted and the music stopped. 'We have a guest! And she's wet!'

Someone threw a towel in her direction, and she did her best to dry herself. While she did this, she looked around. There was more than just one family, she realised, but the light from the camping lamps made it hard to see how many there were.

'The neighbours come when there's a hurricane. We have this big room, cut out of the rock,' someone explained. 'It's storage most of the time, but when there's a hurricane —'

'It's a party house!' said a young woman.

Cass began to take in her surroundings. Across the room, just in front of Cass, there was an older couple, three or four grown men, some teenagers, a couple of women and some little children. There was even a dog. It was crowded but they'd taken her in.

She was introduced to her new companions. There was Irma, wife of Garvin, who was the oldest of the men. There were two sons, Sammy and Usain, who was the one who had rescued her, and there was a very pretty young woman, the wife of one of the sons. But Garvin and Irma seemed to be the senior couple, and the hosts.

After accepting some cocoa-tea (made over a camping gas stove) and some bananas, Cass began to feel better. She sat on the floor next to Usain. All the time she kept one hand on her bag.

'What I want to know,' she asked him, 'is how on earth you knew I was there? I would almost certainly have died if you hadn't rescued me.'

'You were lucky, girl. I was fixing a shutter before the hurricane really hit when I saw the vehicle on the road, way down below where I was. I knew when it would reach here and thought I'd check to see if it had got that far. Not the day to go driving.'

'I know!' said Cass. 'And believe me, it was not my choice. Had I known I was travelling with a madman I wouldn't have gone.' She stopped. She had known, really, that Austin was unstable — certainly erratic. Why had she got in his pick-up when she knew it wasn't safe? To get Bastian's work into the competition on time. She sighed. She'd risked her life for something that now wouldn't happen.

'So you wanted to get away real bad?' asked Usain. 'From Bastian's house?' He seemed incredulous.

'How did you know where I'd come from?' she began and then subsided. Of course he knew. Everyone knew everything about everyone on Dominica, it seemed. 'Not because I don't like Bastian,' she said. 'I think he's amazing.'

'I don't think there's a person on the island who doesn't feel grateful to him for some reason.'

'I know,' said Cass. 'Which is why I was so desperate to help him.'

'Runnin' away with a man in a pick-up may not be the best way of doing that.'

She laughed. 'I know. I really shouldn't have gone with him. But he was blackmailing me — well — not actually . . . he wanted me because he . . .' It was all so garbled and ridiculous-sounding that she stopped trying to explain. 'Austin didn't believe there'd be another hurricane so soon after the last one.' She groaned. 'I am such a fool.'

She thought of Bastian's house, people going about their business and finding her notes. They would be cursing her, she realised. They'd be glad that Austin had gone, but they would have wanted her to be sensible and stay.

'Stop lecturing the girl!' said one of the women.

'Let me show you the 'facilities',' she went on. 'Best to use it early in the day as it'll only smell worse as the day goes on.'

The facilities consisted of a tiny room lit by a camping light. There was a chemical toilet, a plastic bowl and a container of water. There was even a mirror pinned to the wall.

Frightened of what she might find, Cass freed her daypack from her waistband and looked inside. It was all pretty much as she hoped it would be, and she felt a surge of relief. She washed her face as well as she could when she saw how muddy it was. The cool water against her skin was soothing.

'Relax a little,' said Usain as she sat back down with the others.

'I feel such an idiot —'

'We all do foolish things, especially if the heart is involved. Calm down, breathe: we've got hours to spend together.'

'I didn't run away with Austin because I loved him!' Cass said urgently. 'Anything but.'

'Chill, girl,' he said.

'The boys wanted to start on the rum,' said one of the young women. 'I said not until lunchtime.'

'Early lunchtime,' said the other young man, Sammy. He grinned. 'Can we turn the music back on?'

'But quietly please, us older ones want to talk.'

The party atmosphere returned. One of the children, a boy of about five, demonstrated his break-dancing skills while his sister clapped her hands and jogged around. They both had a good sense of rhythm, Cass noted, and loved having an audience.

When everyone seemed to be looking at the children, Cass took out her day bag and looked inside.

She opened the box of tampons and took out the top layer of them. Underneath, folded and wrapped in plastic, were the last pages of Bastian's work. Her drawings were underneath. Then she took out her little pot of moisturiser. Inside, there was a tissue on the top and underneath was a memory stick containing the bulk of Bastian's book. Well, it might not arrive at the competition in time but at least Austin wouldn't get his hands on it.

She knew — or was nearly certain — that Austin had thought all this was in her larger rucksack, the one he had driven off with, the one with her father's camera in it. Keeping Bastian's work with her was an idea that had occurred to her when she realised how desperate Austin was for her to go with him. He didn't need her to help get him on a plane; what he wanted was Bastian's work to be destroyed. Then Bastian would have no chance of getting the prize money. If it wasn't for her father's precious camera, wrapped in her clothes in her rucksack in the back of the pick-up, Cass would have been happy.

But being right wasn't as satisfying as she'd thought, she realised. Here she was, no chance of getting off the island for days if not weeks, while Austin might find the airstrip, get on a plane and escape to where there was internet coverage.

Or he might be killed by a falling tree, washed into a river by the rain, or fall to his death in a landslide. Cass realised she believed all these bad endings were more likely than him jumping on a plane to a hurricane-free island. And although she loathed him, she didn't want him dead.

Eventually, food was passed round, bowls of rice and peas covered in well-worn plastic wrap. She was handed a cup of rum punch. She sipped it and gradually began to relax. It was hard to stay tense and anxious when everyone around her seemed to be in party mode.

The young women were dancing now, circling their hips with amazing flexibility. They barely had room to move but they looked marvellous.

'Come on,' said one, holding out her hand. 'Put down your bag, no one's going to touch it. Dance! We may be here for a long time!

'This is called the butterfly,' said her teacher. 'Move your knees, open and shut, open and shut like a butterfly. Then with your hips —'

Cass had had no idea her hips could move like that and while hers were very stiff compared to those of the young women, they did move. And as the rum took effect, she stopped feeling so self-conscious and let herself go.

'Hey, girl!' said one of the young men. 'You're good!'

'Thank you,' she panted in reply. 'But I need to sit down now.'

While she was sitting, some of the younger children came over, curious about this new person in their midst.

'Hello,' they said.

'Hello!' she replied. 'My name is Cass. What are your names?'

It didn't take long for them all to become the best of friends, and soon Cass got out her notebook and began making little sketches of the people around her. She showed them some of the other sketches in her book and they all gasped, wondering at such a lifelike drawing emerging from just a pencil with no high technology at all. Cass was quite sorry when the children's mother appeared and took them off so they could sleep.

Eventually everyone settled down. Some people slept, others chatted quietly, everyone seemed calm, resigned. Cass realised that hurricanes were part of their lives. They weren't easy to live with but live with them they did.

The hours passed. From the hurricane shelter, built into the rock, Cass found it difficult to calculate how hard the wind was blowing. She settled into a comfortable position; someone gave her a cushion. She closed her eyes and dozed.

* * *

When she awoke she realised the atmosphere had changed. People were more wakeful, stretching and talking in low voices. Tea was being boiled over the camping stoves.

Usain came in. Cass hadn't been aware of him leaving but everyone looked to him for news.

'Not too bad,' he said although no one had asked him the question. 'We got away with it well. The road has more or less gone but it wasn't much of a road in the first place.' He grinned at Cass.

'Will I be able to get back to Bastian's, do you think?' she asked.

He nodded. 'I'll take you.'

'Oh no!' said Cass, crushed with guilt at this suggestion. 'You need to be here. I'll be OK. I'll just follow the road — what's left of it — down. I'll find the house.'

Usain shook his head. 'Nuh-uh. I'll take you.'

Cass took a breath to make her argument again but

he held up his hand. 'The whole island has a reason to be grateful to Bastian, but this family has a special reason. Your man rescued a little cousin of ours. Without him, he would have been killed,' Usain said.

'Bastian's not my man —' Cass said, a bit overcome.

'Figure of speech, honey,' said Usain with a wide smile.

20

After lots of goodbyes, complicated handshakes, hugs and from Cass many, many expressions of gratitude, she and Usain set off. She had the walking stick again although Usain seemed to manage without one. Eventually they got back to the road, which now had no surface; it was all scree. It was not easy to walk down but the air was very clear, the sky blue and the day was full of promise.

'It's like this after a hurricane,' said Usain. 'It's like the island's been through the washing machine with a fast spin. It's really shaken up, but it's clean.'

'It's hard to believe how it was yesterday.'

'I know. It's like the world was made fresh again, with a new start.'

'I don't think it's a new start for me,' said Cass, aware how devastated the thought made her. 'I think this is the end of the road for me. But I'll always love Dominica.'

'It gets into your heart and bones, doesn't it?'

She nodded, suddenly unable to speak and reluctant to let him see she was crying.

After a few stumbling steps down the hill which was now like a riverbed without the river, Cass had no more time to feel sorry for herself. She needed to think about every step. Usain took her arm and she found she was leaning on him for balance. Then they came across a huge crater and paused.

'It'll be easier around the edges,' he said.

They stumbled on for a few steps when suddenly Usain said, 'Listen!'

Cass listened but couldn't hear anything.

'A vehicle! There. It's stopped now.'

Cass wasn't sure if Usain had incredible hearing or she was just unable to focus but she stayed quiet and still anyway. Then she heard a car door slamming.

'They've run out of road,' said Usain. 'Whoever it is, is walking now. Let's just wait.'

Once she let herself relax and just be in the moment, Cass enjoyed the peace and quiet. Sounds from the forest were all there was to hear and tuning into them made her calm.

Then she heard a roar. 'Cass!' came a voice.

She saw Ranulph, running up the slope towards her as fast as the slippery surface would allow. She found herself moving to meet him and in seconds she was in his arms.

'I thought I'd lost you!' he murmured into her hair. 'I thought I'd never see you again.'

The feeling of his arms around her, holding her so tightly she could hardly breathe, was so wonderful she could barely take in what was happening.

'I thought you'd died in the hurricane,' he muttered, not letting her go. 'When we realised that you and Austin were gone, we spent the whole night thinking you were both dead.'

He gave her a final squeeze and then released her.

'Usain came out of the forest and rescued me,' Cass said.

Ranulph took Usain's hand and shook it. 'How did you know Cass was out here?'

'You can see the road from my house,' he said. 'I saw the pick-up, and came out to check it wasn't in a ditch and I found Cass.' He smiled broadly. 'She's a great girl to spend a hurricane with!'

'I was so lucky,' said Cass, looking at Usain.

'Far luckier than you deserved to be,' said Ranulph, moving from relieved to stern with horrifying speed.

'I did what I thought was best, Ranulph,' she said stiffly. She had regretted her actions for what seemed like a lifetime and didn't want to be told off about it now, however justified the telling-off was.

He sighed deeply. 'Let's get you home. I have Bastian's pick-up to get us there.'

'Bastian lent you his pick-up?' said Usain. 'Man! That boy would lend you his heart and both his kidneys before he'd let that pick-up out of his sight.'

'I drove it quite a bit too, when I was first here,' said Cass.

'Hey? Well, he must think a lot of you,' said Usain. He turned to Ranulph. 'When did the road run out?'

'It's OK until this bit,' said Ranulph. 'There's been a lot of rain but as far as we can tell this early, no really bad damage.'

Usain wanted to see what the road was like so the three of them went down to where Bastian's pick-up was parked.

After some chat about the state of the island, Usain declared it was time he was getting back. Cass climbed into the pick-up and Ranulph started the engine.

Embarrassment flooded over Cass like the rain had the previous day. It was not helped by Ranulph being tight-lipped and quietly livid next to her. How could she have been so stupid? She had risked her life. Surely not even Bastian's paper was worth that.

'Is Bastian's house all right?' she asked, desperate

to break through the atmosphere in the pick-up.

'Very little damage. It wasn't a bad hurricane. Only about a two.'

'It seemed quite bad when I was out in it.'

The words were only half out of her mouth before she regretted them.

'You shouldn't have been out in it!' he snapped.

'I know! I've said I'm sorry.'

'There's no point in apologising to me! I wasn't the only one who stayed awake all night worrying about what had happened to you!'

She muttered, 'I'm sorry,' again. It was so similar to being told off by a parent or a teacher.

Had Ranulph ever been a teacher? she wondered. At that moment she was glad she'd told her father she didn't want to train as one. She loved playing with children but didn't want to have to lecture them. She reminded herself she must remember to cancel her college course.

Beside her, wrestling to get the pick-up down the damaged road, Ranulph exuded anger. She wondered why he was going on feeling angry, even after she had been discovered safe and sound. She really hoped Bastian didn't behave in the same way; she had been almost killed — pushed on to the road out of a moving vehicle by Austin — for his work, she really didn't want that thrown back in her face.

* * *

Bastian also hugged her when she got out of the car. 'We were worried,' he said. 'But when we realised the hurricane wasn't too bad, we relaxed. At least, I did. I thought there was a good chance that you were all right.'

'Let the girl come in,' said Delphine, who apparently had walked over from her house early. 'She'll want a shower and some food.'

Cass did feel a lot better after a very quick shower that included washing her hair but then realised she had no clean clothes to change into. All her clothes were with Austin, wrapped round her father's camera. The thought made her shudder almost as much as the prospect of putting her clothes back on: cold, muddy and full of grit. She washed out her bra and pants and put them on while they were still wet. There was only one towel she could wring them out in and, although she'd done her best, it wasn't that effective.

She wrapped the towel around her and sidled into the kitchen. 'Delphine! I've got nothing to wear. Austin went off with my clothes.'

Delphine pursed her lips but refrained from expressing her feelings about Austin. 'I'll find you something.'

She found a dress, a bit shorter than Cass would have liked given that it seemed years since she'd worn anything except combat shorts and T-shirts.

'Suits you!' said Delphine. 'Someone left it behind once. You can keep it. It's too short for me.'

Half an hour later, Cass was sitting at the table on the veranda, surrounded by people wanting to hear her story. Becca was there as well as another couple of people from the dig. Ranulph was elsewhere. He'd heard her story and he obviously didn't want to hear it again.

'So!' said Becca. 'Spill!'

Cass looked at her and realised that Becca was quite annoyed too.

She took a breath. 'First of all, I want to apologise to everyone. I realise you've all been worried sick about me. At the time I just thought I had to leave. I didn't realise the hurricane had actually hit until we were in the pick-up.'

'Ran was beside himself,' said Becca. 'We came up for breakfast and discovered you were missing—'

'We found the notes,' said Bastian. 'I understand why you went but it was a bad decision.'

'I know that now. In fact I knew that about three minutes after we set off, but I couldn't get Austin to turn back.'

'That man was on a mission,' said Delphine. 'My brother said he was on at him all the time to hurry up, get the pick-up fixed.' She paused. 'He paid my brother a lot of money to get it done.'

'He was very keen to get off the island and put a lot of pressure on me to go with him.' Cass gave a wry laugh. 'Although he seemed quite eager to get rid of me shortly afterwards!'

'What kind of pressure?' said Becca.

Cass glanced at Bastian. 'He said—he said he'd ruin Bastian's reputation academically if I didn't go with him. He needed to submit his book and to do that he had to get off the island. I wanted to submit Bastian's paper so I had to get off the island too.'

'Thank you for making the copy of the last section,' said Bastian. 'That was very kind.'

'I couldn't bear the thought of there only being one copy, and considering how near I came to losing those last pages, it was probably one of my better decisions!'

Bastian said, 'Thank you, Cass. You risked your life for my work.'

'I'm sorry, I don't understand,' said Becca.

'Most of my paper was on a memory stick,' said Bastian. 'It's how I back up.'

'I took it with me,' said Cass. 'Plus the last section. I was going to scan the pages, and then email them with the contents of the memory stick to the judges of the prize as soon as I could. And also scan my drawings.' She hesitated. 'I didn't want Austin to get his work in on time and not Bastian's. And it was Bastian's father's work too,' she added.

Bastian smiled. 'It was. It meant a lot to me. Thank you, Cass.' He looked across the table at her and Cass saw real gratitude.

Behind her, Ranulph cleared his throat, announcing his presence. 'Howard has been on the radio. Again. He's been on and off all morning.'

'Oh! The connection wasn't lost? Can I speak to him?'

'Of course,' said Bastian.

'He doesn't know you weren't here last night,' said Ranulph, who obviously still hadn't forgiven her. 'I thought I'd spare him the anxiety.'

'Give it a rest, Ran,' said Becca. 'The poor girl knows she made a mistake but she had her reasons and they were very commendable ones.'

Ranulph humphed. 'I'll take you to the radio,' he said.

The little shack that contained the radio was small and very crowded with other things. There was really only room for one person but Cass and Ranulph crammed two chairs in the space and sat down.

It took a while for Ranulph to connect but at last he handed Cass the earphones.

Cass found herself emotional talking to her father

after so long. She hadn't meant to tell him about her close encounter with a hurricane but it came out. 'We don't know what happened to Austin,' she said when she had given him a toned-down version of events. She hadn't the heart to tell him about his camera.

'I should have suspected that bastard had his own selfish reasons for wanting to leave Dominica but he made out it was you who were desperate to get home,' said Howard. 'But I heard that he survived.'

'How?' said Ranulph.

'The people with the plane I was trying to arrange for you two got in touch to tell me they couldn't fly. They said there was another man desperate to leave. Turned out to be Austin. So I knew that he had turned up at the airfield but you hadn't, Cass.'

'I'm so sorry. Were you worried about me?'

'I didn't know you'd gone with Austin. I assumed you'd stayed at home, safely behind shutters.'

Even with the limitations the radio produced, Cass could hear the irony in her father's tone.

'Anyway, I'm safe now.'

'Good, but I want you home. I'll ask Eleanor to make arrangements this end. I want you back safe and sound.'

21

A couple of days later, Ranulph came in from where the radio was to announce that he and Cass would be leaving the following morning.

Cass, who had been sweeping the veranda of the detritus left over from the second hurricane, looked up.

'But there's still so much to be done here,' she said.

Yet in spite of her words, she suddenly really wanted to leave. She wanted to curl up on the sofa at her mother's house and watch something mindless on television. Or be with her father on a Scottish island and look at the ever-changing view of the sea and the mountains beyond.

'You must go home,' Ranulph said, in a more gentle tone than he'd used for days. 'You've worked very hard. You've done everything you came to do. You can stop now.'

She nodded. 'And we still need to get Bastian's work into the competition.'

'You do know that Bastian has a long-term female friend, don't you?'

Ranulph was still being gentle with her, and Cass suddenly realised what he was implying. 'I did know that, yes,' she said.

'You're far too young for Bastian. He's even older than I am.'

'I did know that, thank you. I read his CV,' she said. 'I know to the day how old he is.'

'It's just a crush, Cass. You'll get over it if you don't see him every day.'

'I know that too!' she said with a rueful smile. But what Ranulph didn't know was who her crush was on.

* * *

'We'll miss you,' said Delphine the next morning. 'You're part of the family now.'

They were just finishing breakfast. Ranulph and Cass were meeting a fishing boat in the early afternoon. Suddenly Cass felt tearful. 'I feel part of it and will do my best to come back soon.'

'Make sure you do!' said Delphine, sounding almost cross.

'Are you sure you don't want this dress back?' She indicated what she was wearing. 'I know you told me someone just left it here —'

Delphine interrupted. 'You keep it and think of our time together when you wear it. It looks good on you. I've noticed the guys looking at your legs.'

'I'll wear my shorts to travel in,' said Cass, hating the thought of her thighs being on show for that long journey. 'I'll be getting in and out of boats a bit.'

Becca appeared with a large cotton wrap. 'Put this in your bag,' she said. 'It can be chilly on planes and it'll be cold when you get to the UK. This will help.'

'That is very kind. I can post it back —'

'Don't bother. You lent me clothes when I needed them.'

'And you returned them. Goodness knows where they are now!' she laughed. 'I hope someone who needed them found my backpack wherever Austin chucked it, and found a use for the contents.' She didn't mention the camera; she knew if she did she would definitely cry.

'So, what's your route back?' asked Becca.

'Fishing boat to Martinique. We'll email Bastian's work and everything from there. Bastian has told us where to go to do all that. And then we'll fly to Paris, and a quick hop to London, where my mum will meet us, according to the messages we've had from my dad. He's arranged all the tickets.' She paused. 'I just hope it all works and I can pick up all the emails on my phone when I get to somewhere with a signal. But there's time to sort out new tickets if not.'

For some reason she thought back to that time, several lifetimes ago, when she and some friends almost failed to catch a flight to Ibiza. Now she was facing the thought of a much more complicated journey with complete calm. Travelling with Ranulph would make it all easy.

While they waited on the beach for the fishing boat, Cass said, 'It seems like years since we arrived, so much has happened.'

'I know. We hardly knew each other when we set off but now it seems we're old friends.'

Cass was grateful they were both looking out to sea. She didn't want to be Ranulph's 'old friend'. 'We may have fallen out a few times,' she said, 'but we travel well together.'

For a moment Ranulph seemed about to say something but then he said, 'Ah! This is our lift, I think!'

A fishing boat, looking horribly small, was steering its way through the waves. The sight of this plucky vessel, knowing it was going to take her away from Dominica, caused a lump in Cass's throat. She coughed.

And as Cass walked through the soft sand and the warm water so she could climb into the boat, she couldn't help wondering when she would be in Dominica again.

⋆ ⋆ ⋆

The trip to Martinique was fairly calm and Cass found looking at the waves hypnotic. She couldn't help contrasting herself with the frightened, nauseated young woman she'd been just a few weeks earlier. She'd learnt so much, done so much and faced so much. And yet a part of her remained the girl who had a crush on an older man — a man who had declared himself to be too old for her.

Should she tell Ranulph that he was wrong about Bastian? That she had never fancied him; that he would always be someone she liked and respected enormously, but he was not a love interest? But would that lead on to her admitting her feelings for Ranulph? No, she could never do that. It would be beyond humiliating. Looking at his profile now, while he too looked out to sea, she realised he would never be hers. He didn't want her, and although in her heart she felt she loved him enough for both of them, her head told her this couldn't ever be sufficient. Somehow she would have to get through the long journey to France, and then to England, by his side but not with him.

He had certainly seemed very fond of her when he'd found her after the hurricane. He had hugged her long and hard. For a few ecstatic moments she had hoped that he cared for her in a romantic way. But they were short moments soon to be cut off. She shuddered slightly at the memory of his sudden change of mood.

'There we are,' said Ranulph. 'Martinique for orders, as my seagoing father would have said.'

* * *

Cass's first impression of Martinique was how like France it was. The cars were French, parked all over the place as they often were in French towns, the people all had a sort of French elegance about them and the shop signs were in French. Of course, as a French island, this was as expected but somehow it was all a bit of a surprise to Cass.

'I suppose we should put our phones on. I've got a tiny bit of battery left,' said Cass, stopping in the street. 'It'll seem so strange, being back in touch with the world again.'

Almost instantly seemingly a million emails flooded into her phone. 'Oh,' she said. 'I wish I hadn't done that.'

Ranulph laughed. 'I'll have to charge mine first. But you can decide if you want to go through them all, or just delete them, en masse.'

Cass thought for a second or two. 'I think I'll go through them, but not yet. Maybe I'll wait until we're in England.'

'I'll delete mine. People will always email you again if there's anything urgent.'

Cass nodded. She didn't want to say what was probably blindingly obvious: she was too needy to do anything like that. She cleared her throat. 'Shall we get Bastian's book emailed then? And my drawings scanned?'

Ranulph had clear instructions where they should

go to get this done. But in spite of these, he still needed to ask the way a few times. Soon, however, they found themselves climbing the stairs to an office above a bakery that smelt of heaven.

'I actually really like the food we've been eating,' said Cass, 'but the thought of a good croissant is making my mouth water.'

'We'll get some on the way out,' said Ranulph. 'And maybe some macarons.'

'Fancy!' said Cass, but he didn't hear.

A charming, elegant woman, who seemed to know Bastian well, did everything that was necessary and it wasn't long before they were out in the street again.

'I'm very glad that's done,' said Cass as they emerged. 'It seems as if getting those papers off has been my mission for years.'

Ranulph smiled a little wryly. 'I'm glad to get them off myself. You risked your life to do that and now I don't need to worry that you'll do so again.'

Cass smiled. He was teasing her but she couldn't think of a snappy comeback. 'I'm starving!'

'Me too. Let's find somewhere for a late breakfast — or early lunch. Then we can find the flat that Bastian has arranged for us to borrow until the flight tonight.'

'I am looking forward to a proper shower, I must say.'

'Would you like to have that first? Before we eat?'

Cass shook her head. 'No, I'm used to feeling a bit grubby. Let's eat first.'

They found a charming café that could have been in any town in France and ordered quiche and salad and drank wine.

'I'll pay for this,' said Ranulph, when they'd finished. 'It seems like a charming novelty to be able to use my credit card.'

'Yes, we really are back in civilisation.' Cass paused. She was about to say that she wanted to buy something to wear to travel in, but Ranulph was suddenly engrossed in his phone.

He looked up. 'Sorry! That's very rude.'

'I understand. We haven't had an internet connection for ages.'

Ranulph nodded. 'And I'm afraid I've got to run some errands for various people. I'll take you back to the apartment and then go and do them.'

Cass opened her mouth to speak but then closed it again.

'The flight is just after nine so we'll need to be at the airport by six. We haven't got as long as we thought.' He smiled at her. 'You go and relax while I hunt down a generator for the dig.'

She nodded. She'd shower, and if there was time, go and find a dress. She had very little money in her bank account but that was why you had credit cards, wasn't it? You could buy things without having the money.

However, by the time they'd found the little apartment, got in and had coffee, Cass had lost the will to go and hunt for outfits. Ranulph had a shower and then went out. She had one too, standing under the warm water for far longer than she had been able to recently. On the island she'd just soaped and rinsed as quickly as possible. Now she took time to wash her hair properly, and put conditioner on it. When her hair was thoroughly clean, she found the hair dryer.

Feeling very different, she went through to the sitting room and turned on the television.

No sooner had she discovered a programme she could understand she fell asleep. She only awoke a couple of hours later when Ranulph shook her awake.

'Sorry to wake you but it's nearly time to leave for the airport.'

Cass instantly began to panic. 'We'll have to clear up here before we leave. I hate rushing when I'm travelling.' They'd had a conversation about this lifetimes ago.

'You looked so . . . peaceful, I couldn't bear to disturb you. I've done the washing up. We haven't left a mess.'

Ranulph seemed a bit awkward but Cass, feeling thoroughly caught out, didn't have time to try and work him out. She was now desperate to leave for the airport.

'We really do have plenty of time,' said Ranulph. 'The airport is nearby.' He put his hand on her shoulders. 'Now calm down and breathe.'

She removed his hands; however hard she'd been fighting it, him being too near her, touching her, still made her stomach flip.

* * *

'Right,' said Ranulph when Cass was satisfied they'd left the flat perfect. 'Have you got everything you need on your phone? Here.' He held out his hand and, meekly, Cass passed it over.

'I bought another phone charger,' said Ranulph. 'To replace the one that Austin ran off with. You should be fine.' He took another look at her phone, scrolling down to check the tickets and the online check-in details.

It all seemed to be taking far too long. 'Let's go, please!'

The taxi ride was indeed extremely quick and it wasn't long before they were at the airport. There was no baggage to check in.

'Come on, Ranulph,' Cass said, heading to the machine to scan their boarding passes.

He didn't follow her. 'Erm, Cass?'

What was the problem? 'What?'

'I'm not coming with you.'

Her heart did a somersault. 'What do you mean?'

'I'm not going home now, Cass. I'm going to stock up with things we need and go back to Dominica. You've got to travel home on your own.'

Cass felt sick, hot, cold and faint, all at the same time. 'Why the hell didn't you tell me sooner?' she demanded as anger came to her rescue and made it possible for her to respond. 'Why leave it until now?'

'I didn't want you to worry about the journey until I couldn't avoid it. I know you have travel anxiety —'

'Fine!' she said, furious suddenly, turning away from him and walking as fast as she could to where she hoped she needed to go. 'Bye, Ranulph,' she muttered to herself. 'Have a nice life!'

But the thought that it would be a life without her in it cut like a knife.

22

It was only a little later, when she'd been through several sessions of showing her passport, her phone and various other things, that Cass found herself being shown to the business-class lounge.

'Oh no, I don't think so,' she said, smiling at what was clearly a mistake. 'Do I look like a business-class traveller?'

'Check your ticket, ma'am,' the lovely woman said. 'It's definitely business class.'

Cass checked. 'I had no idea. My father bought me the ticket,' she said, to explain her extreme lack of attention to the finer details.

'He's looking out for his daughter. Now go through that door and help yourself to drinks and snacks. You'll be called in plenty of time for your flight.'

She found the Ladies' restroom immediately and fashioned the wrap Becca had given her into a skirt. She still looked incredibly shabby, and knowing her daypack did not look remotely like executive luggage added to her feelings of being in the wrong place. But Cass was determined to enjoy every minute of being in business class, despite being so hurt by Ranulph not telling her he wasn't coming with her.

She was able to sleep for much of the journey and made the transfer from Paris to London easily. She knew she was taking 'travelling light' to a level she would have preferred not to sink to, but it did make her journey very easy to negotiate.

She emerged into the arrivals hall at Heathrow aware that she was cold and was utterly delighted to see her mother waiting for her. She fell into her arms and tried very hard not to cry.

'I brought a coat for you,' said her mother. 'I knew you'd be cold and it's a chilly evening.'

Cass slipped on her mother's old linen jacket.

'And a scarf,' her mother added, wrapping a cashmere scarf round her daughter's shoulders.

When Cass was better dressed she hugged her mother again. 'It's so good to be home!'

'It's lovely to have you home. I can't wait to hear all about it. And your dad is equally impatient to see you.'

'Will a phone call do or will he need a visit?'

'He's definitely hoping for a visit.'

Cass sighed. Her father's house was intrinsically linked to Ranulph in her mind.

'I have got some very good news for you, though,' said her mother, leading the way through the car park.

'What?'

'Rosa is back! I met her mother in Waitrose. She's finished her course and is now home. She wanted to come over tonight but I said we'd see how you were feeling.'

'I'd love to see Rosa! I've missed her so much since she's been away.' She didn't add that Rosa was the perfect person to help her through her heartbreak. 'I'll call her now and tell her to come over.' She got out her phone.

'Could you perhaps wait till we've had an evening together first, darling? I want to hear all about your adventures.'

Cass realised she'd been a bit tactless. 'Of course. I

want to spend time with you too.'

'Jolly good. None of your half-siblings are staying so it's just us. I've got a lasagne in the oven and a bottle of wine. It's going to be lovely!'

As her mother drove them home Cass realised she was very glad there wouldn't be anyone there to mock her for her mistakes. Yet she now felt very much better able to hold her own: she had made mistakes, of course she had, but she'd also sewn up a bad cut and the wound had been fine, found the petroglyph which in anthropological terms was very important, as well as ferried supplies to people in need over very bad roads. Now she thought about it, she felt proud of what she'd achieved.

They didn't talk much on the journey home but when they arrived Cass had a long, hot bath. Feeling like a teenager, or Bridget Jones, she found the big old sloppy T-shirt she always used to sleep in, worn-out bunny slippers, and pull-on cotton trousers she'd had since she was twelve. The softness of the fabric was comforting. She went down to the kitchen to the welcoming smell of lasagne and garlic bread.

'So!' said her mother when she'd served up and they both had glasses of red wine. 'Tell me all about Dominica. I don't suppose you have photos, do you? You wouldn't have been able to use your phone, would you?'

'No,' said Cass, having finished her first delicious forkful of her mother's cooking. 'But I do have pictures. I'll show you after we've eaten.'

'Oh good! Did you buy them?'

Cass shook her head. She'd kept her fondness for drawing secret for so long it was quite hard to bring it into the open. 'I . . . I drew them. And just as well

I could because . . .'

Bit by bit the story came out. Cass's mother's eyes opened wider and wider as she heard of her daughter's exploits and achievements.

'And Bastian was able to find the petroglyph because you redrew the map?' her mother asked.

'More or less. I'd also tied a shoelace to a nearby tree.'

'That was clever thinking.'

Cass shrugged.

'I must say, Cass darling, you may look about twelve but actually you're turning into a very capable young woman.'

Cass frowned in thought. 'I don't usually look that young, do I? When I'm not wearing my favourite 'at home' sleeping things?'

'You always look very young. Don't knock it! You'll be grateful when you're my age!'

'Actually, Mum, you look very young for your age, too.'

Her mother shrugged off the compliment but it was obviously one she'd received before. But it made Cass wonder if Ranulph knew how old she was. How young did he think she was?

'Now, pudding? I've made tiramisu. Your favourite.'

Cass felt her stomach was fully extended but the thought of her mother's creamy coffee- and marsala-flavoured dessert made her nod in agreement. 'Isn't it funny how one can be full as an egg, but still manage pudding?'

'I think you've lost quite a bit of weight since you've been away. I'm allowed to fatten you up.'

They took their pudding into the sitting room so Cass could find her drawings to show her mother.

She laid them all out on the coffee table and sat back and ate while her mother looked through them.

'You did these?' her mother said at last.

Cass scraped the last bit of alcoholic creaminess from her bowl. 'I did. I've always liked drawing, Mum. I think you knew that.'

'Yes, but when I last saw anything you drew you weren't as good as this!'

'I was probably about ten! It's hardly surprising. It's the thing I like doing best in the world. I think I really worked that out when I was in Dominica.'

'Your dad is very keen for you to go and see him as soon as possible. He's been so invested in your trip. He'll be thrilled to hear how you discovered the petroglyph,' her mother said, changing the subject.

Cass nodded. 'I want to spend a few days here with you, if that's all right. Catch up with Rosa, decompress a bit, and then go and see Dad.'

'Well, don't leave it too long.'

As her mother said this, Cass suddenly realised that she was right: she shouldn't leave it too long or Ranulph might leave Dominica and go back home. She really didn't want to risk running into him. She felt too raw, too hurt by the fact that he didn't tell her she'd be travelling alone until the very last minute because he didn't think she could cope with the thought. It was insulting.

'I really want to see Rosa. And find a job. I've got no money.'

'Your dad would happily pay for your fare to see him —'

'Good! But I can't be penniless. I must find something.'

Her mother became thoughtful. 'You know at one

time you'd have asked to borrow money from me and not expected to pay it back. You've changed.'

'I have! And while we're on the subject of change, I no longer want to become a teacher.'

Her mother frowned. 'What would you do instead?'

Cass had been dreading this question. 'Ideally, I'd go to art school. Or if I can't do that, maybe I could illustrate children's books or something. I did the drawings for Bastian's thesis, after all.'

'But if you were a teacher, you could do all that in your spare time. You couldn't have a proper career in illustration, surely.'

'Keep my drawing as a hobby? I don't think so, Mum. Teachers work incredibly hard. They have to love it. Teaching is too hard for it just to be something you do to earn money. I want to do something I love.' She paused. 'Take Bastian, for instance. His life and his work are more or less the same thing. He writes about the islands he knows more about than anyone else. It's not just about the money for him.'

Her mother sighed in a way she had sighed many times before. This time, Cass felt annoyed. She was old enough to make her own decisions. 'I'll make it work somehow.'

'How many artists earn money from what they do?'

'I don't know. But it's what I want to spend my life doing. I never was any good at academic stuff, Mum. You know that.'

Her mother pursed her lips. 'Well, it's your choice.' Then she smiled more warmly. 'And as you've already put yourself in your pyjamas you should probably have an early night!'

Cass laughed. 'Are you offering to read me a bed-time story? I'll just message Rosa, to make a plan, then

I can't wait to get to bed.' She hugged her mother. 'I know you only want what's best for me, but I think it's time I decided what that is.'

23

Cass arrived on the Scottish island a few days later. It was late afternoon.

'Cass!' said Eleanor, with her hands on Cass's shoulders. 'You look beautiful! Dicing with death on a daily basis obviously suits you.'

Howard, coming up behind Eleanor, laughed. 'I don't suppose you were dicing with death, were you? I would never have suggested you go if I thought that.'

'There were a few hairy moments, I admit, but most of the time I was perfectly safe.'

'Now, what would you like? Tea, or a proper drink?' Eleanor seemed very much the lady of the house now. 'I think you should have a meal and a bit of a rest before we grill you. Although your father is dying to.'

Cass smiled. 'The hop up here from the Cotswolds was easy compared to coming back from Dominica. A cup of tea would be welcome —'

'And then a stiff drink,' said her father. 'Come on through.'

Eleanor insisted that she should be given time to visit the bathroom and to make herself tidy but her father seemed very impatient by the time Cass joined him and Eleanor in the sunroom.

Eleanor handed her a mug of tea and her father a large whisky.

'Thank you so much for the business-class ticket,' Cass said when she was settled in a comfy chair overlooking the Atlantic. 'If the air steward hadn't pointed it out to me, I wouldn't have believed I'd be turning left instead of right when I got on the plane. I would never have found my seat.'

Howard smiled expansively. 'You deserved business class! I'm just surprised that Ranulph didn't take advantage of it. He'll have to pay for his own plane ticket now.'

'So, you bought him a business-class ticket too?'

'I offered it to him but he declined.' Howard regarded his daughter. 'Why might that have been, do you think?'

Cass sipped her tea and shrugged. 'He said he still had work to do.' She cleared her throat. 'He met someone he used to know, when he was in Dominica before —'

'An old flame?' suggested Eleanor tentatively.

'Probably. Anyway, the hurricane uncovered a really interesting archaeological site. It showed that the Kalinago people and Dutch pirates cohabited, which has never been seen before. So they were both well into that.' Cass was glad that this unexpected fact stopped Howard and Eleanor looking at her so intently. 'And on the plane, the crew were terribly nice to me, in spite of me looking so scruffy.'

'That's really interesting about the pirates and the Kalinago,' said Howard, who always behaved if he belonged wherever he was, unabashed by the wrong clothes or anything else.

'It was. Bastian said it had never even been suspected before. He discovered some shards of very early delft pottery next to Kalinago artefacts. He felt it could only have belonged to pirates who landed to escape the law, or indeed the weather.' She smiled, hoping to move on. She hadn't paid very close attention to the archaeology at the time because she'd had other things on her mind. She picked up her tea.

'Eleanor? Is it all right if I ask her about the petroglyph now?' said Howard.

'Of course,' said Eleanor. 'She's had an opportunity to wash her hands, she's had most of a mug of tea. Now you can give her the third degree.'

Everyone was laughing now. 'Please! Put an old man out of his misery. Tell me about how you found the petroglyph? I want all the details.'

'Although,' said Eleanor, 'dinner is ready. Let's go through and Cass can tell you while she eats. Otherwise there's a danger of her starving to death halfway through her story.'

'It won't take that long,' said Cass. 'But I am hungry.'

'Now will you tell me!' said Howard, when everyone was seated and had plates of Chicken Marengo in front of them.

'Put him out of his misery, Cass,' said Eleanor.

Cass took a breath. 'Well, it was only by chance I was on the expedition to find the petroglyph really. Ranulph would have been more use than me —'

'I don't think so!' said Howard. 'But why didn't he go?'

'He'd cut his leg, really quite badly. It was a good thing we had those first aid kits.'

'Did it need stitches?' asked Eleanor.

Cass nodded. 'I had to sew him up. He was amazingly brave.'

'You had to stitch him up?' Howard was incredulous. 'But you're not qualified! Wasn't there someone else who could do it?'

'I did do St John's Ambulance exams, you know,' said Cass, although sewing people up hadn't been covered in the course. 'And there was no one else. It was fine. The wound is healing up nicely.'

'OK, so you went with Bastian?'

'And Toussaint, and Austin. He insisted. He said there was no petroglyph. His whole thesis depended on there not being one.'

'Tricky,' said Eleanor.'

'He's a dreadful man,' said Howard. 'I spoke to him on the radio. He always insisted no one else was available to talk to me.'

'He wouldn't let anyone else into the hut where the radio was,' said Cass. 'Anyway, we set off. Luckily, apart from a few fallen trees the hurricane didn't seem to have done too much damage in the forest and we got along OK. Then we stopped for a break.' Cass paused. She wasn't looking forward to telling her father this bit. 'Austin threw the camera into the bushes.'

'What?' Howard banged the arm of his chair in fury. 'Couldn't you stop him?'

'No. He sort of unhooked it from my wrist. I was about to take a picture to discover which settings I needed. He pretended it was an accident. Of course it wasn't.'

'That's absolutely outrageous,' Howard began. 'I should bloody well sue him!'

'He'd just tell you to claim on your insurance,' said Cass.

'It's not the money!' Howard was almost shouting.

'Don't get worked up, darling,' said Eleanor, her hand on Howard's. 'And let Cass finish her story.'

Cass was grateful. She so wanted to tell her father

that the camera was safe and the more she thought about it, the more she realised if she hadn't got into that pick-up with Austin, it would have been. She hoped that the fact she'd found the petroglyph would somehow make up for him losing it.

'For a little while after I lost the camera, I went with them but at a certain point, I stopped. I said I was tired.'

Her momentary pause made her father ask, 'Why? Were you tired?'

'I was, to be honest, but that wasn't why I stopped.' Cass paused to think how best to explain the next part of her tale. 'I wanted to be alone, for the others to get ahead.'

'Why?' demanded her father again.

'Howard, darling,' said Eleanor soothingly. 'Do let the poor girl tell her story.'

'It's OK,' Cass said. 'I'm just thinking how best to explain it. You remember the map?'

'Of course!' said Howard.

'Well, you know it was pretty fragile. I had to trace it so there'd be one that wouldn't fall apart if it was used.'

Her father nodded.

'I don't know if you recall, but tracing a document the old-fashioned way, with greaseproof paper or whatever, means you actually draw it several times. By the time I'd finished, I knew the map more or less by heart.'

'And?'

'I actually drew it wrong. I added on a bit. To get everyone out of the way.'

'Goodness me, Cass,' said Eleanor. 'I am so impressed!'

'But why?' said Howard.

'I wanted to find the petroglyph, if it was there, when Austin was out of the way. I thought the place I had stopped was more or less where it should have been except there was a river on the map, and no river where I was.'

This time she was allowed to pause without her father badgering her. 'I thought I'd sit a while with my eyes closed. I was tired, as I said. And it was while I had my eyes closed that I heard water. But it was a trickle, not a gushing river.'

'It was such a long time ago that the map was drawn,' said Howard. 'The landscape would have changed.'

'Anyway, I think I did actually doze off for a few seconds because I woke up when there was a bit of a breeze suddenly and the sun fell on my face. I sat up and looked at the rocks which the others had looked at and walked past. With the sun shining in the right way I could see a face in the rock.'

'The petroglyph,' whispered Howard. 'Oh, my dear girl!' He got up and came over to Cass's chair. She got up and he hugged her. 'You're so clever!'

'But that's not the end of the story, Dad,' said Cass when everyone was sitting down again.

'You had no camera,' said Eleanor. 'You couldn't record it.'

'But I could! I did. I had my trusty sketchbook and pencils. I slipped them into my pack just before we left, in case.'

'But you can't draw, can you, darling?' said Cass's father.

'I can draw well enough,' said Cass, feeling defensive. 'And I had the means to do so with me. I drew the petroglyph and as many of the plants and trees around it as I could. But I knew that wouldn't be enough so I tied my shoelace round a tree really near it.'

'Cass! You are so ingenious,' said Eleanor.

Cass shrugged, smiling.

'This calls for whisky,' said Howard. 'Let's break out the good stuff.'

'Howard, you only drink the good stuff,' said Eleanor. 'You said that life was too short to drink blended whisky. I said it was too long not to.' She laughed, teasing him: 'But you are older than I am so perhaps you're right. We'll have it after dinner though.'

Howard's good spirits had deflated and he suddenly looked his age. 'Of course it was wonderful that you could draw the petroglyph, sweetheart, but I'm still sad about the camera. It was a present from my father.'

Cass put her hand on Howard's. 'Actually, I got it back that time. Toussaint, who was with us, found it and gave it back to me. It was unharmed.'

'What do you mean 'that time'?' asked Howard.

This bit was going to be very hard, Cass realised. She felt so ashamed. 'Erm —'

'Why don't you let Cass get to the end of her story?' said Eleanor, her hand on Howard's again, stroking it a little. 'It'll be quicker in the end.'

Howard nodded, and topped up everyone's wine glass. There was a short time of silent eating before he put down his knife and fork and looked at Cass.

'Much later, when Austin was so desperate to get off the island, he said I had to go with him, and that if I didn't he'd destroy Bastian's reputation academically — and his father's, which was worse really.'

'Go on,' Eleanor prompted.

'There was another hurricane threatening, but Austin wouldn't wait. As soon as we set off I knew it was a terrible mistake. The weather was getting bad and the road, which wasn't good to start with, was turning into a river.'

She'd spared her mother and Rosa some of the details of her journey with Austin, but she felt her father needed the whole truth.

'I kept begging him to stop but it was only when we were quite far away from the house that he did. I think that was so it wouldn't be easy for me to walk to shelter.'

'So you got out of the car?' Her father sounded horrified.

'He pushed me out. He leant across me and opened the door and then shoved me so hard I fell out. He had driven off before I had time to make sure I was out of the way. I had my daypack on my knee, so I was able to grab it, but my backpack, with everything else, including your camera, disappeared with him into the wind and rain.'

'Oh God, Cass!' Howard was horrified. 'I can't believe I put you in that dangerous situation.'

'It was me, Dad! I was the fool who let herself be persuaded to leave.' The realisation of what she'd done, how terrified and stupid she'd felt, came rushing back to her. She shook her head slightly to rid herself of the feeling. 'It was all my fault.'

There was a pause and then Eleanor asked, 'What did you have in your day bag? Why did you need to keep it so close?'

'It had my passport and things in it, but also a memory stick with Bastian's thesis on it. And the sketches I'd done of the petroglyph, among other things. I'd hidden the memory stick in a pot of moisturiser, and the sketches were in a box of Tampax, folded carefully.'

'So you suspected Austin would try to take them?' asked her father.

Cass nodded. 'If only I'd had your camera in that pack too —'

Her father shook his head. 'No. If you'd had too bulky a day bag he might have looked in it. Then he could have seen the other things and he may well have taken them too. Him leaving with your clothes and the camera was fine, really.'

There was a thoughtful silence until Eleanor broke it. 'Why don't you two go through to the sunroom? I'll bring coffee, tea, whatever, and chocolates. I'm afraid there is no pudding.'

It was a glorious June evening and almost full daylight. Cass and her father had reclining chairs overlooking the sea.

'One thing I missed in Dominica was twilight. The sun seems to drop out of the sky leaving pitch dark behind,' said Cass.

'I remember that,' said Howard. 'And the looking for the Emerald Drop. Did you see it?'

Cass laughed gently. 'No, although we looked a few times. I'm not sure I believe it's real.'

'It definitely is,' he said. 'But it's rare.'

'I'm so sorry about your camera, Dad,' Cass said.

'I hope I've taught you better than to be hung up on things, Cass. They're not like people, who do matter. I hadn't used that camera for years. Don't worry about it.'

In spite of his reply, Cass realised he was upset,

which made her even more upset herself. And also, right at the back of her thoughts was the realisation that he hadn't asked about her drawing.

24

Possibly because it was still so light, Cass couldn't get to sleep. She sat up and decided now was a good time to go through her emails. She hadn't had the courage to delete them all, nor had she had the inclination to go through them. Now was the time.

She'd deleted a good few adverts from websites she'd once bought something from and then came across a message from an email address she didn't recognise. Because she was taking her time, instead of deleting it automatically, she read it.

Hi Cass

You didn't reply to my earlier emails which makes me think you must still be on the island. This is my third email. I won't try again.

I have your dad's camera. Do you want it back? I'll give it to you if you come to London to collect it. Otherwise I'll sell it. I have someone interested in it. I'll be in London at the end of July. Let me know.

Cass didn't hesitate. *Dear Austin,* she typed. *I would really like my dad's camera back. I'll come and collect it from you.*

After she'd sent this, she lay back on her bed and then put on the silk eye mask that Eleanor had left there for her. Would she ever get to sleep? It was so light and she had such a lot on her mind. Austin was quite capable of wanting to sell her Howard's camera — demanding a ransom would be a better description — and she had no money. Could she ask her father for the money when it was her stupid fault it was in Austin's hands?

* * *

After Cass had helped Eleanor clear away breakfast the next morning, Eleanor said, 'You never had much of a chance to see the island when you were here before. Would you like a tour? It won't take long. It's very small.'

Cass laughed. 'I'd love that! As you say, when I was here before it wasn't long before we dashed off to Dominica.'

Eleanor took Howard's Land Rover — a far newer one than Ranulph's — driving at a pace which made it easy for Cass to admire the views.

'It really is stunning here, isn't it?' Cass said. 'And what's really weird — and I keep having this thought — is that the sea is the same sea as we looked at in Dominica. The Atlantic.'

'Isn't Dominica in the Caribbean?'

'Yes, but it's also on the Atlantic. There's a spit apparently. One side is the Atlantic and the other is the Caribbean. Where Bastian lives is Atlantic.'

'That is rather amazing.' Eleanor drove on in silence for a little way. 'Now, while I do want you to see the island — this one, not Dominica — I have an agenda.'

She pulled into a passing place where the view of the sea and other islands beyond was uninterrupted.

They looked at the view for a few moments.
'What's your agenda?' Cass asked when she could bear the silence no longer. 'The last time I was in a — well, OK, a fairly beaten-up pick-up that wasn't a bit like this well-turned-out vehicle, and the driver had an agenda, it didn't end well for me.'
Eleanor laughed. 'This might not end well for me!'
'Oh?'
'It seems ridiculous, but I suppose in a way I'm asking you for your father's hand in marriage.'
It took Cass a few seconds to work this out. 'You want to marry Dad?'
'Yes. How would you feel about it? I know if you were remotely uncomfortable, Howard wouldn't do it.'
'Oh, Eleanor! I'd be delighted. I want Dad to be happy and I think you're amazing — putting up with him is fairly amazing — but if you actually want to do it, that's brilliant.' She cleared her throat. 'Are you and he — in love?'
'We are. Strangely.'
'You know he's always been a bit of a —'
'Ladies' man? Oh yes. I'd be going into this with my eyes wide open.'
'I suppose now he's . . . a bit older —'
'Age doesn't really change basic behaviour, but we really are in love and I think he knows if he wants to stay on the island — and he does — he needs someone beside him — someone who is in love with him. That's me.'
Cass rubbed Eleanor's arm, not knowing quite what else to do. 'That's lovely. Very romantic.'
This made Eleanor really laugh. 'Actually, it's a lot more romantic than I make it sound. What will your

mother think about it?'

'She'll be happy. She and Dad get on pretty well.'

'Great! We would still have got married if your mother didn't approve but we'd much rather everyone was on board with the idea.'

'Er — I'm not an only child, you know,' said Cass. 'I have stepbrothers and a stepsister. Although of course it's none of their business, they would have an opinion.'

Eleanor laughed gently. 'If we wanted a blessing from everyone we'd never get it. My sons from my first marriage are being a bit sniffy about Howard, but if the people we really care about are happy, than so are we.'

'Happy to confirm I'm happy!' said Cass.

Eleanor smiled and started the engine. 'Well, that's my love life sorted, now let's pay attention to yours.'

'Agh!' Cass's protest came out louder and wilder than she'd intended. 'No, really, Eleanor, I don't have a love life.'

'When people are in love with people — even if they only think they are — they go two ways. Either they talk about them all the time, find every opportunity they can to bring them into the conversation, or they carefully never mention them at all.' She pulled away and headed off down the road. 'You and Ranulph shared a massive adventure and yet you seem to have completely edited him out of the picture. And anyway,' she persisted, ignoring Cass's squeak of protest, 'I remember seeing you look at him — just once, no one else would have noticed — before you both set off.'

'God, I hope he doesn't know how I feel.'

'He probably doesn't. Men are awfully dense sometimes. I thought you might like to see his house.'

Cass gasped in shock. 'He's not there, is he?'

'No! He's still in Dominica. He'll tell me when he's coming back. I buy groceries for him. I just thought you should know where he lives.' She paused. 'I have the key if you want to go inside.'

Just for a second or two, Cass was tempted. 'No. That would be wrong. But I won't say no to a quick peek at the outside.'

It was delightful, Cass thought, once they stopped outside it. Traditional, lovely views and very secluded.

'What you have to think about is,' said Eleanor, 'could you live here? It's not for everyone.'

'I don't know,' said Cass after a few moments. 'My heart says I could live anywhere Ranulph is, but could I? It's academic anyway because he's never going to fall in love with me, even if I agreed to live with him in a dungeon. And this is far from that.'

'Why have you given up on him? Why do you think he'll never fall for you?'

'I'm too young for him, although he didn't actually say that. He said I was too young for Bastian, who I really like, but only as a friend. But they're roughly the same age. If I'm too young for one, I'm too young for the other.'

'You don't think he was trying to put you off Bastian when he said that?'

'Well, yes. He thought I was in love with him. He was telling me why it wouldn't work. And that Bastian had a girlfriend. Which I knew.'

'Don't you think there's a chance that he was doing that because he wanted you for himself?'

'What a lovely dream that would be! But no. When he found me, after the second hurricane, he hugged me for ages and for a few blissful moments I thought

I was in heaven. Then he put me down and started telling me off. He won't ever fall for me, Eleanor. He thinks I'm a child — even though I am twenty-five. I can vote and everything!'

Eleanor laughed. 'Don't despair, Cass. There's an Irish expression that says: 'What's for you won't go by you.''

'We'll see!' said Cass with a smile she didn't mean.

They drove in silence for a few moments and then Eleanor said, 'Tell me about your drawing. I don't think I knew that was one of your talents.'

'I don't know if I'd call it a talent . . .'

'I'd definitely call it one. Why doesn't Howard know about it?'

By the time they got back to the house, Eleanor had heard more about Cass's drawing than either of her parents had ever cared to know.

'Well, I think it's wonderful. Of course, being a teacher is a safer option, but you need to be happy in your work,' Eleanor said.

'Thank you for understanding!'

'It's easier for me to understand than possibly it will be for your parents. I see you as a younger friend, not as someone I've brought up and looked after all your life.'

'My mother isn't thrilled about it, I must say. She thinks anything arty is insecure and she worries about me.'

'Mothers do. My own children would say the same about me.'

They drove home in thoughtful silence.

* * *

As Cass finally said goodbye a couple of days later, Howard said, 'I've put a few quid into your bank, darling. It may be a while before you're earning again, and you changed all your plans for me. It's a thank you.'

'Dad! I was happy to go! You know that.'

Eventually, Eleanor said she had to get Cass to the mainland so she could start her journey down south. Father and daughter hugged. She was going to miss him and Eleanor and the island.

25

Cass had been back at her mother's house for a couple of days when she took a trip to her favourite shop. It was the art shop and as a child she had taken her pocket money and bought special colouring pencils, one at a time, until she had a set. She loved everything they sold, from the watercolours in little cubes (half pans) to fit into metal boxes, the vast array of pencils, charcoal, brushes so fine you could hardly see them, and of course wonderful blocks of paper. There was every type of paint Cass had heard of and a couple she didn't know about, and beautiful wooden boxes with spaces for everything, like treasure chests filled with colour.

Cass decided to spend a little of the money her father had given her to buy another sketch pad, some pencils and a really soft eraser.

She was queuing up to pay and noticed that only one till was in action. When it came to her turn, she said, 'You seem a bit short-staffed.'

'Yes!' said the charming but harassed woman dealing with the till. 'My colleague has had to go away and I can't get cover for her, which leaves just me.'

'I'll do it!' said Cass instantly.

The woman paused. 'But it's likely to be only for a couple of weeks — three maybe. And it's part time — three days a week — not really worth —'

'I'd love to do it. Working here has been my dream since I was a little girl.'

'Oh,' said the woman. She was in her early forties and she looked like an artist. 'Are you sure?'

'I'm between jobs. It'll be fun to have my dream job just for a little while.' Cass smiled, hoping she didn't look too desperate. She realised this was just what she needed. She'd have to concentrate — there was a lot of stock to learn about — and yet she wasn't committed for too long. If Austin summoned her to London to give her the camera she could probably be available.

'Er — let me just serve these people and we'll have a chat. I'm Sarah, by the way.'

'Cass. Short for Cassiopeia.'

'The constellation? Nice!'

Cass inspected the birthday cards while she waited for Sarah to be ready to see her. She hadn't known the job was available ten minutes before, but now she did know, her heart was set on it. She took the fact that she didn't have to explain her name as a good sign.

'Do you have much retail experience?' Sarah asked, having invited Cass into her office, a room at the top of the building which was part of an old mill.

'No,' said Cass. 'But I'm a quick learner and I do love art. Drawing in particular, but I'd love to get into watercolours. I just love all the kit!' Cass realised this probably wasn't the most mature reason she could give for wanting to work in an art shop but she felt she should be totally honest. After all, if it was only for a couple of weeks, Sarah, her possible new boss, didn't have a lot to lose.

'We do art classes here in the evening. Free classes are part of the deal if you work here.' Sarah laughed. 'The wages aren't huge, I have to admit. Minimum wage, in fact. I know it's not good enough. I'm working on it.'

'Well, from my point of view, my dream job and free classes is brilliant.' She bit her lip — she'd made it sound as if she was only keen on the classes because she wouldn't be paying for them. 'But of course I'd pay for the class once I'm no longer working here.'

'That may not be necessary. It's possible your job might become permanent, if my colleague doesn't come back. Anyway, I must get back downstairs. Come with me and I'll show you round, customers permitting.'

Another perk of the job Sarah hadn't originally mentioned was the staff discount.

'It's just possible I might spend all my wages on paints,' Cass said as Sarah rung up a haul of materials she hadn't been able to resist. 'But worth it!'

'Not if you have to pay rent, frankly,' said Sarah.

Cass suffered a pang of guilt. 'Currently I'm living with my mother, and she's not charging me. That will have to change.'

* * *

Cass was about to bring up the tricky subject of her paying rent when she got home after work a few days later but her mother got in before her with a tricky subject of her own.

'I've got the rest of the family coming for dinner tonight,' she said, knowing the news wouldn't be popular with Cass. 'They're longing to see you. They want to hear about your trip to Dominica.'

Longing to tear me to shreds about it, thought Cass. 'OK,' she said aloud. 'I haven't got an art class tonight, I'll be there.'

Her mother shook off Cass's comment about the art class with a tut and a shake of the head.

'Go and wash your hands and then set the table.'

While she was washing her hands Cass reminded herself how lucky she was to be living at home, rent-free, in great comfort. While she was drying her hands she wondered how long she and her mother could live together without getting annoyed.

'So!' said Cass's brother Martin when everyone had arrived and had a drink in their hands. 'Tell us all about your Caribbean holiday, Cass.'

Cass smiled sweetly. At one time, not that long ago, she'd have jumped on her brother for this dismissive remark, but not now. 'Gorgeous, darling! I highly recommend Dominica just after a hurricane. It is really at its best.' Then she paused. 'Actually, there is a wonderful clarity in the air then.'

Martin, faintly annoyed by his sister's refusal to rise to his teasing, said, 'So what was it like then?'

'Should you really have gone?' said Caroline, the eldest and bossiest family member.

'Do you think we could eat before you all lay into Cass?' said her mother, rather to Cass's surprise. 'I've done a roast. Family favourite.'

'And I made a crumble for pudding,' said Cass.

Although the meal did stave off the criticism for a while, Martin couldn't keep quiet very long.

'What were you doing there, and how on earth did you manage to lose Howard's camera?'

'I really don't think Mum wants to hear the story all over again,' said Cass. 'I got in a vehicle with someone I shouldn't, and when I got out again —'

'She was thrown out!' said her mother. Cass wasn't

entirely sure she'd told her mother this but she may have been talking to Howard. 'She could have been killed!'

'And the camera was in my bag in the back, which wasn't thrown out,' Cass finished.

'Really, Cass, you haven't got the sense you were born with!' said Caroline. 'Surely you know better than to get in a car with someone you don't know.'

'I did — do know him,' said Cass calmly. 'And I wanted to catch a plane. This man wanted to catch it too. It was a mistake because there was a hurricane brewing —'

'Surely the hurricane had happened by then,' said Caroline, confused.

Cass laughed, thinking of Delphine and her reply to this question. 'Hurricanes aren't like Christmas, you know,' she said to her older sister. 'You don't have one and then know there won't be one for another year. There's a season for them.'

Caroline didn't like being wrong so she didn't comment.

Then, unexpectedly, James spoke up. Younger than Martin and Caroline, he was the nearest in age to Cass. 'It seems you've done some pretty brave and exciting things, kid,' he said. 'Why don't you tell us everything?'

For once, Cass's siblings didn't interrupt and let her tell her story, which included sewing up Ranulph's leg. Although this wasn't really part of the narrative, Cass couldn't resist adding it. She was proud of her achievement.

'Well, I must say, you do seem to have done the family proud,' said James.

'Agreed,' said Martin. 'Never thought you would.'

'Although she did lose Howard's camera,' said Caroline. But then she obviously felt she'd been small-minded and gave Cass's arm a pat.

'So, who's for pudding?' said their mother. 'It looks delicious, I must say.'

'Have you learnt to cook as well as do first aid?' asked Martin.

Cass smiled and shrugged. She had every confidence in her crumble.

26

The days passed and Cass realised she loved her new job. She loved the customers, the busy, vibrant shop and being surrounded by artists' materials. Sarah was an appreciative, if somewhat vague boss. But as her wages were basic, Cass also got a job in a wine bar a couple of nights a week.

As she explained to Rosa, 'I want to earn as much as I can and I love being busy.'

It was Cass's first night working at the wine bar and Rosa had come in early, so she and Cass could chat when there were only a few customers.

'I thought you said your dad had given you money?' said Rosa.

'Yes, but I want to get his camera back. Bloody Austin might make me buy it and he could charge me a fortune. Besides, I want to go to art school, and I would really like to pay for at least some of that myself.'

Rosa was still focused on the camera. 'It's as if he's kidnapped it and is demanding ransom money.'

Cass nodded. 'Exactly like that! And currently I'm the desperate parent waiting for the kidnapper to get in touch.' Cass paused in her wiping of the counter. 'I don't want to have to use Dad's money if I can avoid it. I lost the camera and I feel it's up to me to get it back.'

Rosa took a breath to protest and then let it out again. 'Have you got a nice pale rosé? Something from Provence?'

Cass smiled. 'Certainly, madame. What size glass would you like?'

'A small. Can you join me?'

Cass shook her head. 'Not while I'm working; plus Mum has lent me her car so I'm driving home.'

* * *

Free art classes for employees being one of the perks of the job at the art shop, Cass had been very excited, and had intended to sign up for everything she could.

Annoyingly, when she had asked Sarah how to join the classes she received disappointing news.

'Most of our classes start in September. We don't have very much over the summer.'

This had been a bit of a blow. She had been hoping to cram as many classes in as possible, so, come September, she could apply for some sort of full-time art course.

'But we do have 'Flower painting in watercolours',' Sarah had said, obviously seeing Cass's disappointment. 'That any good to you?'

Suddenly feeling churlish, Cass had smiled. 'That would be great! I've always wanted to do watercolours.'

'I teach the course,' Sarah had said.

'Will I need to bring my own materials?'

'Of course. But don't forget you get a staff discount. I'll give you a list.'

By the time Cass had bought a professional watercolour kit, several brushes, a large block of watercolour paper (she accepted she could have bought smaller paper, of a lesser quality) as well as pencils and various other bits and pieces, she realised she would have to work for at least three of her part-time weeks for nothing.

The class was, to put it politely, small. There were only two other people in it. One, Delia, was a jolly elderly lady who described herself as 'having all the gear but no idea', and the other was an elderly man who didn't say much but did beautiful work.

Cass, the youngest by several decades, sat behind the other two so she could make her mistakes in private. There was a jam jar with some wildflowers in it for them to copy.

Sarah was quick to notice that Cass had a very good feel for the paint.

'I've only ever done drawing really,' Cass explained, 'which is why I've drawn the flowers and then painted in the colour. It's probably not the best way.'

'It's not the established method but it's very attractive, seeing faint pencil lines under the watercolour.'

Delia, the elderly lady, was extremely enthusiastic about Cass's work. 'If you cared to give me that painting, it would be the perfect card for a friend of mine. I always struggle to find her something suitable.' She paused, possibly registering Cass's look of utter disbelief. 'Would ten pounds be insulting, do you think?'

'Ten pounds for my first attempt at watercolours?' said Cass. 'That's ridiculous! I'll give it to you!'

The argument went on for a bit and in the end it was agreed that Cass would accept a fiver and Sarah would turn it into a card for Delia, for a bit more money.

Although there wasn't a lot of tidying up to do, Cass stayed behind after class to help.

'You do have a real gift for watercolours,' said Sarah.

'Do you think,' Cass began tentatively, 'that if I added paint to my sketches of Dominica —'

'Where?'

'It's an island in the Caribbean, one of the Windward Islands. I've just come back from there.'

Sarah nodded.

'I could make them into paintings? I could even redo them. Delia wanting my painting as a present gave me an idea. I'd love to make the sketches I did there into proper paintings.'

'I'm sure you could. Let me know if you need any help.'

'I think now I've got the kit I can copy the drawings and then add splashes of colour.'

Sarah smiled, obviously keen to get home. 'I'd love to see them when you're finished.'

* * *

With two jobs, her art class and her new mission, which was to make a set of paintings from her sketchbook, Cass had almost every second of her time accounted for. Sadly, it still left her plenty of time to wonder about Ranulph, and what he was up to.

On a rare evening out with Rosa, they discussed it. 'I think I'd know if he'd gone back to his home on the island where my father is living in Scotland, because Eleanor would have told me.'

'Well, have you looked on his socials?'

'I don't think he's really into social media.'

'But hasn't he got a female friend?'

'Becca,' said Cass.

'What's her other name?' Rosa asked, already

keying 'Becca' into her phone. 'And you're friends on Facebook?'

Cass nodded. They'd agreed this in Dominica, so they could share photos.

'Oh.' Rosa sounded disappointed a few seconds later. 'Not very exciting pictures. They're just of people scrabbling round in the sand. Oh — isn't he your man? He's got that distinctive colouring you mentioned.'

Cass inspected the photograph of some pieces of pottery in the sand and saw Ranulph in a group shot. Even this slightly out-of-focus image was enough for her heart to leap and then sink as she realised his arm was round Becca.

'It doesn't say anything about who's in the picture, it just goes on about ancient pottery.' Rosa paused. 'But Becca's status is 'in a relationship',' although it doesn't say who with.'

Cass shrugged, trying to pretend she didn't care. But to her it was clear: it was Ranulph. Otherwise why would there be a picture of Becca with Ranulph's arm round her?'

'Well, don't give up,' said Rosa. 'Keep the man in your sights and stop at nothing to get him!'

This made Cass laugh.

'Seriously, Cass! If you don't do something about your feelings, you'll end up being an old maid doing watercolours and living with her mother.'

* * *

Time passed and Cass suddenly noticed the date. It was going to be Bastian's birthday in a few days' time. As she had mentioned to Ranulph, she'd read his CV back in Dominica and happened to remember the date.

On impulse she decided to turn the sketch of the petroglyph into a watercolour painting and email it to him as a birthday card. On one of the evenings when she wasn't working at the wine bar or at her class, she set herself up with a table at home that looked on to the garden.

She knew that one of the reasons she was thinking about her time in Dominica was because it felt almost the same as thinking about Ranulph, which she did pretty much all the time anyway.

'Oh, that is very pretty,' said her mother, coming up behind her to see how she was getting on. 'You'd almost think there were faces in that rock. Very basic ones, of course. But it's a nice picture.'

Somehow Cass couldn't bring herself to explain about the petroglyph again. 'Do you like it? I'm going to send it as a birthday card to Bastian. You know? Who Dad knows?'

'Oh yes, I remember. When you've done that, I'd be thrilled if you could do something similar — maybe roses? For Edna? It's her birthday next week.'

'OK,' said Cass. 'That would be a pleasure. I'll finish this, then maybe we could pick a nice bunch of roses out of the garden. You could give her the flowers and the painting. Fresh ones, obviously.'

'What a brilliant idea!' said her mother. 'That would give her huge pleasure.'

So when she wasn't doing anything else, Cass painted. She did another couple of cards for her mother, and in between she worked up her sketches until she had a nice portfolio of paintings. If it hadn't been for Rosa's teasing about her being an old maid already, before she was even thirty, Cass would have been more or less content.

She also had a thank you email from Bastian.

Dear Cass

Thank you so much for my delightful birthday card. You have a real talent for painting — not just drawing.

I'm planning to come to London to meet my publishers who are planning to turn my paper into a proper book, with extra material of course. To celebrate this, and something else, I will be hosting a little gathering and would be delighted if you could come. More details to follow.

Sorry to be so mysterious, but nothing is certain yet!

Very best wishes
Bastian

Cass was delighted for many reasons, but her heart quailed after she had told Rosa this during their regular catch-up at the wine bar, because Rosa said that if Bastian had a party, Ranulph was bound to be there.

Cass did not know how she felt about this. Partly she longed to see Ranulph but she was also very nervous at the prospect.

Rosa was sipping her glass of rosé slowly, watching Cass processing her dilemma and knowing she'd have to order another one sooner or later, or Cass's boss would purse his lips and look hard done by.

'On the plus side,' said Rosa, draining her glass. 'It looks as if Bastian must have won the award, or whatever it is, or why would he be celebrating 'something else'?'

'I would jolly well hope he's won it, after I risked my life to get his work in on time!'

'No more news from Austin about the camera?'

'No.' A horrible thought struck Cass. 'He won't be at the party, will he? No, of course not! Why did I even let myself think that for a second?'

'Because you have literally lost your senses,' said Rosa. 'But never mind, you've time to get them back before the party. I wonder when it will be? What will you wear?'

The day after this discussion came an official invitation. It was a reception to celebrate the official presentation of the prize.

With it came another email. *If you can come, please bring any other watercolours of flowers you have done. I want you to meet my publisher. I have an idea! It's only an idea at present, but I'm optimistic.*

A day later there was another email from Bastian.

There are complications, I'm afraid. Instead of just inviting you to a party, I now have to ask you for a huge favour. Austin has challenged my winning of the prize. There has to be an inquiry, although generally things are looking OK for me. Could you possibly come to London and give evidence? It won't be in a court of law, but it would be wonderful if you could explain how you came to find and see the petroglyph, using the map my father had. You could also tell the committee how Austin tried to prevent you from getting the work off the island in time to get my entry in, after the second hurricane. It's on 30 July at 9.00 a.m.

Cass felt a bit sick at the thought of having to do this but then remembered what she'd done at the time to protect and then email Bastian's work. Relating her story to a few people in smart suits would be easy in comparison.

When she got home from her shift at the wine bar later that evening she also saw the long-awaited email from Austin. *Hi, if you want your Dad's camera, come and collect it from me at 9.00 a.m. on 30 July, at the Alexandra Hotel, Paddington.*

No niceties, no real sign-off, just the bald statement. For exactly the same time as she was supposed to be giving evidence against him. And while Cass didn't know London well, she knew that Bastian's publisher and Paddington were many miles and an awful lot of traffic apart.

It couldn't be coincidence that he chose that time, and that location. Austin would have known about the inquiry and he did not want her giving evidence for Bastian, that was pretty certain.

Although she wasn't expecting a positive response, Cass emailed to ask if Austin could see her at another time.

If you want the camera, be there then. Your choice.

Cass did not know what to do. She'd risked her life for Bastian's work (although she hadn't thought this at the time) and she knew her father wanted his camera back however much he said that he didn't.

Then, without letting herself think about it too much, she emailed Ranulph. She had his email address from when they first set off to Dominica together: she just never thought she'd use it.

Dear Ranulph

I've been asked to tell Bastian's publishers what I know about the petroglyph and how it was found.

Austin has been in touch and says I can collect my dad's camera, in Paddington, at exactly the same time. I asked if he'd change the time and of course he wouldn't. He obviously knows about the meeting with Bastian's publishers and doesn't want me there.

What on earth should I do? Sorry to involve you in this, but I didn't know who else to ask.

Best wishes
Cass

She hadn't known how to sign off her email and 'best wishes' seemed the best bet. Or was it too formal after all that she and Ranulph had been through?

She closed her laptop and went downstairs. She chatted to her mother for a little bit before declaring she was going to bed. Once she had a plan of how to deal with the situation she would probably tell her mother but while she was unsure, she'd keep her worries to herself.

She hadn't intended to check her emails again but couldn't resist it, and to her surprise, Ranulph's name was in her inbox. Her heart leapt. Just seeing his name there made her stomach turn over, just as it used to when she saw him in the flesh.

She made herself calm down. His reply would be short, formal and unhelpful: she couldn't allow herself to expect more.

Dear Cass

Great to hear from you although shame about the circumstances.

Of course you must testify for Bastian, but you don't necessarily have to do it in person.

I'll be in London then and I suggest we meet up in the morning (although it will have to be early) and I record what you want to say about finding the petroglyph. I'll ask questions if I think there's anything you haven't said. Then you can collect the camera. But you mustn't see Austin on your own.

Yours
Ranulph

Cass's heart was racing. Ranulph had responded immediately. And he had found a solution to her problem. Although Cass knew, without even asking, that Austin wouldn't tolerate anyone coming with her to see him.

She took a few breaths before replying, firstly so she wouldn't say anything too crazy, and secondly so it would look as if she'd given her answer some thought.

Thank you so much for your suggestion. It's brilliant [was this going too far?] and very kind. I'll try to get someone to come with me although I don't think

Austin would accept anything other than me coming to see him alone.

Cass x

It was only after she'd pressed 'send' that she realised she'd added a kiss. It was such a habit; she even did it when she wrote notes to herself reminding her to do something.

The emails went back and forth, becoming friendlier and friendlier. At last, when the final arrangements were made and a meeting place confirmed, Cass signed off for the night. There were two kisses this time.

As she brushed her teeth she remembered she had yet to work out how to get to London in time for an early morning meeting without having to buy a train ticket that cost the same as a deposit on a small flat.

27

The following morning, she gave her mother a very toned-down version of what had happened the previous evening. She explained that she had to talk to the publishers about finding the petroglyph and, while she was in London, she would collect Howard's camera from the man who had it. It was true, and it shouldn't send her mother into a spiral of anxiety.

When she mentioned train tickets, her mother reminded her that she had a brother who lived in London.

The thought of involving Martin was not appealing: it would involve too many questions and besides, he lived on the Northern Line and she didn't want to travel too far on the Underground during rush hour.

It was Rosa who provided a solution. 'You can sleep on my sister's sofa. She lives in Paddington.'

'I thought she lived on a boat?' said Cass.

They were in their usual spot in the wine bar, Cass on one side of the bar and Rosa the other. By now, the owner quite liked the situation. They were both attractive young women and he felt they gave the right vibe for his establishment.

'She does live on a boat,' said Rosa. 'And the boat is in Paddington! Paddington Basin actually.'

'Oh, perfect! But would she mind?'

'Of course not. It may not be super comfortable on her banquette but it'll be handy and she'll be happy to have you.'

It was perfect, Cass realised. She could arrive the night before her meetings, either have a meal with Susie, Rosa's sister, or maybe take her out somewhere, and be up early in the morning. She'd meet Ranulph, record her story about finding the petroglyph and then go back to Paddington to collect the camera. Then she'd get on the next train home that she could using her cheap ticket.

Her mother had not approved of the plan. 'Why don't you go and stay with Martin? He's got a very comfortable spare room and he'd love to have you.'

'Mum, he lives in quite the wrong part of London for my morning meeting. I'd have to cross London in rush hour to get there and it would take ages.' This was all true but it didn't mention how much Cass didn't want to stay with her big brother.

Her mother nodded. 'I can see that would be tiresome. Remind me again why you have to explain about how you found the petroglyph? And why the man couldn't give back your dad's camera at another time?'

Cass wished she hadn't mentioned why she was going up to London. But she hated lying and had felt she'd explained it in a way that didn't make the whole venture sound mad, which of course it was.

'He's just not very obliging, Mum. Anyway, it'll be fine. I'm popping up to London the evening before and staying with Rosa's sister — you remember Susie? The actress?'

'She had a part in that crime thing set in Orkney?'

'That's her. I expect I'll be home the next day, but I'll let you know.'

'Well, just don't tell Martin you stayed in London

and not with him!'

'I won't if you won't,' said Cass.

* * *

A few days later, Cass took a train which got her to London in the early evening.

She did know Susie, Rosa's glamorous older sister, but not terribly well. But thanks to Rosa, Cass knew how to find Paddington Basin, and once there, finding the narrowboat would be easy.

Sure enough, Cass was soon making her way along the towpath, the Eliza Doolittle in her sights.

Susie was standing on the bow waiting for her with a big welcoming smile.

'Cass! Lovely to see you! Come aboard. Wait a tick, I'll give you a hand.'

Cass, who'd spent the journey looking out of the train window, too anxious about what was ahead of her to be able to concentrate on reading her book, instantly began to feel better. She handed over her basket, which, apart from a change of clothes and her overnight things, now held two bottles of Cava and a couple of bags of crisps which declared themselves to have been hand-fried in small batches.

'Oh, you shouldn't have!' said Susie, spotting the Cava. 'But I'm awfully glad you did. And it's chilled. What a good guest you are!'

Soon they were sitting in the front of the boat in the evening sunshine, sipping what passed for champagne.

'This is lovely!' said Cass. 'It feels like you're in the country when you're in the middle of London.'

'I love it,' said Susie. 'It's just about affordable and

it's convenient. I'd never be able to afford a flat in London. An actor's life is very 'feast or famine'.'

'Had you always wanted to act?' Cass asked as they watched a family of ducks paddle past.

'Oh yes. Although of course the parents thought it was a dreadful idea and told me I must be mad to even think about it.' She laughed. 'So far, nothing has happened to change their opinion, but we only have one life so you have to make the most of it. And who knows what the future will bring? We only have today. So although it's been quite tough thus far, I don't regret it.'

'And you have had some jobs? You were in that detective thing — ?'

'Yes! And the next job may be the one that changes things for me.' Susie looked at Cass more seriously. 'I do think it's better to take a few risks in life even though you may suffer for them, because otherwise you'll have no exciting memories.' Then she laughed. 'Here's me giving you advice about taking risks! Rosa has told me about what you did after that hurricane in the Caribbean. Amazing! You obviously know all about risk taking!'

'In some ways, yes, but you've made me realise it's better to have a few regrets about mistakes you've made than wonder how things could have been if you'd been braver.'

Susie nodded. 'There's nothing like a few chilled bubbles for turning us into philosophers but you're bang on with that. Good for you!'

'I haven't done anything yet!'

'No, but you might. And if it involves a lovely man, seize the day but use a condom.'

Cass started to giggle. 'I'm going to embroider that

on to a cushion and send it to you.'

'I'll hold you to that! Now, I thought we'd eat out here. I've got a friend coming to join us. Hope you don't mind.'

The Cava, blotted up only by some crisps, had gone straight to Cass's head. 'Of course not!'

'But before he comes, and we eat, tell me about this man Rosa says you're in love with.'

'So much for Girlfriend Confidentiality,' said Cass ruefully.

'She knew I'd be interested and it's good to talk about these things.'

'You mean it's fun for other people to talk about them?'

Susie laughed. 'True. Now what are you going to wear tomorrow?'

Before Susie's friend, Bill, arrived for supper, Cass's choice of outfit (jeans and a stripy top) for the next day had been rejected.

'You need a dress!'

'I didn't bring a dress —'

'I have dozens of dresses. Your man knows you can do the rough-tough capable-woman stuff, but needs to get a different impression of you. Here, try this on.'

Susie's wardrobe was crammed behind a curtain, but she knew where everything was. She had found the dress she was looking for and handed it to Cass.

'It's summery, knee-length, floral and pretty. Best of all, I won't want it back. As you see, I have far too many clothes.'

'But I can't wear a bra with it,' said Cass a couple of moments later.

'You don't need a bra, but you can have this little cardi if you feel too naked. There. You're decent but sexy. Take it off now so it's clean for tomorrow. Would you like me to do your make-up?'

Susie's professional hands made Cass's eyes enormous and gave her cheekbones more definition. 'The thing is,' said Susie, blending in a touch of blusher, 'that you're not actually wearing very much make-up. All the more effective.'

There was a thump and an 'Anybody home?' from on deck.

'That's Bill. Join us when you're ready.'

Cass was left in the bedroom, most of which was filled with a double bed and Susie's clothes, to get her own clothes back on. But she knew already that wearing Susie's would give her added confidence the following morning. And she'd need every bit of that confidence.

'Don't forget you're being filmed,' Susie had said. 'Or that he will be watching it over and over. You need to have some definition round your eyes. But it's going to be a lovely day tomorrow, so that little sundress will be perfect.'

They ate in the bow of the boat, a makeshift table over their knees. They watched the sun set behind the trees and the large white houses that lined the canal. 'This must be one of the most delightful parts of London to live in,' said Cass. 'Thank you so much for having me.'

Susie did not allow the evening to go on too long. 'Cass has got an early start tomorrow, Bill, so we'll need you to shuffle off now.'

'I'm only staying for tonight,' said Cass, who had stopped being shy of someone she had actually recognised from seeing him on television. 'So you can come back tomorrow.'

Bill and Susie laughed.

28

The following morning, Cass put on the sundress and cardigan Susie had given her. She had her straw shopping basket which held her overnight things and a little cross-body bag with her valuables. She felt elegant and chic, maybe even a little French. And she liked feeling different: it made her braver somehow. Although she knew that she'd been through real danger in Dominica, London and the meetings for this morning seemed far more terrifying.

Although Cass had been given instructions as to how she should put on her make-up, she just put on what she usually did, which wasn't much, and fluffed up her hair. She couldn't check her reflection because Susie was sound asleep with the boat's only long mirror in her room.

Cass didn't wake her. It had been arranged that she would slip off early for her appointment with Ranulph and the camera he would need to film her report. She climbed off the boat and on to the towpath, fully intending to take the Circle Line to South Kensington where she was meeting Ranulph. Susie had warned her that at eight o'clock in the morning it would be crowded. But when she found herself back on the street after the comparative peace of the canal towpath, she couldn't face it. She decided to use the Uber app that Susie had insisted she put on her phone, and 'damn the expense', as Bill had expansively put it the night before.

She'd asked her driver to drop her off on the corner of the street so she could walk to the house number that Ranulph had given her. She hadn't wanted to arrive in a fluster of finding her phone, and generally feeling like a country bumpkin who'd never taken an Uber before.

And so she saw Ranulph standing by the gate to the garden that was for residents only from several metres away. He was wearing a pale linen suit but the collar of his shirt was undone and his jacket swung open. His hair was quite ruffled and somehow the combination of the suit and the untidiness was incredibly sexy.

Cass gasped with the shock of seeing him again at the same time as he turned and saw her. She found herself smiling with sheer joy.

He set off towards her as she set off towards him and within seconds his arms were round her, hugging her so tightly she was lifted off her feet.

'Oh, Cass, how I've missed you,' he said into her hair.

And then he was kissing her. For a few blissful moments she was kissing him back, losing herself in the joy of it.

But then he pulled away. 'I'm so sorry. That wasn't supposed to happen. Do you mind following me? We need to get this filming over and done with. We haven't got a lot of time.'

Bereft and deflated, she followed him through the gate into the garden.

It was beautiful. The lawn was like a bowling green, the sun catching drops of dew, making it sparkle like jewels. The borders were full of peonies, roses, lilies and dahlias, set off by simpler cottage garden plants.

Pergolas were covered in fragrant climbers as well as roses and clematis and it looked perfect. The residents of the London square obviously spared no expense when it came to their bit of green space.

But Cass couldn't enjoy it. Ranulph was kind and professional and yet she felt rejected. He sat opposite her on the bench, his phone at the ready. 'Do you want to tidy your hair or anything?'

Cass burrowed in her bag and found a mirror in with her make-up. She looked at herself and pulled at her hair a bit but really she was wondering what on earth had just happened. Why was Ranulph behaving as if he'd done something wrong? And why couldn't she take the initiative and say, 'Please don't stop kissing me, I really like it!' But then it occurred to her — maybe he wasn't pulling back because of her, but because of him? Maybe he and Becca had made a commitment to each other? Her spirits plummeted even more. Either he'd just been mildly unfaithful, or he hadn't. She had no way of telling and she couldn't ask.

'I think that's OK,' she said, having tweaked her hair a bit and wiped a bit of mascara that had ended up under her lower lashes. 'Oh, maybe some lipstick.'

When she had applied some, she put her shoulders back and focused on looking confident and positive for her film.

He looked awkward suddenly. 'Erm — you don't seem to be — erm — aren't you cold?' he said.

'It's very hot in London,' she snapped, not looking at him.

He was disbelieving. 'Oh come on! You've been in Dominica, in the summer. This is nowhere near as hot.'

'It's different! Anyway, let's get on and do this recording. I can't risk being late for Austin.'

Ranulph frowned. 'Where are you meeting him? I want to be there when you see him.'

'You can't. You'll be late for the meeting with Bastian and the judges. Anyway, you know what Austin's like. Everything has to be done his way or he'll call the whole thing off.'

Ranulph pursed his lips but didn't speak.

'It has to be just me, at the right time, at the hotel.'

'Are you meeting him in public? I don't trust him.'

'I don't trust him either, but I don't have much of a choice! Now can we do this recording?' She rummaged in her bag again, unsure how they were now arguing when minutes ago they'd been in each other's arms. 'I've written out what I want to say in case I forget something.'

Rosa had rehearsed this with her so many times she knew it by heart, but she wanted the paper there, to give her confidence.

She had settled herself on the bench and had read through her little speech when Ranulph said, 'Have you got a scarf or something you could put over yourself?'

'Why?' she demanded.

'You don't appear to be wearing a bra,' he said, even more awkwardly.

'Oh!' She found the cardigan Susie had given her and put it on, mortified when she realised her nipples were on show. For Austin she would button it up to the neck.

Eventually they were both happy with what Cass had said about the petroglyph and how she had found it, and Cass looked at her smart watch.

'Oh my God, I'm going to be late for Austin! Will an Uber be quicker than the Tube, do you think?'

As she checked the time she couldn't help noticing that her smart watch reported that her heart rate was extremely high. She took a few breaths to try and calm herself.

'Take a cab,' Ranulph said. 'Do you want me to book it for you?'

Only briefly did she consider that this was the man who had let her fly back across the Atlantic on her own with no warning. 'It's fine. I'll call an Uber.'

Feeling like a proper Londoner, she keyed the hotel address into her phone.

A few agonising minutes later, her joy in being like a Londoner was dampened somewhat when her phone rang. It was the Uber driver calling to check the pick-up address.

After some annoying repetitions, and Cass having to ask Ranulph exactly where they were, the driver announced he was on his way.

'Now I'm really worried I'm going to be late,' she said.

'I know Austin's made things as difficult for you as possible,' said Ranulph, 'but he wants to see you, to give you the camera, so he'll wait.' He paused. 'Had it occurred to you that he might want money for it?'

'Of course. Although I'm not going to pay for something that's mine unless it's the only way I can get it. It'd be a ransom.'

'The man is a complete bastard,' Ranulph said.

'Yes,' said Cass. 'But there's nothing we can do about it.'

'You must avoid going into a private space with him. You'll promise me not to do that, won't you?'

'Yes, of course. We're meeting in the hotel lobby. It's all arranged.' Though as Cass said it, she realised this wasn't strictly true. He'd just told her to come to the hotel.

'I should come and get the camera for you —'

'At last! Here's the Uber. Honestly, I'll be fine.'

It was a relief to be away from Ranulph in some ways, but in others it felt as though she'd been ripped away from her chance of happiness. And she couldn't even indulge in reliving the kiss, because he was obviously regretting it already.

29

Cass got into the Uber with barely a wave at Ranulph and settled herself as comfortably as she could.

Soon they were crossing Hyde Park, then going up a wide street full of large houses near Paddington Station, nearly all hotels of some description. None of them looked like a place Cass would want to stay in, she was convinced.

The car finally pulled up outside a hotel with a neon sign with only half its letters lit. For a moment she considered asking the cab to drive on, but then she braced herself and got out. She said goodbye and thank you to her Uber driver, with whom she had exchanged barely a word, feeling he was her best friend in the world. Now she had to enter the building where Austin awaited her.

She pushed open the door to the hotel. There was a man on the desk who was engrossed in his mobile phone. She didn't think she could befriend him if things got difficult. She really wished she had not been talked into the sundress without the bra. She felt practically naked, even after she had put on the cardigan and done up all the buttons.

'I'm here for Austin Gilmour,' she said. 'Can you call him and tell him I'm here?'

The man glowered but picked up the phone. 'I've got a woman here for you,' he said. Cass exhaled, trying to keep calm. The man looked at her. 'He wants you to go up. Room Nine.'

'Sorry, can you tell him that he needs to come down here to see me? I'm not going into his room.' She spoke firmly and with authority.

The man sighed and picked up the phone. 'She said you have to come down here.' He was silent for a couple of seconds and then put the phone down again. 'He says unless you go up to his room, you won't get what you came for.' This time he stayed looking at her, as if trying to work out what that was.

Cass's mouth went dry. What on earth should she do? She'd gone to a lot of trouble trying to get her father's camera back: could she abandon it now for reasons of personal safety? Her father would definitely say yes, she should just leave, get out of there, and forget about the camera.

Memories of the day of the second hurricane flooded back to her. Thinking of the danger she'd been in then — danger that she'd had to cope with — was going into Austin's hotel room so much worse? She couldn't decide.

The telephone on the desk rang. The man picked it up, listened, nodded and put it down again.

'He says if you're not in his room in the next two minutes you can kiss goodbye to what you wanted.' He paused. 'He sounds angry. I'd hurry up if I were you.'

Now Cass was sweating. Things were getting worse, not better. But a fragment of the conversation she'd had with Rosa's sister the previous night came back to her. Something about taking risks. She cleared her throat. She had decided what to do.

'Tell him I'm on my way, please,' she said and quickly texted Ranulph, giving the address of the hotel.

After a thumb had been jerked in the direction of what Cass had to trust was Austin's room, she added, 'And if I'm not out in ten minutes, I want you to call the police.'

Cass was not surprised by his look of utter disbelief, but at least she had taken this precaution.

As she walked along the dark corridor with holes in the carpet she wondered why Austin had made her meet him somewhere so vile. Was he really that short of money? It was possible, and she realised that the cash she had concealed in her bag, separate from everything else, might not be enough to get the camera back.

A couple of cockroaches scuttled along the gap between the wall and the greasy carpet as she knocked on the door.

Suddenly, Cass and Austin were standing toe to toe as he pulled it open.

'Well, well, well, don't you scrub up well!' he said. 'Last time I saw you, you looked like a drowned rat.'

'And you know why that was,' said Cass. 'Hello, Austin.'

He beckoned her into the room, and she followed him, trying to make sure she was nearer the door than he was. Annoyingly, he was too quick for her. She put down her basket.

'I don't suppose you could make me a cup of coffee, could you?' she asked. She was very conscious of him being between her and the door and this would give her a bit more space.

Not that she'd dream of drinking the coffee. This was the sort of establishment that inspired urban myths about what people did with electric kettles in hotel rooms. She hadn't believed them before; now they all seemed possible, likely even.

Austin came over to the kettle and started searching through sachets looking for coffee.

'This isn't the sort of place I thought you'd stay in, Austin,' said Cass, determined to get the upper hand. 'It's a bit low-rent for you.'

'I don't need it for long.'

'So, you're just going to give me the camera and I can leave?'

Austin thought this was funny. 'Surely not even you are as naïve as that.'

'You want money? You want me to pay for what's mine?'

'Possession is nine-tenths of the law, and yes, I want money. You lost me money, a lot of money. I want some of that back.'

'How did I lose you money?'

'If you hadn't been so quick to get Bastian's thesis to the judges for the prize, I'd have won it, no question.'

'You left the island before I did. Why didn't you get your own book off so quickly?'

'I hadn't finished writing it!'

He seemed annoyed and Cass thought she'd better not risk him getting angry. 'So how much do you want for the camera?'

'Less than what I'd have got for it if I'd sold it, which I think is more than fair.'

'How much?'

'A thousand pounds.'

Cass felt sick. She'd got out as much money from her bank account as she could, but it wasn't that much. 'That's ridiculous!'

'It's a bargain. The going rate for a Leica M3 is

higher than that.'

Cass found her lips had gone dry. She had no idea if this was true; he could easily be lying. In the forest he'd said it wasn't very valuable. She knew her father's camera was a Leica, but she didn't know the number. It was just her dad's camera, although she knew he'd added a lens he had to adapt himself to fit.

Sweat pricked along her hairline and, without thinking, she undid a few buttons of her cardigan and unhooked her little crossbody handbag. 'Can you prove that?'

'I'll show you on eBay.' Austin went to the small desk where his laptop lay. It took him a few moments to find what he wanted and Cass realised two things: firstly, there would be such a range of prices on an auction site he could find the number he wanted, and secondly, she could escape while his attention wasn't on her. But she needed the camera first.

'There,' he said.

Cass took a couple of steps nearer. Sure enough, there was a camera going for a huge amount of money. But was it her dad's camera? Would Austin realise she didn't know the model number?

'OK, but do you actually have my father's camera? Showing me pictures on the internet is all very well but it's not proof that you've got it.'

'I knew you'd be difficult about this. You always were annoying.' He went to a corner of the room, rummaged through a bag and produced a camera. 'Here!'

'That could be any old snapper you've found somewhere.'

His horror at this suggestion encouraged her to believe it was the right camera. 'Here! See for yourself.'

Holding the camera was a wonderful feeling. And yes, it was the right camera; it was familiar in her hand. But whether it really was worth a thousand pounds, she couldn't say. 'OK. That's the camera you stole from me. I'll take it now. Thank you very much.'

She was across the room in seconds, but he got to the door first. 'Oh no you don't. You can't just take it after I've gone to all this trouble to get it to you.' He pulled the camera out of her hand but she'd wrapped the strap round her wrist so he couldn't get it free.

'Give me back the camera,' demanded Cass, although the strap was cutting in painfully. 'You know you stole it.' By now she was angry as well as frightened.

But he had hold of the camera so Cass was pulled up against him. She was suddenly aware of how vulnerable she was, her body pressed against his.

'Nothing is free in this world, sweetheart. I want something in return.'

'I'll get the money out of the nearest cashpoint —'

'I've rather lost interest in the money. I could let you go and get it and you could just run off. No, I'd rather have what's right in front of me. The bird in the hand, so to speak.' He seemed to find his joke very amusing. His mouth came down on hers so she couldn't even scream.

Then, just as Austin had pulled her dress off her shoulder, there was a banging on the door, followed by a loud scraping noise and another crash as the door was forced open.

Ranulph burst in and pulled Cass away from Austin, unaware that her wrist was connected to the camera. Then he punched Austin in the jaw, sending him, the camera and Cass crashing to the ground.

Cass ended up on top of Austin.

'The camera!' she gasped. 'It's under him! We have to get it out!'

Austin was fighting back. Cass couldn't get up until she'd managed to release the strap of the camera which was really hurting now. Once Austin realised he had Cass where he wanted her, unable to escape with the camera, he stayed down.

Ranulph pulled him to his feet and Cass released her wrist. She tried to grab the camera, but Austin was keeping a firm hold on it.

There was a struggle as Cass, still furious and made braver by Ranulph's presence, grabbed the camera and ran out of the room on to the landing and down to the street.

Ranulph followed soon after her.

'I've got the camera,' she said, panting. 'But he's got my basket and handbag.'

Without speaking, Ranulph turned and went back into the hotel. Cass was leaning against the railings when he came out again, holding her straw basket and her bag. 'Here.'

Cass was feeling dreadfully faint. Suddenly she was aware of Ranulph's arm around her, holding her up. 'Have you eaten today?' he asked softly.

'I can't remember,' she said, her head still spinning.

Ranulph half carried her to a little café that had an outside table. He set her down on a chair and disappeared inside. He came out again soon afterwards with a tall glass of orange juice.

'Drink this. It'll give you some sugar and make you feel better quickly. I've ordered some food.' He gave a rueful smile. 'I hope you like it.'

A few sips of orange juice and Cass's brain began

working. 'You don't think Austin will see us here?'

Ranulph shook his head. 'No, I don't. He was calling a cab when I went back to the room and looked pretty fed up. I think he knows he might as well just go back to America. He's probably on the way to the airport by now.'

'He surely didn't come to England just to try and blackmail me over the camera? That would hardly have been cost effective, even if I'd paid up!'

Ranulph laughed. 'He had other reasons for being here. Remember he'd been to see Bastian's publishers and was trying to discredit what Bastian wrote about the petroglyph. He was after that prize, and for that he'd have to disprove Bastian's theories about Dominica's earliest inhabitants.'

'Oh my God! I'd forgotten all about that! You were supposed to give evidence —'

'I didn't have a lot to say. Yours was the important evidence and I got the recording of how you found the petroglyph to the publishers a few minutes after you left.'

At that moment a plate of waffles, a jug of maple syrup and a bowl of whipped cream arrived, along with a bowl of strawberries and blueberries.

'Would you guys like tea or coffee with that?' The waiter was young and tattooed, with a hipster beard and a warm smile. 'We have a large range we can offer you and an equally large range of the white stuff. Cow's milk, goat's milk, any variety of plant milk —'

Cass opted for builder's tea with cow's milk. Ranulph went for the sort of coffee that made Cass's heart rate increase just to think about drinking it.

She took a breath and from somewhere found her social skills and a need to confess. 'Thank you for rescuing me. I should have known Austin would never have just given me the camera in the lobby of a hotel, however hard I tried to make that happen.' She paused, feeling awkward. 'I knew I was taking a risk going to his room, but I'd been through so much for that wretched camera. I felt I just couldn't walk away from it at the last minute.'

Ranulph put his hands on hers. 'Oh, Cass! I can't bear to think what might have happened. Thank goodness you texted me the address of the hotel. I'd swing for that man, honestly, I would.'

From somewhere deep inside Cass came a chuckle. It was lovely feeling the warmth of his big hands round her own small ones. 'You did take a good swing at him.'

He was rueful now. 'That's not something I do often — if ever — but I was prepared to make an exception for you.'

Just for a moment, Cass caught a look in his eyes that made her heart flip. Suddenly shy, she looked away.

The waiter came with their drinks, Ranulph let go of her hands and the moment passed.

Cass finished her orange juice and poured her tea. To fill the silence, she said, 'So, what are you up to now, Ranulph? Generally, I mean. Have you a glamorous assignment in a far-off city to go to?'

He laughed, taking a sip of his coffee.

'Not glamorous, no. But I do have an assignment which should be interesting. And it is quite far away — in Africa, actually. What about you? What are you doing when you're not eating pancakes in the sunshine?'

'Oh, I'm just pottering along in my home town in

the Cotswolds. Nothing exciting. I think my exciting days are over, left behind in Dominica.' She frowned. 'At least I thought I had until just now!' She shook her head, still a bit embarrassed by what had happened.

'So what are you doing these days? Anything fun?'

'Yes! At least I think it's fun. I'm learning to do watercolours, of flowers and foliage mostly.'

'Oh?'

Glad to be talking about something that didn't make her embarrassed, Cass went on. 'I wish I could say it's a long-held ambition of mine, but the answer is far simpler. I work in an art shop and they have classes there. As an employee, I get lessons for nothing. And it happens to be watercolours for flowers.'

'That sounds perfect for you.'

Cass nodded. 'You know I like drawing. I've worked out a technique where there's a very rough sketch and then the paint goes on top.' She laughed, feeling so much better after a couple of waffles and maple syrup, with Ranulph across the table from her. 'My brother has always referred to my drawing as 'colouring in' — now I really am doing colouring in.'

He was indignant. 'But, Cass, you're a very talented artist. Think of the drawings you did in Dominica.'

She shrugged. His praise made her feel awkward. She was sitting in the sun and it was hot. She was about to remove her cardigan but stopped. She had a lot of cause to regret wearing a dress without a bra that day and she wasn't going to risk showing off more than she meant to again. She sighed more loudly than she'd intended.

'What's the matter? Are you all right?' Ranulph was instantly concerned. His hand went across the table back to her hand. 'Oh! Your wrist. It's very red.'

'It's where the camera strap cut in.' She took a sip of tea with her free hand. She didn't want to be seen as a victim. 'But I'm fine. I was just a bit faint with not having breakfast, that's all.'

'So why the sigh?'

She looked at him, wishing she was brave — or even brazen — enough to tell him the truth. That she was sighing because she knew she might never see him again. But she wasn't either of those things.

'I'm just wondering how I'm going to get the camera back to Dad. After all this . . . trouble. I was so intent on getting it from Austin, I forgot about the final part.' She smiled. That sounded completely convincing! And like all lies, it was all the stronger because it was mostly true.

'I'll take it back for you. I've got to go back to Scotland to sort things out for this big trip I'm going on.' He paused. 'Don't you want to take it up to Howard yourself?'

She shook her head. 'I've only just been up to see him and I don't want to take too much time off from my jobs.' She smiled. 'It's called a portfolio career, having more than one job. My other job is working in a wine bar.'

'Do you enjoy it? Retail doesn't sound all that exciting after what you got up to in Dominica.'

'You think I should retrain as a doctor and sew people up for a living? How is the leg, by the way?'

'Good as new, thank you. But I will have your signature on my leg forever, in the form of some really quite neat stitches.'

She laughed, taking a strawberry from the bowl and putting it into her mouth. 'Of all the scary things I did in Dominica — and since — I think sewing you up was the most terrifying.'

'I'm very surprised. You were so brave.'

Cass thought about it. 'I did frightening things, yes, but I didn't have time to think too much. Taking a curved needle to your leg — I had plenty of time to think about how much I was hurting you, how it could get infected, all those things. With the other stuff, I just sort of held my nose and jumped in.'

'So does working in an art shop not seem a bit — dull?'

'I'm not qualified to do much and I love the art shop. But I do have a side hustle.'

'Of course you do! What?'

'Well, I've only done a couple, but my mum picks a bunch of flowers from the garden — she's very good at flower arranging — and I paint them. So her friend gets the bunch of flowers and a painting of them as a birthday card. It's fun. I let myself have a bit of artistic licence. So far I've only done it for my mother, but I think it has potential.' She took another strawberry. 'I also think if I had some printed, the shop would take some of my paintings as cards.'

'And the wine bar?'

'Is great for meeting people.'

'People your own age, I imagine.'

Ranulph seemed to want confirmation of this. Cass remembered him lecturing her about how Bastian was too old for her.

'All ages. But my friend Rosa often comes early and we have a catch-up. The manager doesn't mind. He says we add glamour to the place. It's fun for now, anyway. I might try and go to college to learn illustration properly later. Is your work fun? On the whole?'

Ranulph smiled but Cass got the impression he

wasn't as happy about her answer as his smile implied.

'Journalism is what I know. My next assignment is based around another early civilisation. It'll be a way of making money out of archaeology, which I've never been able to do before — of course I don't usually write about that.' Then he smiled. 'This new mission will involve a lot of travel.'

'Which is interesting? Broadens the mind and all that?'

He nodded. 'Sometimes I get fed up with it.'

'Is there anything — other than journalism with a side of archaeology — you'd rather do?'

He was silent for a moment. 'I'd love to focus on writing that biography of your father, get enough of it done so we could approach publishers.'

'So you could spend time at home?' She thought of Ranulph, sitting at his laptop, looking at the rugged coastline and the sea pounding away below.

He nodded.

'I don't blame you for wanting to do that,' said Cass. 'You live in a very beautiful part of the world.'

'But it's very far away from everywhere else. It can feel a bit cut off.'

'Do you mind feeling cut off?'

He laughed. 'Not at all. I like it. But it's not for everyone.'

'I think it could be for me. The last time I saw Dad I thought: This is just beautiful. Although of course it's colder than Dominica. I think I must love places that are difficult to get to.'

'To visit? Or to live in?'

Cass shrugged. 'I don't know, to be honest, but I think I'd like to live somewhere like that.' Then she laughed and looked around her. 'Although London suddenly seems like fun.'

Cass realised she felt a bit euphoric. She had been through a horrid, dangerous situation and come out the other side. Everything and anything was possible. She found she was smiling.

Ranulph looked at her questioningly. 'Do you have a train to catch?'

She shook her head. 'As long as it's off peak, I can get any train. Even one tomorrow, if I need to.' She didn't add she'd left it so she could stay a couple of nights with Rosa's sister if she needed to. She had wanted to stay flexible — just in case.

'Then would you like to go across town and see if Bastian is still at his publishers? I did say I'd be there and I would like to see them.'

'Oh, I'd love that! And if we went, I'd stop feeling guilty that it was my fault you couldn't go when you were supposed to.'

'Not really your fault, Cass,' said Ranulph. 'Right, I'll go and sort the bill and then I'll hail a cab.'

'No, I'll call an Uber,' said Cass. 'I have the app!'

30

If anyone had described paradise as sitting in the back of a hot car that smelled quite strongly of Lynx, listening to an extreme-pop music station on a poorly tuned radio, in barely moving traffic, Cass would have thought they were mad. And yet here she was, thinking she'd gone to heaven.

She didn't want to talk. She couldn't say what she was feeling anyway; she was just happy sitting next to Ranulph. She closed her eyes. An aphorism, something she'd heard Susie say, floated into her head. 'It's the things you don't do that you regret.'

She moved her shopping basket next to her on the seat and leant against Ranulph. If it weren't for the butterflies doing cartwheels of delight in her stomach, she might have drifted off on a cloud of bliss. Although she didn't know how Ranulph was feeling about this closeness, he didn't pull away.

At last Ranulph leant forward to alert the driver: 'This is Hennings on the left,' and they were outside the publishers' in Bloomsbury. They got out and went into the building.

A multi-pierced young person directed them to the first floor, and, shortly afterwards, they were opening the door to what appeared to be an imposing boardroom.

There was a bit of a party going on inside. Bastian was there, with a very elegant woman Cass identified as his significant other. There was an older man who was obviously in charge, and a few more people.

'Cass!' said Bastian. 'And Ranulph! You made it! Come and join the celebrations.'

Everyone was delighted to see them and Cass was charmed to see Bastian looking so elegant in his suit, a contrast to the casual shorts and shirts he wore in Dominica.

Cass in particular was something of a heroine. It was her account of finding the petroglyph and marking its location for Bastian that had saved Bastian's work as well as that of his father. His father's lifetime of scholarship was going to be repaid at last.

There was talk about Austin, too. Apparently, the previous day, he had come in with slides and a PowerPoint demonstration trying to prove that his was the true account and there was no petroglyph. Although he'd already lost the prize by then.

The older man (who was called Michael) said, 'He had obviously done very little research himself and was mostly relying on the work of other people. Bastian here, and of course his father before him, had studied everything to do with the islands and knew the history, the flora and fauna, the traditions, the folklore, everything. He was an obvious choice for the prize.'

Cass found herself with a glass of champagne in her hand. 'And this is the heroine of the hour!' declared Bastian. 'Without her cunning with the map, redrawing it so Austin would go off track, and actually spotting the petroglyph, I might well not have won.'

'I'm very interested to meet you,' said Bastian's friend. 'I'm Loretta. I live on Barbados. I've heard a lot about you.'

Cass returned this woman's friendly smile. She

had the distinct impression that Loretta had felt a bit threatened by her but now she could see how young Cass was, she was happy to be charming.

'I've heard about you too,' said Cass, feeling far less shy now she had a glass of champagne in her hand. 'How you won't live on Dominica and how Bastian won't live on Barbados.'

Loretta laughed. 'That's true, but it's a way of life that works well for both of us.'

Next, Cass found herself next to a young man with glasses that had one round frame and one square. It wasn't a surprise to discover he worked for the art department.

'Your drawings are amazing!' he said, possibly a little extra enthusiastic because of the champagne. 'Somehow they're more realistic than the photographs Bastian took.'

'Don't say that to my dad!' said Cass. 'He's Howard Blakely and quite well known.'

'Oh my goodness! He's really famous, I'd say. But you're not a photographer yourself?'

'I would have been if my dad had had his way. But really, I prefer drawing — and watercolours, but that's just recent.'

Cass found herself chatting to this pleasant young man until Bastian appeared at her elbow. 'There's a table booked for lunch. Hennings would be thrilled if you and Ranulph would join us. If you hadn't had to be somewhere else, you'd have been invited anyway.'

Across the room, Ranulph gave her a questioning glance. Then he came to join her. 'Do you fancy lunch? Or do you have to get back?'

Cass thought she'd told him she didn't have to go back. 'Lunch would be lovely.' She glanced at the clock on the wall. 'Although it's late for lunch.' It was nearly half past two.

'I think it's been booked for three so it will be fine.'

Ranulph put his arm round her as they left the room. She had never felt so happy.

* * *

Lunch was a long table covered in dishes. There were cold meats, exotic charcuterie, salads, pasta, smoked salmon, oysters, prawns and heaps of crisply fried vegetables. At the centre was a plate of fried plantain.

'This is our gesture to Dominican cuisine,' said Michael, the publisher.

'I'm touched,' said Bastian.

Cass found that she was suddenly quite weary. She enjoyed the food but had only had one glass of wine since the meal began, although bottles were circulating. As the volume of the conversation increased, she felt worn out entirely.

She had learnt that Hennings hadn't provided the money for the prize that Bastian had won, but were only administrating it. However, they took their duties very seriously and had read all the entries submitted very closely.

She had chatted to the art director who had really liked her drawings and she had had a long talk with Loretta about how important Bastian's work was to him — which of course she knew already.

Ranulph caught her eye and came over to her. 'Would you like to leave?'

Cass got up immediately and in no time had located her straw basket. Then she and Ranulph said goodbye to everyone.

Out on the street, Ranulph summoned a black cab. When they were in it, he said, 'Do you have a train you want to catch?'

Cass was totally disorientated. 'Erm, I can't remember which trains I can catch on my ticket —'

'Or you could spend the night here. You must be tired?'

Cass nodded. She *was* tired, but it wasn't this that made her want to stay. Her conversation with Susie the previous evening was still with her. You had to take a few risks — emotional risks, not just those involving hurricanes or sordid hotels and cameras. This was her chance to make love with the man she had been in love with for so long. He didn't love her in the same way, she was fairly sure of that. But he liked her and cared her about her being safe. He had got into a fight with Austin for her, after all. And he did want her, she could tell. She had made her decision.

* * *

The cab took them to a block of serviced apartments. 'It's like a hotel,' Ranulph explained in the lift. 'But there's a kitchen and a sitting room. Also a balcony. I always stay here when I'm in London. It's a different apartment every time I come but this time we have an incredible view over the river.' He swiped his key card and opened the door.

The room was warm and Cass took off her cardigan as she went to the double glass doors, drawn by the view beyond. There was a balcony with a table and two chairs. They were right over the river.

'This is possibly the best view in London,' said

Ranulph. 'Or at least, the view with the most famous landmarks.'

'Can I go out on to the balcony?'

'Of course.' He opened the doors.

'Wow! You're right about the landmarks. Big Ben, Houses of Parliament, the London Eye — they're all here.'

'And a few others as well. You can see the Shard on a good day. Would you like a drink?'

Cass nodded, feeling she was saying yes to more than a glass of wine.

'Sit down,' he said, putting a glass on the little table.

'This apartment must be terribly expensive!'

She was relieved to hear Ranulph laugh. It was a very naïve statement, something she could think but should not have said. She had never associated Ranulph with money. Besides, she wanted him to think of her as a contemporary, not a teenager who made childish comments.

But Ranulph didn't seem to mind her frankness. 'It is, but I don't come down often and it's convenient and comfortable.' He paused. 'Where I'm going after this isn't going to be comfortable. And I'm going to be there for a while. I thought I'd enjoy the amenities of a power shower and good sheets while I could.'

'What's the assignment? Are you allowed to say?'

'I don't know very much about it but it'll involve a series of articles that one day I may turn into a book.'

'Great.' She smiled. 'And of course there's the biography of my father.'

He smiled. 'Yes, that's the one I really want to do but Howard hasn't absolutely agreed to let me do it. These articles will pay me now, so that's what I need to do first.'

To save herself from having to look at him, Cass concentrated on the view. In spite of her firm decision to let the evening go where it led, in the hope that it would lead her into bed, she felt quite shy about it. 'It really is stunning here, isn't it?' She paused. 'London is so beautiful. It's absolutely my favourite city. But although I said it was fun earlier, I couldn't live here.'

He added wine to her glass from the bottle on the table. 'No?'

'Not for more than about a week,' she said. 'I need countryside. Even where I live now, in the Cotswolds, isn't really wild enough for me.' She paused. 'I think Dominica has spoilt me a bit. It's so rugged and challenging — although that was probably the hurricane — but I loved the drama of it. This is dramatic' — she made an expansive gesture — 'but in a different way.'

'I do agree with you. I'm always excited to be coming to London but I love going home the best. I need the hills and mountains — the heather even — to keep me grounded. I think it's because I have all that at home that I can cope with my tougher assignments.'

'Do you know how long this next assignment will take?' Cass hoped this just sounded like a general enquiry and not as if she was burning to know when he might be back in the UK again for personal reasons.

'Months, probably, although you can never tell until you're there.'

'It sounds exciting and pretty terrifying.'

He brushed this off. 'Exciting yes, but you take all the precautions, make sure you know what you have to do, have a good support team on the ground and it's not terrifying.' He laughed properly. 'Although I was terrified the first time I went to this part of Africa. But it's like it was in Dominica — it was all unknown and a bit nerve-racking to begin with, but we soon found our way around.'

'True.' Thinking back, Cass realised it hadn't been long before she had started to settle into Dominica.

'Come inside and sit on something more comfortable,' he said. 'Unless you'd like to stay on the balcony and go on enjoying the view?'

'You're right. These chairs are very attractive to look at, but actually, they're quite hard.'

She followed Ranulph back inside and sank on to the sofa, kicked off her shoes and found a cushion for the small of her back. 'This is much better.'

Ranulph sat down next to her.

'Are you hungry? There's room service, or there's a nice little restaurant not far away.'

'I'm not hungry now as I had such a lot to eat at lunch which wasn't that long ago. Perhaps a snack from room service? I won't have to put my shoes on to eat it.'

'True. You're full of wisdom, Cassie.'

'No one calls me Cassie any more.'

'Except me. Do you mind?'

Cass considered. She'd been very keen to throw off the more youthful Cassie when she was a teenager. Cass sounded edgier, more grown up. But hearing his dark, low voice saying it seemed perfectly fine. More than fine. Almost erotic. 'No, it's all right,' she said, thinking she should fight the feelings he was stirring in her. They were dangerous — maybe Susie's advice was all wrong? Maybe sleeping with him would be a horrible mistake? Maybe she would never get over the inevitable heartbreak that it was bound to cause?

Seizing the day was dangerous.

His arm went round her shoulders. Feeling his hand on her bare shoulder made her stomach flip. She'd had relationships previously but whereas before her erogenous zones were clear, now every part of her seemed on high alert.

He didn't move his arm and she realised he was waiting for her to make the next move. He wanted to be in no doubt that nothing was happening that she didn't want. She reached up and kissed his cheek. Then his mouth came down on hers.

'Shall we move to the bedroom?' she breathed into his ear. 'This upholstery is scratchy.' She still had her dress on but there wasn't much of it.

He got up and took her by the hand.

'Oh my goodness, what an enormous bed!' she said, distracted for a moment.

He pulled off the bed cover and the several scatter cushions that decorated it. He turned to her, panting very slightly. She went into his arms and let him take off her dress. A moment later she was naked, lying on very good-quality sheets.

Then she forgot about the sheets . . .

31

She hadn't been aware of sleeping until Ranulph woke her. 'Hey? Are you OK? It's eight o'clock and I'm ravenous. Do you fancy a look at the menu?' He put it into her hands. 'Unless you have to rush off?' He sounded distressed at the thought.

'No. I'll call my mum and Susie — I need to tell her I won't be coming back for another night with her — and I'll stay here with you. If that's all right,' she added, suddenly shy. She pulled the sheet up over herself although she realised it was a bit late for that.

'Please stay!' he said. 'I really don't want you to leave now.'

She smiled warmly at him, her heart and mind still fuzzy with love and lust, and took the menu.

'I think a steak sandwich . . .' she began.

'Agreed. With chips. Chocolate brownie and ice cream for afterwards. Now, is wine OK? Or would you like something else to drink? I have a couple of bottles of beer and there's a minibar.'

'Have you got water? I think I should drink water from now on.'

He nodded. 'I have sparkling or still. I even have ice.'

'Sparkling with ice, please. And could I use the shower?'

'Of course! They have very nice toiletries here.'

Cass was very tempted to drag the sheet with her to the bathroom like people did in films but she had always thought it ridiculous when they did it, and felt it was ridiculous for her to do it now. It was too late to be having hang-ups about her body, which most of the time she was perfectly happy with.

She came back wrapped in a large towelling robe, smelling of verbena and citrus. She had washed her hair (by mistake) and felt very clean and very lacking in make-up. But it would look crazy to apply more now. Besides, Ranulph was used to her being covered in mud, so just being clean would be an improvement.

'The food should be here any minute,' said Ranulph. 'It always seems to take ages, although it probably doesn't.' He cleared his throat. 'That's a very fetching robe you're wearing.'

Cass caught his glance and looked away quickly. It was wonderful to be so desired, but it suddenly made her shy.

The food arrived and Cass tried not to feel embarrassed as the waiter brought it in and set it out on the desk. It wouldn't matter to him who she was, after all.

* * *

They ate their steak sandwiches sitting on the balcony, enjoying the panorama of London. But then they took the brownies and ice cream to the sofa. Cass couldn't say what made them want to do this, but she agreed with the decision.

'I think we should find a film to watch,' said Ranulph, taking the remote and clicking through the channels.

'Good idea,' said Cass, relieved and only a little disappointed at this wholesome suggestion.

After the dishes were set aside, and Cass had accepted another glass of wine in spite of her resolution to only drink water, Ranulph pulled her to him. He found her breasts and then loosened the tie on her robe, saying, 'That is a very fetching bath robe, as I said, but would you mind terribly taking it off?'

Moments later he was carrying her back to the bedroom and she was in heaven again.

* * *

It was pitch dark when Cass woke up. The expensive apartment had very efficient blackout blinds and she had no idea what time it was. Feeling her way, she reached the sitting room and found her phone. It was 4 a.m. There was a Facebook notification, and for some reason this made her think of Becca.

She sank on to the sofa, all her happiness crashing down around her. She felt horrendous guilt — she hadn't checked whether he was in a relationship with Becca but she was kidding herself by pretending she didn't know. Facebook had certainly implied that. Why hadn't she asked him outright? Deep down she knew why: she didn't want to hear the answer. What kind of a woman did that make her? Not one she'd want to know, that was for sure. And while the sex had been far beyond anything she'd ever experienced before, she hadn't bargained for this awful come-down.

She had experienced it before. If she had a bit too much to drink a very happy time would be followed by terrible remorse. And this remorse wasn't only caused by too much wine.

She went into the bathroom and sat on the closed

lid of the lavatory. Seizing the day, having a night of passion with the man you loved was good in theory. But Ranulph didn't love her in return. Soon, she knew, she would be remembering each touch, each moment of passion. But now she just felt full of desolation and guilt.

She had to go home, immediately. She was too unsettled to have a lovely morning eating croissants in bed with Ranulph, getting jam on the bedding and maybe showering together. She'd had the sex and enjoyed it with every part of her, but she hadn't had what her heart needed: Ranulph's words of love, the commitment.

She got dressed as quickly and quietly as she could and then went back into the sitting room. She couldn't just leave, she realised, she'd have to write a note. Luckily there was writing paper in a drawer.

Dear Ranulph,

Sorry for running off like this. I suddenly remembered I had to be in work today. I've left the camera. I would be so pleased if you could deliver it to Dad.

Thank you so much for all your help with this whole business. And thank you for last night. It was lovely. I think it's better that I leave without us saying goodbye. And let's not keep in touch. We don't really have more than a friendship and a lot of experiences in common. You're going to be away for a long time. It's better that we move on.

With all my good wishes and some very fond memories,

Cassie

She was crying as she let herself out of the apartment. Would she have felt any better if she hadn't taken Susie's advice? She would never know.

She walked all the way to Paddington. It took her over an hour. She was exhausted when she arrived and still had to wait for the first train. It was vastly expensive but Cass didn't care. She just wanted to be home.

She'd texted Rosa and, like the true friend she was, Rosa was at the station, although it was only just past eight.

'Oh Cass! You poor thing! Come and let's get you coffee and a pastry. Burt's will be open.'

'It was so cold on that train!' said Cass. 'The air con was up to the max and I didn't really have enough clothes with me.'

Rosa pulled her into a hug and soon the two friends were sitting in a café that was warm and smelt of coffee, bacon and pastries.

'When did you last eat? I really fancy a bacon roll.' Rosa paused. 'It looks as if the situation calls for one.'

'That sounds good. And tea.'

Although Cass could tell Rosa was dying to hear everything, she waited until they both had breakfast in front of them. Then Rosa said, 'Are you ready to talk about it?'

This made Cass smile, something she'd felt she'd never do again. 'I know you're ready to hear about it! But actually, I do want to talk. It's been such a trauma — well, no, that's far too strong a word —'

'You slept together?'

Cass nodded. 'I thought I'd regret it forever if I didn't. I was seizing the day, like Susie said I should. And it was really, really lovely at the time, but now I feel broken.'

'Why?'

'Because I may never see Ranulph again! He's going to Africa on some assignment and has no idea when he'll be back. And . . .' Cass took a deep breath. 'I've done a really dreadful thing. I slept with him because I wanted to, but I was — am — fairly sure he's in a relationship with Becca. Remember, we looked on Facebook?'

'Hang on. You're feeling guilty in case he's in a relationship? What about him? He should be the one feeling guilty, surely?'

'Yes, but I'm not a hundred per cent certain.'

'What makes you think he's not single? He doesn't sound like the sort of man who'd cheat.'

Cass sighed. 'We did kiss, earlier, when we first met again and he pulled back from the kiss. I didn't know why at the time, but now I think perhaps he was feeling guilty?'

'Honey! You're overthinking this.'

'I'd hate to think I'd slept with another woman's man. Becca is a really nice person and it's against the Code.'

Rosa laughed. 'The Code!' It was something they'd decided on as twelve-year-olds. 'I'm not sure I can remember everything that was on it now.'

'I do remember it was OK to get the same item of clothing as someone else, but not OK to wear it if the other person had said they were going to wear it first. And it was definitely wrong to snog someone else's boyfriend,' said Cass. She sighed. 'And we did far more than just snog.'

'I never liked that expression,' said Rosa. 'But anyway, you may be imagining things. Maybe he's not in a relationship.'

'I still feel awful. I thought I'd be having a lovely time, doing something I'd remember forever, no matter who I end up with, but I just feel horrible.'

'Would you feel horrible if he wasn't going away and you could see him, say, next week?'

Cass considered. 'I don't think I'd have snuck off like that if he wasn't going away.'

'So really, you're feeling bad because he's going away for a long, unspecified time and you're going to miss him.'

Cass exhaled. 'I suppose it's that too. But I'm just not totally sure he was a free agent when I went to bed with him.'

'I still say that's for him to worry about, not you,' said Rosa firmly.

* * *

Cass was feeling a lot better when Rosa dropped her home a little later although she knew she was in for a long bout of missing Ranulph. She couldn't decide if it would have been better not to have slept with him, if she would miss him less. But then, to think she might never have had the opportunity seemed so desolate.

'Morning, darling!' said her mother. 'You're back earlier than I expected you. Did it all go all right? Did you get Howard's camera back?'

'Hi, Mum. Yes, I got an early train.' No need to tell her how much it had cost her. 'I did get the camera and I gave it to Ranulph, who's going to give it to Dad.'

'That all seems very satisfactory. And did you visit

the publishers?'

Cass had given her mother a much-expurgated version of her plans. She had left out any hint that what she was doing might be dangerous in any way. 'I did. They were great. They complimented me on my drawings and said how they'd helped Bastian.'

'You are good at drawing. And now you're home, I can pick the flowers for our next assignment. It's a leaving present for the president of the WI, so quite prestigious. Have you got time to paint them?'

Cass sighed. She had all the time in the world now. She had no interest in socialising with people she didn't already know, or looking for a boyfriend. If she couldn't have Ranulph, she didn't want anyone.

32

The summer faded into autumn and soon Cass had a range of Christmas cards for sale at the art shop. Her mother bought a lot of them too. When she thought back to the spring, when she had first set off to Dominica with Ranulph, she realised her life had been so exciting, so full of possibility. Now she seemed to have the life and career of a recently retired teacher — her position at the art shop had become permanent — who had a couple of jobs to keep themselves busy and a flower-painting hobby. While she had now applied to go to a couple of art schools, she wasn't expecting to hear back from them immediately.

But at the end of October, when she was at her busiest (she'd developed a good line in poinsettias which she touched with the slightest hint of gold pen) she had an email from Bastian's publishers.

Dear Cass

We all enjoyed meeting you very much back in the summer and, as you know, we greatly admire your talent as an artist and illustrator.

So much so, in fact, we are wondering if you would consider being the illustrator for Bastian's new project, which is to be an illustrated guide to Dominica and could possibly become a series?

If you think this might interest you, would you care to come and see us in London to talk about it?

Very best wishes
Michael Masters
Publisher
Hennings

Cass had to sit down for a few moments before giving her answer, which was a very strong yes. Going to London, to Hennings, was going to be a visit full of memories, and would make her sad in many ways. Yet she had to grasp this opportunity. She gave herself a mental shake. She had to live her own life, without Ranulph, and this new project seemed like a good beginning.

Shortly after this sensible decision, and just before she went for her shift at the wine bar, she texted Rosa. This was news she needed to share with more people than just her mother, although her mother was absolutely delighted.

'All that colouring in seems to have got you a job, Cass!' her mother had said when Cass told her. 'And not just painting pretty pictures for my friends.'

* * *

'I don't know why you're so surprised,' said Rosa half an hour later, sipping her Virgin Mary. 'Your drawings are brilliant.'

'I assume the publishers will want colour and not just line drawings. They haven't seen any of the watercolours that I've done, I don't think. Although, thinking more about it, I did send Bastian a card that

I'd painted — just an email version — maybe they've seen that?'

'Whatever! It will be different and a lot more fun than all this spinster-woman-with-cats type stuff you've been doing!'

'In case you've managed not to notice, we're in a wine bar, where I also work. And I haven't got a cat. I suggested it to Mum but she wasn't keen.'

'Cass! You know how worried I've been about you. You just moon over Ranulph —'

'I haven't said a word about him!'

'I still know you're doing it though. Those very nice men tried to pick us up the other night and you wouldn't even let them buy us a drink.'

'There was no point —'

'You could have gone along with it for my sake!' Rosa was indignant.

'I'm sorry. You should have said.'

'Not with them standing within earshot!'

'Seriously, I won't let it happen again. If anyone tries to pick us up, I'll let them. For your sake.'

Rosa sighed. 'Look, I'm just pleased you've got this new thing in your life. Hey! Why don't I go up to London with you? We'll spend the night with Susie, and have a blast.'

'Oh, excellent!' said Cass. 'I will find it a bit triggering, you know? Going to London on my own.' She paused, suddenly worried. 'You won't want to come in with me to the publishers, will you? I won't be able to let you —'

'Of course I don't want to come in with you. But we could have fun afterwards. Susie would love it, I know!'

And so, with a bit of job juggling for Cass and Rosa,

the following week, the two friends set off for London. They went on the first affordable train with, among other things, a heartfelt blessing from Cass's mother. Apparently she had been really worried about her daughter's nun-like ways. 'You were a bit wild when you were young, Cass,' she had said. 'But you've only ever been out for work or a drawing class recently. It's not normal.'

* * *

Rosa was getting off at Paddington and Cass was transferring to the Underground to Holborn. She had her route planned, her phone well charged and her laptop in her cross-body bag.

She was early for her appointment with Hennings so she sat in a little café nearby. It was not unlike the café in Paddington where Ranulph had fed her breakfast after the drama of getting her father's camera back from Austin. And of course she thought about Ranulph. But as she left to go to her meeting, she accepted she would always think about Ranulph. He was in her mind, like a screensaver. Whatever else was going on in front, in the background he was there, whirring around in her imagination.

Although she'd met Bastian's publishers before, she felt a bit shy. Last time she'd been with Ranulph, a couple of glasses of champagne down, and she was just a hanger-on. Now she was the main attraction. She was greeted at reception, and sent up to the second floor. She put on a smile as the lift doors opened.

There were several people there to greet her. Bastian's publisher Michael Masters, the art director with his quirky glasses and a couple of people from Sales and Marketing. Everyone was friendly and seemed pleased to see her.

'Cass! It's so kind of you to come. We're all very excited by this new project and we'd love it if you were willing to be part of it,' Michael Masters said.

She was ushered into the room and offered both hot drinks and cold. 'We're hoping you'll have time to come out for a bit of lunch after this,' said the art director. 'Now let me tell you what the plan is. We're imagining a series of illustrated guidebooks to the islands of the Caribbean. Starting with Dominica because Bastian has photos of all the places he'll want to mention.'

'But if you've got photos, why would you need me?' Cass laughed. 'You haven't got me muddled up with my father, have you? He's the one for photography.'

There was general laughter. 'We don't want photographs because, although of course they are works of art in their own right, we want something more . . . creative. Bastian has a wonderful writing style which really makes you see what he's describing. We want something as lyrical as that for the illustrations.'

'Have you seen any of my paintings? It's quite a new . . . direction for me.'

'We have!' said the art director. 'Bastian actually had the original idea for this. He sent us the birthday card you did for him. We were very impressed.'

'And of course we know all about the drawings you did of the petroglyph,' went on Michael Masters.

'We felt that the drawings really added something, and as you can add a bit of colour, we think the end result would be delightful,' the art director said. 'It would be almost a coffee-table book, something you'd flick through and think, I'll go there!'

Cass cleared her throat. 'Well, I have images of what I've been doing lately. Mostly it's been paintings of bunches of flowers — not really bouquets — as presents. My mother picks the flowers and makes them look gift-worthy and then I paint them. The picture is a permanent version of the flowers which by their nature are transient.'

She was quite proud of this phrase. She opened the document and handed her laptop across the table.

'These are charming!' said Michael Masters.

'Just the sort of thing we'd be looking for,' said the art director. 'You might need a bit of landscape to go behind the pictures of the flowers —'

Cass retrieved her laptop. 'Here are some landscapes I painted from photographs, of where my father lives. And I've worked up some of my sketches of Dominica into paintings. They should give you an idea —'

'These are perfect,' said the art director. 'We'd love to take you on as our illustrator. Don't you think, Michael?

'We'll pay for your fare to Dominica — of course you'll have to go. And we'll pay you a fee, of course. It won't be huge but —'

Cass interrupted. 'It sounds wonderful, I must admit. But — sorry to lower the tone — will these books sell enough to make you money?'

'We think so,' said Michael. 'The thing is, the same trust who donated the money for the prize that Bastian won wants to promote tourism in Dominica and thinks a book like this will help. They will also help with costs, publicity, distribution, all the expensive stuff.'

'That's brilliant!' said Cass. 'Even if the fee isn't

huge, I get a trip to Dominica out of it.'

'Bastian is very much looking forward to working with you on this,' said Michael. 'In fact, he was so determined he told us it had to be you or no one.'

Cass bit her lip. 'What would you have done if you'd hated my work?'

'We already knew we weren't going to,' said the art director. 'Now, shall we go to lunch? There's a delightful little Greek restaurant just nearby.'

33

Cass left Hennings in an Uber that was paid for by the company. Cass was aware she'd had a little bit too much to drink but didn't care. It had all gone brilliantly, and for a few hours, Ranulph had only popped into her mind a few times. Maybe she was getting over him? Maybe the trip to Dominica would finish the job?

She called in at a little Waitrose in Paddington for Cava and snacks. She knew Rosa and Susie would want to celebrate.

And they did! They opened the Cava immediately and in spite of Cass's insistence that she'd had at least two large glasses of wine at lunch, poured her another one.

'And you've got my favourite crisps!' said Rosa. 'How did you know I loved these?'

'Because I've known you since we were ten?' said Cass, with an upward inflection.

'Oh, OK. I suppose we do know those things about each other,' Rosa conceded.

'We've booked somewhere lovely for supper,' said Susie. 'Just us. It's a bar really, but the food is great.'

'I've been there with Susie before,' said Rosa. 'It's quite edgy. The sort of place our mothers would think we shouldn't go to.'

'Sounds perfect,' said Cass.

'Our table's not until later,' said Susie. 'Now, tell us again what went on with your publishers?'

'My publishers! I can't believe it!' said Cass.
'So grown up,' said Rosa.
'How much are they paying you and have you got an agent?' asked Susie, suddenly businesslike.
'I haven't got an agent, but they are paying me to go to Dominica, so I count that as part of my wages.'
'I'll let you off this time, but if you get any more work from these people, you must get an agent,' said Susie. 'You pay them commission but they earn that by selling rights on the books you illustrate.'
'OK,' said Cass. 'Now, shall we finish this bottle before we go out?'
'Let's,' said Rosa.
'Tell you what, I really want to have a look at this Ranulph,' said Susie. 'See if he's worth all the heartbreak.'
Cass pursed her lips; she was a bit annoyed. 'Well, if he wasn't in Africa, I'd definitely introduce you.'
'Facebook, darling!' said Rosa, pulling Cass's laptop towards her.
Before Cass could do anything to stop her, Rosa had gone into Cass's Facebook account.
'You know my favourite crisps,' said Rosa, 'I know your passwords.'
'Yes, but —' Cass tried to take her laptop back but it was lifted out of her reach — 'I haven't been on Facebook for months.' She hadn't wanted to accidentally see pictures of Ranulph.
'Here we are,' said Rosa, who was showing zero loyalty, Cass felt. OK, she wanted to please her sister, but surely pleasing your best friend from primary school took precedence? 'Oh, Ranulph hasn't been near Facebook for months either.'
Cass exhaled deeply. He was probably trying to

forget her, too, if he hadn't already. After all, he hadn't been in touch with her since their night in London. He was probably overcome with guilt.

'But it's OK because his friend and Cass's, Becca, has been on Facebook!' Rosa sounded delighted until she suddenly said, 'Oh.'

Of course Cass couldn't stop herself from looking. 'Oh,' she said louder.

On Becca's Facebook page there was another of the group shots she favoured. There was a fairly long line of people, obviously in Africa. And there was Ranulph with his arm round Becca. He looked quite possessive.

'Which one is he?' asked Susie. When Rosa pointed Ranulph out, Susie said, 'Yes, well, I see your point.' She closed the lid of the laptop. 'I think we should go and eat now. And if anyone half-decent flirts with us, we should definitely flirt back.'

Cass did her best. She drank more wine. She smiled. She laughed at other people's jokes, and when a group of businessmen wanted to buy them Metaxa, she drank that too.

She did at least fall asleep quickly when they got back to the boat. But she felt dreadful when she woke up.

Rosa was in a bunk opposite hers. 'Are you OK, Cass? Shall I get you some coffee or something?'

'I'm OK,' said Cass. 'Just hungover, which is entirely my own fault.'

Too late she realised Rosa had been referring to her hangover. Cass had been thinking about her heart-break, which had been woken out of its persistent but not acute phase into full-on agony.

Rosa sniffed. 'I think Susie is making us bacon

sandwiches. What a sister!'

'There's nothing a bacon sandwich and a cup of tea can't cure,' said Cass, smiling bravely although her head ached almost as much as her heart.

They ate breakfast sitting in the bow of the boat. Around them ducks and moorhens swam about, carrying on their day. Behind the houses was the faint roar of London, but here on the canal, all was calm.

'This is such a lovely spot, Susie,' said Cass. 'And so kind of you to put me up again.' She thought she sounded normal, as if her head wasn't about to split and she didn't feel like crying until there wasn't a tear left in her.

'Pleasure, treasure!' said Susie. 'It's been such fun having you girls. And it's been a privilege to share your wonderful news.'

For a few seconds Cass didn't know what she meant by this. What wonderful news? Then she remembered. 'Of course! Getting that illustration job and going to Dominica!' she said. Then she became aware of the odd looks her companions were giving her. 'Sorry, the Greek brandy seems to have gone to my brain.'

'It'll come back,' said Susie, giving Cass a knowing look.

* * *

An hour or so later, they were at the station sipping cans of Coca-Cola as they waited to board their train.

'So, do you know when you'll go to Dominica?' asked Rosa.

'If it was up to me I'd go now,' said Cass. 'But Michael said something about travelling with him and his wife, nearer Christmas. It'll be a bit of winter sun for them. As they're paying for my ticket — and it might even be business class — I can't complain.'

'I should think not!' Rosa sighed. 'Imagine, a Caribbean island, blue skies, miles of sandy white beaches, in winter, travelling business class. Bliss!'

Cass couldn't help smiling. 'Dominica isn't quite like your typical Caribbean island. It has something very special about it but it doesn't have miles of sandy white beaches. Although there's nowhere else I'd rather go.'

At last their train was boarding and they could get on. But once they'd found their seats and were settled, Cass said to Rosa, 'I'm going to have a doze, if you don't mind. It was a heavy night!' Really, she just wanted to be alone with her thoughts and not have to talk.

'It was!' said Rosa instantly, possibly understanding this. 'And after a busy day for you. I'll read my book.'

* * *

Rosa's mother picked them up at the station and dropped Cass back home. Cass's own mother was there to welcome her, eager to hear her news.

'Tell me all about it, darling. I want every detail.'

Cass went into the kitchen, having dumped her bag on the hall floor, as she always had. 'Can't do this without more tea!' she declared. 'Want some sort of hot drink, Mum?'

'I'll make it,' said Cass's mother. 'You sit down and tell me everything.'

As Cass narrated her story, it did dawn on her again what an amazing job she'd been given. Without the addition of the disastrous look on Facebook, which had been like a knife to her already wounded heart, it did sound fantastic. She smiled and breathed and pretended the world was her oyster.

'So when will you be going?'

'That is the slight downside,' Cass said, taking one of the biscuits usually reserved for visitors. 'I'd like to go now and get going, but as the publisher is taking me, with his wife, I have to go when they want to go, which is much nearer Christmas.'

'Talking of which, have you got any plans for Christmas?'

This seemed a strange query coming from her mother. Cass had assumed she'd be at home for Christmas, like every other year of her life. 'Have you got plans, Mum?'

'Since you ask, your brother has invited me up to London. Of course you could come too but Martin and Lou would be a bit pressed for space —'

'So they don't really want me?'

'Don't put it like that! But you and Martin do always rub each other up the wrong way . . .'

Cass decided to overlook how keen her mother seemed to stay with Martin, but this was Christmas. She realised that her mother longed not to be in charge and have to cook a turkey she then had to deal with for (seemingly) weeks afterwards. But inevitably, Christmas with Martin and Cass cooped up together would be stressful.

'I'd be more than happy to go to Dad's,' said Cass. 'He's often asked me but I've never fancied it before. But now he's got this lovely house on a Scottish island, Christmas there would be perfect!' She wondered if her mother knew about Eleanor and decided not to mention her.

'I do hope you're not offended, darling—'

'Of course I'm not!' Cass quickly scanned her feelings and discovered that no, she wasn't at all offended. She was twenty-five; she didn't have to spend every Christmas with her mother and her mother didn't have to spend every Christmas with her, either.

'You'd better ask your father if it's convenient,' said her mother.

'Christmas is ages away, Mum!'

'It'll be on us in no time. You mark my words.'

* * *

Cass's call to her father, which was mainly so she could tell him about her job, ended in an invitation to come up and stay for a few days. Although the shop was busy, there were plenty of people looking for extra shifts and it was the same at the wine bar. Cass decided a few days off with her father, while she waited for Michael Masters to decide when they should go to Dominica, would be a good thing. She would invite herself for Christmas while she was in Scotland.

Although the island where her father lived was very different in late autumn, it was still stunningly beautiful. She arrived on a golden day when the sun was low and the shadows were long. The colours of the fading heather and golden bracken looked extra bright against an ice-blue sky.

'Darling!' said her father. 'How was your journey? It's bloody miles from anywhere, this place!'

'But you love it and so do I,' said Cass, kissing him, before going to hug Eleanor.

'He does,' she agreed. 'I'm very glad you do too. Come inside and get warm. It's that last bit of the journey that takes the time.'

'But the trip on the boat is always lovely, especially as it's so calm today.'

'Hmph,' said her father. 'It's not always like that, I promise you.'

'I know, Dad!'

Eleanor led her to the sitting room where a fire was burning brightly, adding a fragrance to the air which was particular and special.

'Tea?' said Eleanor.

'Whisky?' said her father.

'Both,' said Cass.

Later, at dinner, her father said, 'Darling, when Ranulph brought back my camera, he told us a bit more about what you'd done on Dominica. I realised you'd thoroughly underplayed it when you told us about it yourself. Had I known you'd have to cope with even half that, I would never have asked you to go.' He paused.

'Ranulph told us what an absolute heroine you'd been. How much you'd done in Dominica. You definitely gave us the expurgated version, so as not to worry us.'

'Dad! I loved it. I don't mean I loved being in danger or anything, but I fell in love with the island, loved the people, and I loved doing something important. It made me really grow up and I needed to do that.'

'You do seem a different young woman from the one who had dodgy boyfriends and was the despair of your mother. I had a bit more faith in you, I think,' said Howard. 'So tell me — I couldn't work it out from anything that Ranulph said — are you and he . . .

an item?'

In spite of the pain this question caused her, Cass couldn't help laughing at her father's tentative choice of words. 'I'm afraid not, Dad. He's an 'item' with somebody else, an old flame he'd met when he first went to Dominica and who turned out to be still there.'

'Shame.' Howard looked as if he was going to say more but Eleanor interrupted him.

'More cheese? There's pudding —'

'He's a good man,' Howard persisted. 'I think you'd be well suited.'

Cass forced another laugh. 'Sorry to disappoint you.'

Her father made a noise as if he wanted to pursue the subject but Eleanor put her hand on his. 'I don't think Cass wants to discuss her love life with us, darling. Apart from anything else, she's had a long day.

'So, tell us about this illustration job you've got?' said Eleanor when she'd served the pudding. 'And are you pleased to be going back to Dominica? Or has the place become a nightmare to you?'

'Nothing of the sort! I just wish I knew when I was going. I'm travelling with my publisher and his wife. Lovely, but they can't seem to commit to a date.'

'I can't say I'm not a little disappointed that you haven't followed up on your early talent for photography,' said Howard. 'But at least you're doing something artistic. Your half-brothers and -sister are all very staid and sensible in their career choices.'

'So you're pleased I'm going for something freelance and unlikely to make me eligible for a mortgage?' Cass was laughing.

'I wouldn't object to you having a steady income

but it's important for you to enjoy your work. They do say that if you love your job you never work a day in your life, but although I love photography, it can be bloody hard work!'

* * *

The next few days were spent exploring with Eleanor, eating, sleeping and sketching. Eleanor had taken her to the highest point on the island where the view was spectacular.

'Do you ever feel isolated, living up here, so far away from the rest of the world?' Cass asked.

Eleanor didn't answer immediately. 'I'm not saying I don't wish it didn't take so long to get anywhere else,' she said. 'But now I'm with Howard and we're living in the house I built, I'm very happy to be here.'

Cass didn't speak immediately, and Eleanor went on. 'I stopped Howard questioning you last night, and I know from what you said last time that you think nothing is ever going to happen between you and Ranulph. But if you and he did get together, could you live here?'

Eleanor let the pause last. Eventually, Cass said, 'I think I could live anywhere with Ranulph, and if we were settled here, I would be very happy.'

Eleanor put her arm round Cass's shoulders and gave her a squeeze.

That night Cass slept as if pole-axed. She was the perfect temperature, the room was very dark and it was so quiet. She awoke feeling much better. She felt she would always love Ranulph, but she was not going to let this blight her life. She would live it to the full.

To add to her more positive attitude, there was an

email giving her a date for their flight. It was a little close to Christmas, but Cass wasn't going to grumble. She'd just see as much of the island as she could in the time.

'Thank you so much for having me,' said Cass when it was time to leave. 'I feel so much better for having been up here and spent some days being fed wonderful meals with wonderful scenery.'

'Come back soon,' said Eleanor. 'We love having you.'

34

A few weeks later, her mother kindly drove her to Heathrow where she met Michael and Sylvie Masters. They were experienced travellers, and after the formalities of checking in and going through security to Departures, they ushered her to the business-class lounge.

'We thought we couldn't travel business class and put you in coach,' Sylvie explained. 'And Michael is no fun at the airport. He only ever reads things on his laptop, won't go shopping or anything.'

'I'm always happy to shop,' said Cass, although her checked-in case was full of presents, and gifts suitable for small children who lived on an island. 'Even if I don't buy anything.'

Somehow she found herself buying tins of shortbread and chocolates anyway.

'You never know when you might have to give something to someone unexpectedly. Christmas will be on us before we know it,' said Sylvie, looking at what was in Cass's basket. 'Maybe I should get some of those cute tins as well.'

A smile from Michael when they were back in the lounge indicated he was grateful to Cass for keeping his wife company. While he was obviously quite prepared to ignore Sylvie, he did generally prefer her to be happy.

They were sipping a reviving glass of champagne after their shopping when Sylvie explained why she was also on the trip to Dominica. 'We like a little bit of a break towards the end of the year. It makes the winter go past more quickly,' she said. 'So this is business for Michael and pleasure for me. I know this is work for you, Cass, but I do hope you'll enjoy it as well.'

'I've been before. Dominica is a wonderful island you're bound to fall in love with.' Cass stopped. 'Although there had just been a hurricane when I last visited.'

'I don't suppose that made it more lovable, if you don't mind my saying,' said Sylvie. 'If you loved it then, you're bound to like it more now, when things have had time to settle down.'

Cass smiled. 'I do hope you both love it as much as I do.' She realised that she felt possessive about Dominica and would be resentful of anyone who didn't fall under its spell as she had done.

* * *

Although the flight was extremely comfortable and the change at Antigua fine, Cass still felt she had travelled to another world by the time they arrived on Dominica. But when she saw Toussaint, grinning widely and waving, she suddenly felt at home.

The soft air welcomed her like a cloud perfumed with exotic flowers and trees. The sound of the people, all talking rapidly, gesturing, hugging, handing over erratically wrapped baggage, was familiar and welcoming.

Toussaint gave her an enthusiastic hug before greeting Michael and Sylvie more formally.

He stowed all the bags and then they were away,

Cass sitting in the front with Toussaint.

Soon she began to feel herself relax. Although her previous time on Dominica had been full of stress and adventure, she felt it had made her come alive. She'd had to stretch herself, find strength from the deepest parts of her. But it was so great to be back, and she felt embraced by the warm air.

Then suddenly it began to rain. It was hard and heavy and Cass laughed. 'I'd forgotten how much it rains in Dominica,' she said to Toussaint. She turned to Michael and Sylvie in the back. 'Don't worry, it won't last for long.' And that very moment, it stopped. 'You see?'

'It must explain how lush everything is,' said Sylvie, who, Cass felt, may not yet have fallen under Dominica's spell.

'Wait till you see where Bastian lives,' said Cass.

As they drove along the rough and currently muddy track to his house among the trees, glimpsing a vivid blue sea edged with foaming surf, Cass felt a bit like she sometimes felt in Scotland, that she was coming home. Or if not home, to a place where she felt happy, relaxed and knew what to do.

Bastian was waiting for them outside his house, Delphine at his side and Friendly coming forward to meet them. There were hugs, exclamations and greetings. Delphine gave Cass what she felt was a specially warm embrace which Cass returned with enthusiasm.

'Friendly!' said Cass as the dog came up to her. She gave him special attention, crouching down to fondle his ears, thinking how much she liked dogs and how pleased she was to see him.

The others had moved on to the veranda and Delphine was pouring rum punches. Cass smiled to think of how strong they would be, and hoped it wouldn't be too long before lunch, when a shadow made her look up.

Ranulph was standing over her like a character in a superhero movie. Tall and, with his back to the light, dark and expressionless.

Cass thought she was going to faint and realised it was partly because she'd been crouching for too long. She got up and had to steady herself on a nearby chair. She had not imagined she would see him here, and felt furious suddenly. Apart from work, getting over Ranulph was one of her major reasons for coming to Dominica, in spite of the memories. She was convinced that being on the island, doing what she loved — painting — was what she needed.

'What are you doing here?' she said, hardly able to speak from shock.

She could at least see his face properly now. He raised an eyebrow. 'Much the same as you are, I imagine.'

Cass moistened her lips. 'I doubt that.'

Delphine appeared with two tall, misted glasses full of cut-up fruit as well as liquor. Her look as she gave Cass her drink was almost apologetic and suddenly Cass understood. The extra hugs were supposed to be a warning.

She took a gulp of her rum punch, relishing the jolt it gave her. Alcohol wasn't going to save her from this situation but, just now, she was glad of it.

'Do you guys know where you're sleeping?' asked Delphine.

Cass wanted to faint again. Was Delphine's innocent-sounding question an indication that she and Ranulph were supposed to be staying together? They had of course shared a room when they were here before, but that had been entirely different.

'I'm happy to sleep on the veranda, Delphine. You know that,' said Cass stiffly.

Delphine shook her head. 'Ranulph is sleeping in one of the new guest cabins my brother has built. Bastian always has so many people wanting to stay here, it's good to keep them out of the way.'

Cass was grateful that Delphine realised Cass didn't want to be near Ranulph. It could have been the Sister Code that had picked up her feelings, or it could have been that Delphine had spotted the look of horror on Cass's face when she saw Ranulph.

At any other time Cass would have laughed at Delphine's bluntness in telling Ranulph it was good to keep him out of the house and Ranulph obviously saw the funny side of Delphine telling him.

'Where is Cass sleeping?' asked Ranulph.

'She's in the house. She's working on Bastian's new book.'

Bastian appeared. 'Has Delphine told you guys where you're sleeping?'

'We're sorted,' said Ranulph. 'I think Delphine wants to show Cass her room.'

Delphine ushered Cass to a small room usually used as a store but now containing a bed, a small table and a chair; all the rooms in Bastian's house were multi-purpose.

'Will you be OK here?' She looked about the room. 'It's small! But we had to put Michael and Sylvie in the guest cabin, which has a big lounge area. It would have been perfect for you to do your drawing in.'

'I'll be fine here, thank you, Delphine. I can draw on the veranda if I need to.'

'So, what's the problem with you guys? I thought you were in love with each other when you left.'

Cass shook her head. 'I may have been in love with Ranulph but he's still in a relationship.'

'How do you know that?' demanded Delphine, very sceptical.

'I've seen pictures of them together on Facebook.' Cass paused, and then hurried on, feeling the need to confess. 'But I still slept with him when we were in London, even though I knew this.' It was the guilt this memory produced that was making her feel so terrible.

Delphine rolled her eyes. 'OK!'

'I wish I could just turn around and go back home right now,' said Cass. 'But I'm here to work on some illustrations for Bastian's new book and my boss — well, the person who asked me to do the illustrations — paid for my ticket. Business class!'

This made Delphine laugh. 'He's bought you, girl! Now wash up and come and have lunch.'

35

When she could put it off no longer, Cass joined the others on the veranda. They were knocking back rum punch as though it were fruit juice. Cass was far more circumspect. She knew just how lethal punch could be. But it took the edge off her anxieties about lunch, at least a bit.

All through the flying fish, fried plantain and salad that Delphine served, Cass felt Ranulph's eyes boring into her. But when she forced herself to glance up she realised he was talking to Michael about Bastian's book and not looking at her at all.

As she ate she plotted how she could avoid Ranulph while they were both on the island. She couldn't think about leaving until she'd got sketches of everything they might need for the book, or at least photographs so she could work them up at home.

It had been arranged that she would travel round with Bastian, Michael and Sylvie so she knew exactly what illustrations were required. This would keep her out of Ranulph's way during the day. But what was he doing here?

It couldn't just be a holiday, surely. He must be writing a piece about the dig — possibly something about how it had revealed that the Kalinago people cooperated with Dutch pirates in pre-Columbian times. That would be it. The fact that they were both here at the same time was just a ghastly coincidence.

It would be fine, she decided. She would tour the

island, sketching and taking photographs, while Ranulph would be on the beach with his archaeological version of a bucket and spade. She'd get all the sketches and photos she could possibly need and then she could leave. With luck, Ranulph would stay mostly on the site, taking pictures, making notes and maybe writing back in the guest lodge. Their paths would hardly cross.

Delphine didn't let her help clear up after lunch. 'You can help tomorrow, when you're not working,' she said. 'You have a nap now. Get over the jet lag.'

Cass did sleep a bit but most of the time she lay on her bed, listening to the birds and wondering how Ranulph was feeling. Surely he must be feeling even more guilty than she was: he would have known for definite he was with Becca, while she only suspected it.

She stayed in her room as long as she could before people would begin to think she was hiding in there, which of course she was. Listening for voices as she emerged, she decided the kitchen was safest.

Delphine took one look at her and rolled her eyes. 'OK, you can stay in here until it's time to take the afternoon rum punches out.'

As the kitchen bench was covered with limes, nutmeg and a bowl of ice cubes, Cass realised she had only minutes before she had to face everyone. By everyone she meant Ranulph. She was really looking forward to catching up properly with Bastian and to finding out as much as possible about the guidebook. Did he want an illustration on every page, for example, or only the odd one of certain chosen beauty spots?

'I can't believe it's rum punch time already,' she said, glancing at her watch and seeing it was nearly four o'clock.

'With some guests, it's always rum punch time,' said Delphine. She was filling tall glasses with ice and fruit.

'Where did you get all this ice from?' asked Cass. 'Last time I was here there was no electricity.'

Delphine laughed. 'We bought a lot of ice and put it in the freezer. Bastian likes to keep things low-key when it's just him but if he has a lot of guests, he turns the deep freeze on.'

'Luxury!' Cass sighed.

'Why the sigh?' asked Delphine.

'I liked it as it was. Simple. No frills.'

Delphine was scornful and amused at the same time. 'You'll like the rum punches cold, that's for sure. The simple life is fine if there's just been a hurricane but otherwise, it's not so great. You should see the size of the TV I have in my house!'

Now Cass laughed and indicated the tray of drinks. 'Shall I take these out?'

'Yes, please. But try not to drink them all!'

Having a tray to hide behind did give Cass some protection from the feelings of shyness Ranulph's presence caused. She handed out the drinks in a very professional way. She did regularly work in a wine bar, after all.

'Did you have a good sleep, Cass?' asked Sylvie. 'I never sleep a wink on planes, so I passed out like the dead after lunch.'

'I did, yes,' said Cass.

'Our little guest lodge is adorable!' said Sylvie. 'Simple, but it has everything we want except maybe air conditioning.'

Cass waited to hear Bastian's response to this.

'I think you'll find if you open the jalousies, the breeze will blow through and you won't need air conditioning,' he said.

'Oh, yes, of course,' said Sylvie, embarrassed. 'I suppose I'm used to more . . .'

'Tourist destinations?' suggested Ranulph.

'We want Dominica to be more of a tourist destination,' said Michael. 'Hence the illustrated guidebook. It isn't the same as your typical Caribbean island, but that's what makes it special.'

'Of course, darling,' said Sylvie, obviously concerned in case she'd appeared to be being critical of somewhere everyone else obviously loved.

'Dominica is basically a huge mountain covered with rain forest with a few bits round the edge,' said Bastian.

'I think there's a bit more to it than that,' said Cass.

'Our mountainous terrain is what sets us apart from other Caribbean islands,' Bastian said, his expression making it clear how he felt about his home.

'So, what's the plan for the next couple of days?' asked Michael.

'There are a few sights that we must have in the book, I feel,' said Bastian. 'Beautiful places that are not in other books. There are a couple more waterfalls visible now, thanks to the hurricanes. I'd like Cass to see them. With my commercial hat on —'

'Do you have a commercial hat, Bastian?' asked Ranulph.

Bastian laughed. 'I do! And I think Cass could create some wonderful pictures for the book that could also become cards, postcards, posters even.'

Cass, who'd only quite recently mastered the art of delicate watercolours of small vases of flowers, felt a little daunted but didn't comment.

'But as I think Sylvie would like to see some of our more well-known beauty spots, I've arranged to borrow a car from Delphine's brother, and perhaps, Ranulph, you would take her on a tour?' He smiled at Sylvie in a way that obviously made her feel flattered and excited at the prospect. 'My pick-up only holds two comfortably.'

'That sounds excellent,' said Cass, lighthearted with relief that Ranulph would be safely out of the way, during the day at least.

Cass got through dinner, helped Delphine in the kitchen afterwards, refused a nightcap while sitting on the veranda, looking at the stars and listening to the surf breaking gently on the sand below, and went to bed. Once there, she realised she couldn't put off facing Ranulph too long or she'd be spending most of her time in Dominica hiding in what was usually a storeroom. It was fine as a small bedroom but when the sounds and scents of Dominica were outside, being enjoyed by everyone else, she felt like a prisoner. But only she could get herself out of her cell.

36

Cass got up early the following morning and went to look for Bastian in the building where he sorted out Friendly's food.

'You're up early,' said Bastian, measuring out rice.

'Yes! I just wanted to find out what your schedule is for today.'

'Well, I've told Michael I want to set off immediately after breakfast but we'll see. He may be jet-lagged or he may have already gone on to Dominica time and not feel the need to hurry.' He paused. 'I know you'll be ready on time whatever, Cass.'

'Yes. I'm very excited by this project, as I'm sure you know.'

'I do know, and I also know that there is something going on between you and Ranulph.'

'No. I mean yes. There is something going on — or there was — but there isn't now.' She stopped, not sure how much she wanted to explain.

'I hope you're not asking for tips on your love life from someone who can't persuade his girlfriend to share an island with him,' said Bastian.

Cass laughed. 'I think your system suits you both very well. So perhaps I should ask your advice.'

'I'd rather you didn't. I'd feel so responsible if it all went wrong because of something I'd said.'

'Don't worry about that,' said Cass. 'It's already gone wrong; you couldn't make it worse. But I'm not going to insist you talk to me about it. I'll go and help Delphine.'

'Delphine: now, she's your woman for advice on your love life. I speak from experience.'

* * *

'You don't have to help me, you know. I am paid to do this,' Delphine told her a few minutes later.

Cass liked Delphine's forthright manner. You were never in any doubt about what Delphine thought and Cass felt she could be forthright in return.

'I know you are, but I don't mind helping at all, and I want to avoid Ranulph.'

'Hmm. Haven't you been in love with that boy all this long time?'

'Yes! But I told you what happened, and I want to get him out of my head. Him being here was a horrible shock. I don't even know why he is here!' Cass picked up the tray of glasses for fruit juice. 'Shall I take these?'

Delphine nodded. 'Breakfast is formal today. I imagine that will go on for a couple days and then we'll go back to normal ways.'

Cass went through to the veranda. 'Good morning!' she said to Michael and Sylvie, who were already at the table. 'Did you sleep well?'

'Yes, thank you,' said Michael.

'It took me a while to get off and then I was awake a lot in the night,' said Sylvie, who didn't seem to know that 'Did you sleep well?' was a rhetorical question that didn't require a truthful answer.

Ranulph appeared shortly afterwards, and Cass managed to give him a nod in an almost normal way. Bastian didn't come to breakfast and Cass found it all tortuous.

'I must get my things together,' she said as soon as she reasonably could. 'I know Bastian will want to be off as soon as possible.' She smiled at no one in particular, and got up.

It didn't take her long to put a sketch pad and a selection of pencils in her bag. If she needed to take photographs, she had her phone. How different everything was now compared to her first trip to Dominica. Electric light, mobile phone coverage and ice in the drinks. It was almost decadent.

She went outside to stand by the pick-up, where she found Bastian.

'Will you be OK in the back?' he asked, looking a bit guilty.

'Of course! It's part of the Dominica experience, going in the back of Bastian's pick-up!'

Bastian laughed. 'I'll help you up. I hope we don't have to wait too long for Michael. He knows we have a lot to fit in today.'

'Where do you think we should go?'

'We'll explore what we can of the north of the island and then go further south if we have time. Do you have any preferences?'

'Not really. As long as I have something pretty to paint at the end of my time here, I'll be happy. I wonder how many illustrations Michael wants?'

'There'll be some he definitely wants and I will certainly want some from the very top of the island where there are parrots. And waterfalls — very picturesque.'

'What about the petroglyph?'

Bastian shook his head. 'I don't want to encourage people to go tramping through the forest looking for something they may well not recognise.' He paused.

'Here's Sylvie, all ready, I see.'

Cass felt overcome with relief. If Sylvie was ready she and Ranulph would soon be off and she could relax. Then he appeared. After chatting with Bastian for a few moments, discussing where would be good to go and where roads were still nearly impassable, Sylvie, wearing enormous sunglasses and a big sun hat, was ushered into the front seat of the four-by-four.

'Is there anything else you might need?' asked Ranulph. 'Have you got water?'

'Here!' said Cass, holding out a bottle. 'Have mine. I'll go and get some from the kitchen.'

She didn't want anything to hold up Ranulph and Sylvie's departure. She wouldn't mind at all taking a plastic bottle from the fridge and letting Sylvie have her own water bottle, new and reusable.

At last, Sylvie and Ranulph set off but still Bastian and Cass waited for Michael. Bastian didn't often show impatience, but Cass could sense it without difficulty. At last, Michael appeared, full of apologies and explanations.

Cass was aware that sitting in the back she was missing out on Bastian's commentary on what they were passing. She knew he was brilliant at adding life and colour to every little place or vista on the island. They all had stories attached. She remembered when she was driving his pick-up just after the hurricane, they had squashed three people into the front, but if she wanted to join Bastian and Michael, she would be practically sitting on their laps. She had to make do with noting the places she particularly liked as they passed by; she would ask Bastian about them later.

They stopped at the side of the road high up in the

mountains. Cass had been glad of the pullover she'd put in her bag by the time Bastian gave her a hand to get out.

'This is a glorious spot,' she said, joining Michael who was looking far across the forest to where the sea could just be spotted.

'It's one of the places the hurricane was kind to,' said Bastian. 'If you look behind you, there's a waterfall that wasn't visible before the hurricane took down a lot of the forest.'

Cass got out her phone. 'I'll take a picture.'

'I wouldn't mind a chance to stretch my legs,' Michael said.

'Do you want to come with us, Cass?' asked Bastian.

Cass shook her head. 'I want to see if I can sketch the waterfall. As you know, currently I mostly do flowers and very small-scale things. I want to see if I could do bigger things if I tried.'

'Of course you can,' said Bastian. 'We'll leave you to it.'

* * *

Half an hour later, Cass was enjoying herself, drawing across two sheets of paper on a scale she hadn't tried before. She was letting her arm move across the paper, sketching the waterfall, the trees, the ferns and the bromeliads which hung from the branches of the trees. She heard a car just as she was nearing the end of the first sketch, but didn't stop. Only when she'd got everything she wanted on to the page did she let her hand fall.

'That really is amazing, Cass,' said Ranulph.

Cass jumped. She had been so wrapped up in her drawing that she hadn't heard him approach. 'What are you doing here?' she said.

'You've asked me that already,' he said gently.

Cass shook her head to clear it. 'No, I mean here? This particular spot? Miles from anywhere?'

'I asked Bastian where he planned to go last night.'

'So you're stalking me?' She was furious.

'Certainly not! That sounds creepy and sinister. I wanted to get you away from everyone else.' He stopped. 'Sorry, that still sounds creepy and sinister.'

'I don't want to talk, if that's what you had in mind.'

'I know you don't,' he said quickly. 'But we will have to. We can't just pretend our night in London didn't happen. I know —'

Before he could say more, Sylvie came and joined them. 'What an amazing spot! What a good idea to come here, Ranulph. And Cass! That is a wonderful drawing. It should definitely go in the book. The cover, maybe.'

'I've never done anything on this scale before,' said Cass. 'I'm not sure I can.'

'You can,' said Ranulph and Sylvie, almost together.

'Here, Michael,' Sylvie called as her husband and Bastian appeared from between the trees. 'Come and see what Cass has done!' She walked to join them and Ranulph put a hand on Cass's arm.

'How long are you staying?' he asked urgently.

'I don't know.' This was true but it sounded pathetic.

'I'll give you a day to get accustomed to me being here,' said Ranulph. 'But then we need to have a proper conversation.'

37

All through that afternoon, Cass made herself run through in her head what Ranulph was likely to say to her. He would tell her he was in a relationship; that he and Becca were together. He might even tell her they were getting married. Cass had deliberately not looked at Facebook again because she didn't want any of this confirmed. Ranulph would be very kind about it, but he would explain that what happened in London was a one-off, never-to-be-repeated occurrence. He would say that he would have explained all this at the time if she hadn't run off. She was bound to cry, just through tension, and she would look like more of an idiot than she did already. But there was no way round it. She did have to talk to Ranulph, however agonising it would be.

Both her sketchbooks were full by the time they got back, tired and in Cass's case slightly nauseous from being swung around in the back of Bastian's pick-up. She allowed Bastian to steady her as she climbed out.

'Long day,' he said as they walked together into the house.

'Yes. But I got a lot done.'

'You're really talented, Cass,' said Bastian. 'I'm so glad you sent me that birthday card or I would never have known how gifted you are. I would have just thought of you as someone who could handle a pickup over damaged roads, or who could sew up a leg if necessary.'

Cass laughed. 'Thank you. Those first two skills are for occasional use only! Let's hope the drawing is for ever.' She paused. 'But now I'm going to grab a shower before the others get back.'

She heard the car arrive and listened to Sylvie and Ranulph getting out, greeting the others on the veranda, the clink of glasses as the inevitable punch was served. She put on a dress, a bit of jewellery and some mascara before joining them.

'Hey, beautiful girl!' said Sylvie, who was lying flat out on a reclining chair, a misted glass in her hand. 'I am exhausted! But you look fresh as a daisy, damn you. Come and have a drink. Tell me what you and my husband got up to with Bastian.'

Cass perched on the wide arm of Sylvie's chair and chatted about the day, and when Ranulph put a glass in her hand she thanked him but didn't look at him.

Eventually Sylvie got up. 'I'd better sluice myself down before dinner,' she said.

'Actually, Sylvie,' said Cass, following her, 'can I have a word in private? I should have asked before really, but I just wondered when we're booked to go home?'

'Home?' said Sylvie. 'Who wants to go there? But you're not booked, love. I thought you could decide for yourself how long you stayed. It's an open ticket. I'll get it for you.'

'You are so kind, bringing me here,' Cass said as Sylvie handed her an envelope.

'Not as kind as all that,' said Sylvie. 'It's cattle class, I'm afraid.'

'Oh, that doesn't matter! Really! A free trip out here — that's beyond generous.'

'You are the chosen illustrator for the new guide-book,' said Sylvie, brushing off Cass's gratitude. 'And you're working hard. But it's a wonderful island and I can see why you and Ranulph are so fond of it.'

* * *

The next day Cass borrowed a much larger sketchbook from Bastian as well as taking her own. She wanted to do another large drawing — let herself go, as she had before. She'd discovered this new talent for large sweeping scenes and she wanted to make the most of it while she had such wonderful scenery in front of her.

Bastian took her and Michael to a verdant valley where there was another stunning view for her to draw.

Somehow, although in theory she was depicting flowers and trees, rocks and waterfalls, she realised she was painting from the heart, as if she had nothing to lose, and the effect was amazing.

Bastian had hired a boat and a boatman and taken them up the Indian River and Cass never stopped drawing. Buttress roots almost like walls supported huge, old trees. The hurricane seemed to have shown mercy to these ancient natural structures.

'Do you want a turn up front, Cass?' asked Michael when they got back to the pick-up. 'I wouldn't mind a go in the back and I don't think it's far to where we're going next.'

'That would be nice,' said Cass. 'Just for a change. Do you know where we're headed?'

'A little spot only Bastian knows about. It should be interesting.'

It wasn't long before they stopped at an unpromising pull-in at the side of the road.

'Trust me,' said Bastian, although Cass hadn't asked what they had stopped for. 'This is worth it.'

It was. They walked up the track a bit and then into the forest. There was an old mill.

All the buildings were still there: where the owners had lived, the slaves, the hospital. The wheel which turned the stones to crush the sugar cane was on its side, but huge copper vessels used to boil the sugar were all still present.

'What sort of mill was it, Bastian?' asked Cass. 'Sugar? And how old is it?'

'It dates from the 1720s, so it's a French settlement, and in its time it's produced coffee, sugar, rum and even lime juice. That' — he pointed — 'is the only windmill tower on the island.

'I don't think this should go in the book,' said Bastian. 'But I thought it would be interesting to see. I'm not sure if you'd want to draw it, Cass. You can decide. It's the oldest surviving estate on the island.'

'It's very atmospheric,' said Cass, who felt she'd stepped back into the past. 'I'm not sure I like being here. It seems haunted.'

Bastian shrugged. 'Our past is always haunting and often shameful. But history is history.' He took a last look around. 'Shall we go? I'll ring the owner when I get back. He needs to see to the roofs of the houses. Before they fall into disrepair. Do you want to draw it?'

Cass shook her head. She couldn't wait to get home.

* * *

Cass was feeling sombre on the journey back. It wasn't only the old sugar mill that had cast a shadow over her, it was the realisation that she would have to face Ranulph and have their difficult conversation.

By the time they got back she had decided she couldn't put it off. She had to hear the truth, the truth she already knew, from Ranulph's own lips. This feeble behaviour was just that, feeble. She couldn't let herself get away with it.

When Cass got in, Ranulph and Sylvie were already ensconced on the veranda, discussing their day, showing each other photographs they'd taken on their phones, Friendly sitting happily at their feet.

Cass went to her room to tidy herself and then went straight to the kitchen. Delphine put a rum punch in her hand.

'You're at least one behind the others, girl,' she said.

Cass couldn't help smiling. 'Do I look as if I need a drink?'

Delphine didn't answer and Cass went out on to the veranda.

'Ranulph?' she said after she'd taken a couple of heartening sips of punch. 'Could I have a word?'

She'd spoken quietly but Sylvie heard. 'When people say that, you know it's bad news,' she said. 'Although I'm sure Cass hasn't got bad news for you, Ranulph.' She looked from Cass to Ranulph and back again. 'Or maybe . . .'

Ranulph guided Cass away from the veranda on to the short grass with a view of the sea. He didn't speak.

Cass exhaled. 'We need to talk about what happened in London.'

He turned to her. 'Yes! Why didn't you reply to any of my texts and emails?'

She swallowed. 'I didn't read them. I had them sent to a folder automatically.' She realised what utter cowardice this had been.

'Why?' He was obviously furious but keeping it in check.

'Why did you come here?' Cass asked. 'To Dominica? Are you working?'

He shook his head. 'I came to see you, Cass. I heard from Bastian you were coming and got myself a flight.'

'Why?'

'If you'd read my emails and texts you'd know.' He turned away from her.

'I didn't want to read a lot of lies and excuses. We both know what we did in London was wrong. It should never have happened, and I don't think I'll ever be able to forgive myself.' She moved round so she could look at him. 'But I at least had the benefit of doubt. You knew you were in a relationship.'

'What?' He seemed confused.

'You know what a relationship is? It's when you commit to each other and don't sleep with other people!'

'Cass, what are you talking about?'

'Am I suddenly speaking a different language? Is gobbledygook coming out of my mouth? It all sounds perfectly comprehensible to me!'

'But what you're saying makes no sense. Who am I supposed to be in a relationship with?'

'With Becca! You're in a relationship with Becca. And if you've broken up it must be very recent!'

'What?' Ranulph said again. He took hold of her shoulders and then let them go again. 'Cass, Becca and I had a thing when we were both students; since then we've just been friends. Where are you getting your information from?'

For the first time since the beginning of their

conversation, Cass suddenly felt less sure of her ground although she still thought he was lying. 'Facebook. There are pictures of you with your arm round Becca. Her status is 'in a relationship'.'

'I don't do Facebook.'

'If you did, you'd know how revealing it is!'

'It can't reveal what doesn't exist. I'm not in a relationship with Becca! She's happily coupled up with someone else. Doesn't Facebook tell you that?'

Cass shrugged. Her heart was beating hard and she felt she didn't know what to believe any more. She'd been so certain and now she wasn't.

Ranulph sighed. He suddenly looked tired and strained. 'I've been in love with you for a long time, Cass. Ever since I first saw you on that ferry in Scotland. You were lost in your own world and I thought how beautiful you were. I know it sounds ridiculous, but there it is.' He cleared his throat. 'That's why making love to you in London felt completely right, because it was right. There's only ever been you.'

Cass looked at him in confusion. 'Then why didn't you say so at the time?'

He looked away from her and then out to sea. 'I was frightened that you weren't ready for me to tell you I loved you. I just wanted to go with the moment. I would certainly have told you in the morning, but you weren't there.'

He took another breath. 'I see now that I should have declared myself sooner. I suppose I thought my feelings were pretty clear.'

Hearing all this from him didn't feel as convincing as it should have, somehow. 'Rescuing me from Austin was amazing and I'll always be grateful, but hitting a man doesn't exactly say 'I love you'.'

Ranulph swallowed and looked around him again as if seeking help to make her understand. Then he took a deep breath. 'Cass, I really want you to know how much I love you but I see that I made a major mistake and I didn't know that mistake would make you cut me out of your life.' He paused. 'Can I have a second chance? Please? Can I prove my love for you while we're here together, in Dominica?'

Cass felt her feelings had been through an emotional blender. She had been so positive Ranulph and Becca were together, she couldn't just accept that this wasn't true, and that she was the one he loved. Maybe time was what she needed? She didn't speak.

'Or maybe,' Ranulph went on, 'we could just be friends? Give you a bit more time to get used to the idea that it's you I love? If you don't — can't — accept that before we leave, then it will be me who has to accept it. But I want a chance to prove my feelings. I came to Dominica to sort this out, to tell you how I feel. I'm not going to give up without a fight!' He smiled ruefully. 'Although I hope it doesn't have to be with Austin!'

Cass took a few breaths to think about this. She'd spent almost every moment since she first met him believing she was in love with Ranulph. Now it seemed he was in love with her. It should be the best news she'd ever got and yet, somehow, she just felt numb.

38

'Can we change things up a little tomorrow?' asked Sylvie. 'I'd really love to travel with Bastian, and Ranulph can drive Cass anywhere she'd like to go.'

Ranulph laughed. 'I think you'll find that Cass is more than capable of driving herself. After the hurricane she was driving Bastian's pick-up all over the place, on very damaged roads.' He smiled, a little diffident. 'So where would you like to go, Cass? Now that you have the choice?'

Cass didn't have to think. 'I'd love to visit the family who rescued me during the second hurricane.'

Delphine, who had cleared the dishes after dinner, put down a bowl of bananas and some locally made chocolate for dessert. 'If you're going up there you might need a shovel and perhaps a rope. The road hasn't been repaired.' She paused. 'You might need a man, too.'

Cass laughed. 'In which case, I'd better take one. Ranulph? Are you up for it?'

* * *

'You've got a lot of stuff!' said Ranulph the next morning, taking the laundry sack Cass had with her and putting it in the back of the borrowed pick-up.

'It's presents for the family. Only little things but I'm hoping it's something a bit different from what can be got here. And I found a quirky little toy shop full of odd things for the children.'

'It's a lovely way to say thank you for being rescued,' said Ranulph. 'And that's your art bag?'

She nodded. 'I've probably got enough sketches to fill two books, but if I don't bring it I'll see something I'm dying to draw.'

He nodded. 'So do you want me to drive? Or do you know the way?'

'I know the way but you can drive. I can direct you.'

They drove in silence for a while until Cass said, 'The last time I came up this hill, I was with Austin.'

'Oh! That must be a bit triggering for you,' said Ranulph.

'I probably wouldn't have said that exactly, but I am remembering what it was like and it was terrifying.'

'Of course, on the way back, you were with me.'

'Definitely worse!' Cass made a joke of it. 'Maybe I should drive now, to get rid of the bad memories. The weather was so wild and Austin wouldn't turn back. He was mad!'

'But he survived and, most importantly, so did you.'

'And so did Dad's camera.'

She couldn't help thinking how much trouble that camera had caused. If she hadn't had to retrieve it in London, she would never have slept with Ranulph. How much simpler her life would have been. But even as she framed the thought, she realised, in the very deepest part of her heart, she would never quite regret that night, however much pain and guilt it caused.

'Had he but known it, Howard could have sent you here with a sharp pencil and an artist's pad instead.'

Cass laughed. 'Luckily I'd packed those things

for myself.'

He pulled into the side of the road and they exchanged seats.

'What are you going to do for Christmas?' Ranulph asked. 'Will you be in the Cotswolds with your family?'

'No. My mother is spending it in London with my brother. I was invited but really didn't want to go. I'm spending it with Dad and Eleanor in Scotland. I love it up there anyway and was delighted when they invited me.'

'Oh?'

Cass nodded. 'I'm looking forward to seeing it in proper winter.'

'The winters are long, which can be a problem,' said Ranulph. 'And we run out of daylight quite quickly.'

Cass shrugged. 'We run out of daylight quickly here, too. Think how the night comes down immediately the sun has set.'

'True. And in summer up there, the nights go on forever. You can see the Northern Lights.'

'That would be amazing. I've always wanted to see them.'

'I've always wanted to see the Emerald Drop — or the Green Flash, whatever they call it,' said Ranulph.

'That would also be amazing. But I gather it's very rare. The conditions have to be exactly right. I'm not sure I believe it's real,' said Cass. Just for a second she asked herself if her feelings were real, or if they were just an illusion. She hurried on. 'But of course it would be amazing to see it.' She was about to add that it would be a good omen but realised it would take a lot of explaining and lead her to territories where she didn't want to go.

'Are we nearly there yet?' said Ranulph.

Cass shot him a grin. 'It's still a little way. We have to get quite a bit higher.'

'Why did Austin come this way if he was on the way to the airport?'

Cass shrugged. 'Perhaps his plan was always to dump me on the side of the road.'

Ranulph turned abruptly to look out of the window, obviously angry suddenly.

* * *

'Hey! It's Cass!' said a man who emerged from an old ti kai, followed by several small children and a teenager.

Cass realised that before, during the hurricane, she'd never had a chance to look properly at the house. Now she had time to admire the traditional sloping roof and wooden shingles. 'Yes! I've come back. I have presents for some of you,' she said. 'This is Ranulph.'

The man nodded. 'The man who came to get you after the second hurricane. We're Garvin and Irma.'

'That's me,' Ranulph said. 'Thank you for taking Cass in.'

A woman with an ample figure and a wide smile had joined her husband and children. 'You're welcome. Now come in! Have a drink. Rum?'

'We'd love to come in, if that's all right, but maybe we shouldn't have rum—' Cass didn't want to be rude, but she didn't want to drink rum either.

'I have some freshly made sorrel,' said the woman. 'Made from bushes just behind the house.'

Soon they were all sitting on the veranda looking out over the mountain and across to the sea, just visible in the distance.

'This is so refreshing,' said Cass. 'I must find out how to make it.'

'Delphine will show you,' said Irma.

Cass picked up the laundry sack she had stowed between her feet and looked at the children who had gathered. 'Now, you guys? Can you find your brothers and sisters and cousins? I have presents.'

The presents were all opened instantly. There were fidget spinners, high bouncing balls, magic sand, some dominoes, several little cars and some packets of colouring pencils.

The children inspected them with delight and Lola, the teenager, was delighted with her gel nail kit with stick-on gems.

'I didn't really know what to get them, and I certainly didn't know what to get you,' said Cass, turning to Irma. She suddenly felt shy giving a present to someone who was virtually a stranger. 'I hope this is all right?' She handed over an extremely heavy parcel, bubble-wrap under the Santa with his sleigh paper that covered it.

It took Irma a few moments to realise what Cass had given her. 'A set of Pyrex dishes?'

Cass nodded. 'And they all have watertight plastic lids. You can stack them in the fridge.'

'How did you know I needed these?' asked Irma, delighted but suspicious.

'I was in your house for a while,' said Cass. 'I thought they might be useful, when you have a big family.'

'But so bulky in your luggage!' Irma exclaimed.

Cass nodded. 'But I didn't need to bring many clothes so it was fine.'

Irma nodded. 'Thank you.'

She wasn't effusive but Cass knew her present had hit the spot.

After more chat Ranulph got up. 'Cass? I think we should get back. We don't want to be late for lunch.'

'No, you don't,' said Irma. 'That Delphine, she doesn't like it if you're late for meals.'

After the goodbyes were said and Ranulph and Cass were back in the car, Cass said, 'I can't remember how Irma and Delphine are related, but they are.'

'It's a small island, really,' said Ranulph, who was now in the driving seat. 'Shall we go straight back?'

'Yup. Or is there anywhere else you'd like to go?'

'Well, not now, but I'd love to see the petroglyph sometime,' said Ranulph. 'I was sorry to miss it the first time. Except you wouldn't have gone if I had — so it worked out for the best.'

They drove back in silence. Cass was reliving the miraculous moment in the rain forest, alone with her pad and pencil when a chance gust of wind and ray of sunshine revealed the petroglyph.

Just before they turned on to the road that went along the coast towards Bastian's house, Ranulph said, 'If Austin hadn't knocked Howard's camera out of your hand, the petroglyph might not have been discovered.'

Cass gave a wry chuckle. 'Well, it certainly wouldn't have been by Austin or even Bastian — I had altered the map when I copied it.'

Ranulph gave her a smile that was heart-melting and made her suddenly regret her decision that they should be just friends for the time being. 'You're a very clever woman, Cass. Devious, but clever.'

'Just as well, hey!' said Cass glibly, allowing her spirits to fly just for a moment.

39

Everyone was on the veranda when they arrived back and Sylvie in particular seemed in high spirits.

'We've decided to throw a party!' she announced. 'A local launch to celebrate Bastian winning the bursary and his new book.'

Cass looked at Bastian, who caught her glance and shrugged. 'Everyone loves a party,' he said. 'Loretta and her family will come over from Barbados. Lots of local people will come.'

'How does Delphine feel about this?' Cass murmured.

'She loves a party too,' he said. 'And Loretta is insisting on doing the cooking. She's already told me she will bring a turkey and a ham although it's not Christmas yet.'

'Well, that's good,' said Cass.

'It's kinda good,' said Delphine from over Cass's shoulder. Then she came round and handed Cass a glass of punch. 'But she is one messy cook.'

Bastian smiled. 'And Loretta's parents want to come. And her brother. They've never been to Dominica before.'

'They think it's a backward little island where no one goes,' said Delphine. Then she huffed in an impressive way and returned to the kitchen.

* * *

The following days were a flurry of activity. Sylvie was obsessed with trying to buy pretty paper napkins, Michael was trying to buy enough alcohol to render half the island unconscious, and Ranulph and Bastian spent time rigging up the perfect party venue on the beach. This required a very long table, benches, a shelter for the steel band that was booked, a table for food, and a bar made with a huge cable reel on its side.

Cass and Delphine made rooms ready for the guests who were staying over.

Apparently, the original plan had been for Loretta to come the day before her parents and brother, Delphine explained. Now they were all coming at once.

'Loretta still has time to prepare for the meal, but we have to entertain her family for a day longer,' she finished. 'I don't know where we're going to put everyone!'

'I've had a job as a chambermaid,' said Cass, hoping Delphine wouldn't comment on the fact that she was not offering to stay with Ranulph to free up a room. 'I'll help you make up all the beds.'

* * *

Bastian and Cass were in the dog-feeding shack. Cass had offered to boil up the chickens while Bastian was busy building structures on the beach. He had come back so he could feed Friendly himself.

Cass thought she'd take the opportunity to find out more about Loretta's parents. 'Have you met them?' she asked.

Bastian smiled ruefully. 'Yes. I don't think they approve of me as I'm not a millionaire, but they are impressed by my status on the island, apparently.'

'What does that mean, exactly?' Cass stirred the chicken and rice, the smell of which was making Friendly very excited.

'It means they'll drop my name at every opportunity on the journey and try to get through customs without paying any duty on anything.'

Cass shuddered at the thought. 'How embarrassing!'

'Yes. But on the other hand, if anyone discovers that Loretta has a frozen turkey in her luggage, it may be a good thing.'

'Really? Is it illegal to bring food in, then?'

Bastian shrugged. 'It might be. Loretta's mother is worried about it, anyway. She has the ham. Loretta's brother Clyde will make his famous sweet-potato dish, which includes marshmallows. One thing we can be sure of, there will be enough food.'

'That's good! said Cass. 'This all seems to be cooked. Shall I turn off the gas?'

He nodded. 'Come on, Friendly, time for breakfast.'

* * *

Loretta and her family arrived the following day. Cass waited with the others to greet them, and soon realised they were warm and humorous, and if they were a bit thrown by the lack of things they took for granted ('You don't have air conditioning? How do you manage?') they didn't appear snooty. Michael and Sylvie were equally approachable of course and so it wasn't long before everyone was getting on brilliantly.

As she helped Delphine prepare the usual gallon of rum punch, she said as much. 'They're really friendly! It'll be easy.'

'Hmph,' said Delphine. 'You wait.'

* * *

While the new arrivals and Michael and Sylvie were sleeping off their lunch, Cass found the large pad of drawing paper she had purloined from Bastian and took herself to a spot where she could see the whole house. Now everyone was here, she felt at a bit of a loose end. But she had a plan to make use of her spare time.

Quickly she drew the outline, the different rooms and some background. Then she put in the people. She had never drawn people before but this was an experiment to see if she could do them. She got into it. She added detail. She made it so you could see the heated conversation between mother and daughter. She added Bastian in his study, ignoring the discussions about turkey and ham. She put Friendly at his feet, happily chewing a large bone with a bow on it. She put in herself sitting on the edge of the veranda with a huge pile of vegetables, a pile even bigger than the one she actually did peel and chop. Ranulph was there too, carrying a table over his head with one hand, with as many chairs as Cass could manage to fit in hanging off his arms.

When the real Ranulph came up behind her she jumped. 'Is there no end to your talents?' he said. 'That's good!'

Cass inspected her drawing with a critical eye. 'I think I've stopped trying to get things right or to make my work look like someone else's. Since I've stopped caring so much I've got better, I'm not afraid to try new things.'

'Well, good for you!'

He seemed genuinely impressed and Cass's heart swelled with pride for a moment.

'I've bought you a present — not for anything — just a present. I want to give it to you now,' he said.

He produced a crumpled rectangle from somewhere. 'I wrapped it at home, which is why it's looking so battered. Please open it. I've been worrying about whether it's the right thing for ages.'

Cass tore off the wrapping. Inside was a small box and she knew, before she opened it, that it had watercolours in it. She was not disappointed. Twelve full-sized watercolours in a tin she could take anywhere. 'Ranulph! We sell these at the shop, but I've never felt I could afford to buy one. Oh, sorry,' she went on, 'that's probably a bit rude. I love it!'

After the tiniest pause for thought, she reached up and kissed his cheek. 'Thank you!'

'I'm so glad,' he said softly, obviously delighted by Cass's reaction.

'Now I feel dreadful that I haven't got you anything.'

'There's no reason why you should have bought me anything, but if you would take me to see the petroglyph,' he said, 'I'd love that.'

'Of course! You told me it was disappointing for you missing it the first time.' She paused again. 'I've more or less finished this for Bastian. Shall we slip off now? While everyone's asleep? Otherwise someone is bound to want to tag along.'

* * *

'Will you remember the way?' asked Ranulph. 'Should we have brought the map?'

Cass laughed. She was feeling very happy; she was going on an expedition with the man she loved and who she was beginning to believe loved her. 'No, the map is engraved on my mind. We'll be fine.'

Although the undergrowth was a lot thicker since Cass first came with Bastian, Toussaint and Austin, she found the path through the woodland quite easily. It was quite a long climb down through the forest on a path that, very many years ago, had been someone's regular road. The man who used to see the petroglyph almost daily, long since dead, had left traces.

'Maybe it's because I did quite a bit of sketching, I sort of know where I am. Here, for example, is where I stayed behind and the others went on. Dad's camera went flying just about now.'

'What did you do?'

'I lay back on the ground and closed my eyes and I heard water. Then there was a breeze and the sun shone down on to these rocks.'

'And?'

'There it is, the petroglyph.'

She spoke softly, as full of wonder as she had been the first time she saw the carved faces. If that was because Ranulph was so near her, almost breathing into her ear, or because she could smell him, his soap, his own distinctive odour, she couldn't have said. All she knew was that she wanted to make love to him so much she could hardly breathe.

She didn't move but heard him clear his throat and felt him step back. Did he feel the same? Or was Becca standing between them again, invisible but almost tangible?

'We'd better go back,' she said, annoyed to hear a break in her voice. 'It's quite a long walk back up the hill to the car.'

'Yes, let's go. I'd like to take you to Scott's Head and it's a little way away.'

'What's at Scott's Head? I didn't go there when I was staying with that lovely family all those years ago and they gave me my first, whistle-stop tour of the island.'

'It's where the Atlantic and the Caribbean meet. It's a particularly good place to see the sunset.'

'Shall we stay and look for the Green Flash?' Cass was pleased to be able to say something lighthearted, a bit frivolous.

'Of course! It wouldn't be right not to do it there. Mind you, if I'm ever anywhere remotely suitable on Dominica, I look for it.'

They stood in silence for a few moments, looking at the petroglyph, the primitive offering to the gods, asking them to ensure a reliable water supply. She couldn't tell for certain, but she thought that Ranulph felt the same about this spot as she did. Finding it had meant such a lot for both of them, and being here together now felt as if they were somewhere almost sacred.

Neither of them spoke on the long climb up the hill to where they'd left the car. When they got in, Cass felt breathless, not so much because she'd walked up a steep hill quite fast, but for far less sensible reasons.

'Seeing the Green Flash would make today perfect,' she said, when she felt the silence was becoming too meaningful.

'It is very rare.'

'But think how amazing it would be to see it! It would be such a good omen.'

He glanced at her quickly. 'A good omen for what?'

Cass definitely had something in mind but she was not going to tell Ranulph. 'Oh, I'm not fussy. I'm always looking for good omens. They don't have to be for anything in particular. Rainbows are a good omen, for example.'

Ranulph laughed. 'Which is good because they are so frequent here. It rains so much.'

'It's a good system,' said Cass, smiling.

He started the car and then they lapsed into silence.

It was quite a long drive down the coast to Scott's Head. Although it was still daytime, Cass couldn't help remembering how quickly the night came down. They had to reach their destination by sunset.

At last, they got there, parked the car and then walked along a narrow strip of land between two seas. They walked right to the end of the spit. On one side was the Atlantic, with crashing waves, and on the other, calmer and more blue, was the Caribbean Sea.

'I recognise this from Dad's photographs,' said Cass as they looked back at the island, which looked magnificent. 'It is such a perfect spot for photographs.'

'Or paintings.'

Cass nodded. 'It's unusual, I suppose, to be brought up in a household where photography was considered the fine art, and anything using paper and colouring pencils, or even worse, paint, was slightly despised. Not that Dad stayed with us long. I think I was about nine when he left.'

'Hard for a child.'

Cass shook her head. 'It was fine, really it was. Hardest for my mum really. But we survived. She's happy and fulfilled now.'

'Oh look, it's nearly sunset.'

'I hope the clouds shift a bit,' said Cass.

'Trade-wind clouds. They're very distinctive.'

'But I'll be cross if they get in the way of me and the Emerald Drop,' Cass said.

Even without rare meteorological phenomena to watch for, the sunset was magnificent. Huge dark clouds stood out against an apricot sky and the rays of the sun shone down to the sea like strobes.

When Ranulph put his arm round her waist and pulled her close, Cass didn't pull away.

Then it happened. The sun dropped down and for a split second there was a flash.

'Oh my God,' said Cass. 'Did you see that?'

'I did! How absolutely extraordinary. I never thought I'd see it.'

'Nor me.' Cass found herself overcome with emotion. She turned away so Ranulph wouldn't see.

'Now we have to wait for what the good omen was for,' he said after a few moments. 'But I feel hopeful suddenly.' And he smiled at Cass, who suddenly felt full of happiness — and hopefulness, too, that things would work out between them.

'We should go,' she said after several moments.

40

The journey back in the dark was necessarily slower and it seemed to take them a long time to reach Bastian's house. Now, there were several cars parked and the beach was full of light, people and music.

Cass didn't want to go and join them immediately, she wanted to cherish the special atmosphere she and Ranulph were sharing.

'Will they believe us when we tell them we saw the Emerald Drop?' she said as an excuse to keep him by her side.

'You know what? Let's not tell them now. Everyone is already partying. We'll tell Bastian in the morning.'

'Good idea,' she said. 'Now, shall we join the others?'

He took her hand.

⋆ ⋆ ⋆

There were large storm lanterns all down the long table which now had huge bowls of food along the middle of it. There were bowls heaped with rice. Plates of piled-up turkey, ham, vegetables, salad, corn bread, saltfish fritters, dumplings and all manner of things Cass couldn't recognise. There was a steel band playing and Clyde, Loretta's brother, was dancing with a girl in a red dress and matching bandana. Briefly, Cass remembered dancing in the hurricane shelter and smiled.

Sylvie came up to them and handed them drinks. 'You were out for a long time. Have you had a lovely day?'

'Yes, thank you,' said Cass. 'We went to Scott's Head. It was beautiful.' She didn't want to go into details; as Ranulph had suggested, she wanted to keep what had gone on just between the two of them. She raised her glass. 'Santé!'

It wasn't long, though, before they were fully drawn into the beach party. Delphine handed Cass a plate of food. 'Eat it before you have too much rum punch,' she ordered.

Cass took the plate, amused at how bossy Delphine was, which disguised the fact that she cared about people.

Michael and Sylvie were obviously enjoying themselves. The conventional publishing couple from London had become proper Dominican party-goers, drinking, dancing and laughing at everyone's jokes.

Errol, Delphine's brother, came up to Cass and asked her to dance. She got rid of her plate and glass and joined him on the canvas pegged out on the sand, which formed a makeshift dance floor. She was soon remembering some of the moves she had been taught, and really let herself go. She spun from partner to partner, giving the appearance of a girl without a care in the world, even though really there was only one man she wanted to dance with.

She looked up to see Ranulph looking at his phone. Why was he on his phone? she wondered. It was a party! Why didn't he come and join everyone on the dance floor?

She forced herself to stop looking at him. Instead, she thought about the special things they had shared today. One day, in the distant future, could anything feel as special again, with someone else?

Suddenly he smiled and looked up from his phone. He put it in his pocket and caught her gaze. Cass looked away, embarrassed suddenly, but he came over.

'Can I cut in?' he said to Toussaint, Cass's current partner.

'Hey, man, you can claim what's yours,' Toussaint said.

Before she could get indignant about this remark, Ranulph took her arm and led her away from the dance floor and the party to a place where the loudest noise was the sound of the surf crashing on to the shore.

'I've had a message,' he said, obviously pleased. 'But actually, it's for you.'

He handed her his phone and she took it, confused. She looked at the message on the screen.

Hi Cass, I'm messaging via Ran because I don't have your details, but I want you to know that he loves you very much! He and I have never really been an item although I did try very hard when we were on Dominica together. But it was always you for him. I know he thought you were too young for him and was being all old-fashioned and gentlemanly (men, eh?) but he asked me to tell you that he is a free man.

I realised when I checked that on Facebook it might have looked as if we were together. If I'd seen a group shot and Ran's arm was round me and my status was 'in a relationship' I'd have thought that too. But I have my own lovely man now, nothing to do with Ran.

Be happy! And look after Ran. He is a man who deserves all your love.
Love and Happy Christmas! From Becca. Xoxoxo

'What does this mean?' Cass asked him, handing back his phone.

'Come with me and let me explain.'

He took her arm and he took her even further away from the party to where there was a clear view of the starry sky.

'Look up!' he said. 'That constellation there, like a W? That's Cassiopeia.'

'Oh! Like my name.'

'Yes, those are your stars.' He put his arms round her and looked down into her face. 'Cassiopeia — Cassie — you should know by now that I love you, and if you don't, then it's entirely my fault. I do, so much I can't really put it into words, although I'm supposed to be a writer.'

'You're a journalist,' said Cass, gently teasing him.

'I want to be a writer who works from home and doesn't flit around the world so much. I want to write your father's biography — I want you to be able to draw, paint, do illustrations, do whatever you want —'

'Ranulph? Why are you telling me all this?'

'I'm trying to ask you to marry me. I want you to know that being with me wouldn't mean you were isolated on a remote Scottish island, on your own, while I travel. I never want to leave your side.'

Cass couldn't catch her breath. Had he just proposed to her? It didn't seem completely clear.

'Please, Cass, say yes,' he said. 'Then we can take it from there. Do you love me? Do you want to marry me? What's your answer? I need to know!' He swallowed, as if fighting desperation.

It all became clear. He loved her and she loved him. 'It's yes,' said Cass. 'I do love you and have for a while now. And I'd love to be isolated on a remote Scottish island with you.'

He took her into his arms, and they kissed for a very long time.

* * *

When eventually they felt they had to go back to the party, they were greeted with a round of applause.

'That took a long time to happen,' said Bastian. 'But I know you're going to be very happy together.'

'I've got champagne!' said Michael, full of bonhomie. 'This is wonderful!'

Friendly barked with excitement and frolicked around them. Cass thought the stars over Dominica had never shone more brightly and she had never been so happy. 'Seeing the Emerald Drop turned out to be a really good omen,' she said.

'It certainly was for me,' said Ranulph and wrapped his arms around her. 'It brought me my girl, my Cassiopeia, the love of my life.' And then they kissed, oblivious to the whoops of the guests that surrounded them.

Afterword

I wanted to write a book set on Dominica because I have family on the island. In the 1930s my aunt went there with her second husband, the eldest daughter from her first marriage and a boy and a girl from the second. Both girls married on the island and consequently I have dozens of cousins. I have also visited many times and it feels a little bit like home.

The cousins I am closest to, probably because we're of an age, are Sara and Lennox Honychurch. Lennox, more properly known as Dr Lennox Honychurch, features in the book, only I had to divide him into two characters, father and son, because I wanted my Bastian to be in his thirties.

Our most recent trip to Dominica was last Christmas and we took our three children, their spouses, and seven grandchildren. It was not a simple journey because there were too many of us for inter-island planes. But it was wonderful, and we are still talking about it.

Before we went, I knew that I wanted to write about Dominica and I asked Lennox for help. He is the Caribbean expert and has written many books about the area. The Honychurch name is well known on the island.

Lennox told me about the petroglyph; he described how he had helped to find it (there was a hand-drawn map) and he told me about the archaeological site, uncovered by Hurricane Maria, where early delft pottery was found alongside artefacts belonging to the Kalinago people.

It was in 1996, when we first went, that Lennox took me to the deserted sugar mill called Bois Cotlette. At the time it was as described in this book but in fact it was sold to an American family in 2010 and is now a tourist spot. I have never forgotten seeing it for the first time, though, and have tried to do justice to the haunted, melancholy atmosphere of the place.

Friendly, the dog, belongs to Lennox, and the descriptions of what it's like to go through a hurricane come from Sara. Sara also supplied all sorts of details and certainly caught a few errors before they got into the book. Petrea (daughter of Sara) was also amazingly helpful and has written a charming picture book called *Goodnight My Sweet Island* which perfectly encapsulates why I love Dominica. Her sister Marica, a wonderful photographer, did the photos for a fascinating book about ti kais, the vernacular wooden houses of Dominica (*Still Standing: The Ti Kais of Dominica* by Adom Philogene Heron, photographs by Marica Honychurch).

The most important book written about Dominica is *The Dominica Story* by Lennox Honychurch. It gives us the story of the island, why it is different from other Caribbean islands, and what a truly fascinating place it is.

I also mustn't forget my aunt, Elma Napier, who wrote biographies and novels set on Dominica. She was Sara and Lennox's grandmother and, to me and my sister, she was a favourite aunt whose visits to London were always looked forward to.

Finally, my apologies: while I've tried hard to give due credit to this fascinating island I have maligned my cousin Lennox whose wonderful artistic talents I gave to my heroine, Cass. I feel a bit as if I've stolen from someone who contributed so much, so willingly, to this book.

Acknowledgements

They say it takes a village to raise a child. In my case it takes a small suburb to produce a book and I want to thank everyone so much for their enormous help and support.

Naming names, I will start with my Honychurch cousins: Lennox, Sara, Petrea and Marica, who were so generous with their time and information. I will add Polly Pattullo of Papillote Press to the list as part of the Dominica family.

As ever, I must thank Bill Hamilton who continues to be the best agent ever and everyone else at A. M. Heath who look after me so well.

Richenda Todd, whose meticulous copy-editing has been saving me embarrassment for many years.

I have the best editorial team without whom I'd be lost: Selina Walker, Charlotte Osment, Laurie Ip Fung Chun, Sarah Ridley, Hope Butler, Ceara Elliot, Annabel Wright, Olivia Allen, Evie Kettlewell, Helen Wynn-Smith and Meredith Benson.

David O'Driscoll, who researched wildlife photographers for me but who actually supplied everything I needed himself.

Not forgetting my own family who continue to be pretty wonderful, from Desmond, husband of over fifty years, down to the youngest grandchild. Thank you!

We do hope that you have enjoyed
reading this large print book.

Did you know that all of our titles
are available for purchase?

We publish a wide range of high
quality large print books including:
Romances, Mysteries, Classics
General Fiction
Non Fiction and Westerns

Special interest titles available in
large print are:
The Little Oxford Dictionary
Music Book, Song Book
Hymn Book, Service Book

Also available from us courtesy of
Oxford University Press:
Young Readers' Dictionary
(large print edition)
Young Readers' Thesaurus
(large print edition)

For further information or a free
brochure, please contact us at:
Ulverscroft Large Print Books Ltd.,
The Green, Bradgate Road, Anstey,
Leicester, LE7 7FU, England.
Tel: (00 44) **0116 236 4325**
Fax: (00 44) **0116 234 0205**

Other titles published by Ulverscroft:

ONE ENCHANTED EVENING

Katie Fforde

Ever since she can remember, Meg has wanted to be a professional cook. But it's 1966, and in restaurant kitchens all over England it is still a man's world. Then she gets a call from her mother who is running a small hotel in Dorset. There's an important banqueting event coming up. She needs help, and she needs it now!

When Meg arrives, the hotel seems stuck in the past. But she loves a challenge, and sets to work. However, she has reckoned without Justin, the son of the hotel owner, who seems determined to take over the running of the kitchen. Infuriated, Meg resolves to keep cooking — and soon sparks between them begin to fly.

Will their differences be a recipe for disaster? After all, the course of true love never did run smooth . . .

A WEDDING IN PROVENCE

Katie Fforde

1963. Alexandra arrives at a chateau in Provence: old, substantial, its four large towers seeming to grow out of the soil. It is, she thinks, reassuring in its permanence and solidity.

Less reassuring are the three silent children waiting for her inside, her charges for a month: a boy and two girls badly in need of some love, attention, and an English education.

Fresh from London and a recent cookery course, Alexandra has always loved a challenge and feels equipped to deal with most things life throws at her. What she is less sure about is whether she'll be able to deal with the children's father — an impossibly good-looking French count with whom she is trying very hard not to fall in love . . .

A WEDDING IN THE COUNTRY

Katie Fforde

Lizzie has just arrived in London, determined to make the best of her new life.

Her mother may be keen that she should have a nice wedding in the country to a Suitable Man chosen by her. And Lizzie may be going to cookery school to help her become a Good Wife.

But she definitely wants to have some fun first.

It is 1963 and London is beginning to swing as Lizzie cuts her hair, buys a new dress with a fashionably short hemline, and moves in with two of her best friends, one of whom lives in a grand but rundown house in Belgravia which has plenty of room for a lodger.

Soon Lizzie's life is so exciting that she has forgotten all about her mother's marriage plans for her.

All she can think about is that the young man she is falling in love with appears to be engaged to someone else . . .